# VASHLA'S WORLD
## Book 2
## The Ancient Alien Series

Jill Smith

MILES ST PUBLISHING

COOLANGATTA, QUEENSLAND

**MILES ST PUBLISHING**
**Jill Smith Aussie Author**
**Coolangatta, Queensland, Australia**
https://authorjillsmith.wordpress.com/



Book Layout © 2020 Jill Smith and Kate Russell
Cover updated by Kate Russell and Pamela Uekerman@Spiral Designs

**Book Title/ Author Name**. – 2nd ed.
Book ISBN 978-1-8758656-7-3
eBook ISBN 978-1-8758656-8-0

## DEDICATION

I dedicate this book to my writing friends who have encouraged me to be courageous, think outside the box, and most importantly, to persevere.

I also thank my husband Clive for putting up with my many hours on the computer creating other worlds.

ACKNOWLEDGEMENTS

I wish to acknowledge the assistance I received by Kate Russell in completing the cover changes, updated by Pamela Ueckerman of Spiral Designs. And my fellow writers in The Ten Penners, adults writing for children group, who constantly inspire and encourage me. I also thank Robyn Lee Burrows as mentor and guide during my writing journey with editorial advice. This is the second book in The Ancient Alien Series, an adult theme continues throughout.

MAIN CHARACTERS LIST

Name - Planet of Origin

Gardt Ness - Ghaur
Vashla - VaLinta
Agai - VaLinta
Ria and Bru - Ghaur
Commander Dreece Corma - Ghaur
Richard Davidson - Earth
Davrew - Orthama (orbiting space station)
Bill & Pat Davidson - Earth
Zorn - Zamba
Amar - Zamba
Elder Vini - Orthama (orbiting space station)
Rinra - Orthama (orbiting space station)
Colu - Orthama (orbiting space station)
Guhamp - (purple trader) Ozer

# CONTENTS

## CHAPTER ONE

# Gardt's World - Ghaur

On a planet at the other end of the universe, not unlike our own, Gardt Ness looked up at the stars. He knew each constellation formation like his own body. He rested his lean, fit frame on the shovel. It was a beautiful night.

The flood lights that illuminated the yard gave him a view of a half-dug patch of ground that needed turning before morning. It would be a long night. The continual physical activity of digging the vegetable garden that helped feed his family, kept him fit and strong. Leaning on the shovel would not get the job done. He recommenced his digging.

Over the years since his return from the stars, he'd come to appreciate his solitude and ignore the bile of bitterness plagued him when he first landed. He had expected to be heralded as a hero by the public that praised and applauded as they had when they sent him on his journey. His discoveries had been profound and largely ignored.

Turning each sod to welcome the warmth of the sun the next day, Gardt worked his body into a hard-sweat saturating his t-shirt. He moved to the outdoor shower beside the garden shed. He turned off the floodlights as he carefully put his shovel away. The cold water was invigorating as he washed away the grit.

He walked inside the small garden shed and sat on the end of the bed. There was a shelf above with a small lantern beside a manuscript. The bundle of paper represented his latest play that he hoped the local theatre group would agree to perform. They had already staged two of his works and were eager for more. A broad smile spread across his weather-worn face. The plays were his way of telling the people what really happened to him during those two turbulent years in space.

The next morning, he rose early and went into the house. The kitchen was his neutral ground. He prepared breakfast, oats, toast, fruit, and yoghurt and set them on the table. The children jostled as they vied for seats, ignoring him as was the norm. Ria entered in a state of frenzy, entreating the children to hurry and ready themselves for school. He scrubbed the pan hard gulping down his resentment. She did not talk to him. She did not look at him. Her former husband, Gardt Ness, the disgraced space hero.

The children only knew him as the gardener and housekeeper. Bru, their father, appeared wearing a business suit, dangling car keys. He snatched and the cup of coffee Gardt offered, pecked his wife's cheek, and waived farewell to the children.

'Stop that and eat!' Ria chastised the two youngest children who were arguing over where to sit. The older boy slopped the milk into the bowl. The breakfast was as a battleground until every morsel disappeared. Gardt proceeded to clean up.

'Mum, I've got an excursion tomorrow to the ILD to see the Launch Platform. How am I going to get there?' the oldest boy asked.

'What's the ILD?' the youngest nudged his sibling.

'The Immigration Launch Department silly,' the oldest boy rolled his eyes.

Ria looked up at her son, their son, and turned to Gardt, finally acknowledging his presence.

'I've an important meeting tomorrow, so I can't take you, Joss. Perhaps Gardt could take you. I'll be in town at a meeting with your father. Gardt can use my electro car. After all, it's a place he knows well.'

'I used to know it well. Many years have passed since I've been permitted there. I doubt your father will approve of me taking Joss.'

'Hmm, I can't see a problem,' she shrugged, 'I'd best check with Father anyway.'

'Oh, Mum, I'd rather Pa take me. I don't want to be seen with the home help.'

Gardt turned back to the sink and dived into washing the dishes, his shoulders slumped, head down, he took a deep breath to compose himself. That had hurt.

'Okay, Joss, I'll ask Pa. I guess, even after all these years, Gardt may still not be welcome at the ILD.'

'I'm fourteen now Mum, how long do you think it'll be before I can join the Immigration lists?'

'Now Joss, I've told you before, Pa says that it's best to wait for whole families to go. Your father is working his way into a good position to set us all up for passage in the next few years. That would be the best thing.'

Gardt held his breath. They couldn't be serious? He had tried to warn his family of the immense danger they would be in but, he was ignored.

Today he would take his manuscript to the city. He had to do something to warn people. Lately, the newspapers were encouraging registration of families to migrate to space. The dangers he'd experienced would have to have been eliminated for this for this to be possible.

Later that day, Gardt took his hover disc from the corner of the shed and turned it on. This was one privilege they couldn't deny him. He had the right to basic transport to meet the needs of the family. As he suspected, his former father-in-law and mentor had prohibited Gardt going anywhere near the ILD. What was happening? He had to find out.

Today was an important day. He arrived at the office of the local theatre production manager. He knocked and heard the shout to go in, a balding round-faced man looked up at him and grinned.

'Gardt, I'm glad you're here. I've some great news for you.'

'You have?' Gardt smiled back. 'The play has been accepted?'

'Yes, it has,' the bald man stood up and nodded towards the package under Gardt's arm. 'This is the next play?'

'It is,' Gardt said handing it over, 'it's even more controversial than the last one.' He paused and looked directly into the shorter man's eyes. 'Do you think the theatre will get repercussions from the authorities? You know I'm banned from the ILD and virtually have no civilian rights.'

'I don't think so,' the producer rubbed his chin. 'The Title?'

'*Captivated.*'

'I can't wait to read it,' the bald man flipped through the pages then put it on the desk. 'Do you mind if I ask you something, Gardt?'

'Ask away. I've nothing to lose, Mr B.'

'These things you write about are based on real events?'

'Yes, although the authorities would have everyone believing it's safe out there. That certainly wasn't my experience.'

'I've a friend who is a literary agent. He read your first play *'Surviving Space'*. He's looking forward to seeing our production of it. He's coming to rehearsals this afternoon. Can you stay around for a while and meet him?'

Gardt nodded. 'Do you think he might want to do more with my plays?'

'Sounds keen,' the bald man clapped his hands together.

'You know my circumstances. He might not want to deal with me.'

'Perhaps, but it can't hurt trying.'

Several hours later three men watched a small local theatre group rehearse the new play. Gardt was impressed by the quality of their efforts. So was the literary agent.

Mr B introduced the two. 'Mr Kymlah, this is Gardt Ness. He's a non-citizen, a disgrace in the eyes of the authorities and the law. He is also the author of this play, and another I took delivery of today.'

Mr Kymlah raised his eyebrows, said nothing, and continued to watch the rehearsal. When the company took a break, he turned to Gardt.

'Interesting subject matter, or should I say, unique.'

'Unique?' Gardt nodded. 'Yes, it is. Based on truth, as certainly as I stand here, and controversial. I'm impressed by this performance, Mr B, and I'm wondering what you think of it, Mr Kymlah.'

'Impressive.' He turned his steely dark eyes towards Gardt and scrutinised him carefully. 'I'll be in touch. Where do you live Gardt?'

'I have a home a short distance from here. It is mine by birthright, and all I have.'

'I will come to see you there. I understand your family live there also.'

'Commander Dreece would prefer that you not call them my family. They are his daughter, her husband and children.'

'If there is an element of truth in this play, they were your family. Have you had the opportunity to discuss your thoughts with the ILD?'

'They dismissed my findings when I returned and cast aspersions about the whole experience. They chose not to believe it happened and have not permitted me any credibility.'

'If this is not just a work of fantasy, Gardt Ness, then the authorities' version of our potential colonisation of space is greatly exaggerated, possibly flawed. Do you believe there is still danger for the immigrants?'

'I'm certain of it.'

'That would mean that we are being fed propaganda. If we present these plays nationwide by many reputable companies, do you think there will be some backlash?'

'Perhaps,' Gardt held his ground.

'Well, naturally, you must remain anonymous, but you'll be paid a royalty for each performance. Do you have any source of income?'

'No. I grow vegetables and permitted to purchase the family necessities through their credit. I have none of my own. In fact, as you can see, I wear hand-me-down clothes.'

'If you had funds would you be able to spend it?'

'Not directly,' Gardt shook his head.

'Well then, Mr B and I will assist in that regard. This play is full of action and drama and a wicked space pirate with a violent streak. It's controversial, but I doubt anyone will believe it's based on fact.'

Gardt's face clouded over. He could not hide his disappointment.

'You want the world to know this horror exists?'

'Yes, and this may be my only way of letting people know the reality of what is out there.'

The final act was being rehearsed. The whole cast came back onto the stage while the hero made his climactic speech.

'We've won this battle, but the war is far from over.' The hero addresses the cast. In unison, the whole troupe begin to sing an unusual rhythmic chant.

'What is that?'

'It's the space pirate's war chant.'

Mr Kymah raised his eyebrows again and nodded. Gardt left a short while later. Mr Kymah arranged to meet him the next day.

## CHAPTER TWO

# Gardt's World - Ghaur

Gardt had seen the end of another school year. The vegetable crop had been harvested and reworked twice over. He now had a good income from the successful plays being presented throughout the country. Bru, Ria's husband, came out to speak to him while he laboured, again in the evening, turning the soil under floodlights.

'Gardt, I have something to say to you.'

Gardt nodded and continued digging.

'We are going to see Joss in the new play on tonight in the local theatre. He's the lead character.'

'I see in the papers this is quite a successful play.'

'Yes, the whole thing is a bit far-fetched, but entertaining.'

'Far-fetched? But Joss is a good lead?'

'He's wowing the school and showing a possible talent as an actor. Ria is not all that wrapped in that idea.'

'Hmph, I bet she isn't.' Gardt stopped digging and lent on his shovel, 'but that's not why you've come out here. You have something to say to me?'

'Yes,' Bru looked down at his shoes, which he realised now were caked in soil. 'We are leaving this house, Gardt. It's too small for us now, with the new baby coming, and with my new job being on the other side of town, we thought it best to make a new start.'

'A new start,' Gardt stared at Bru. 'That's exactly what I didn't get, Bru. This is my home. I've allowed you and the family to live here because it suited you all to stay. Now you tell me you are moving out like I should be grateful for the fact. Never mind that I've worked for no reward to keep your family. I've done that because of Joss. He is my son. Ria is my wife. Our marriage was never annulled. I was away two years and came back to nothing but the right to continue to live in my home, and cook, clean, feed and assist you with your lives. Well don't expect me to throw a party for you because you've finally decided to try to live without the home help elsewhere.' Gardt started turning the soil again, his anger burning with each turn of the sod. More dirt landed on Bru's shinny shoes.

Bru shook some dirt off his feet, stepped around the mud pile, said nothing more, and walked back into the house. Later the whole family jumped in the electro car and headed to the school auditorium to see the play.

After they'd left, Gardt dared to take a hot shower inside the house and to change into comfortable clothes Bru no longer wore. What would happen when the family moved? Would he be able to buy his own clothes and basic needs? He could only guess. Dreece, his former father-in-law, although retired still had a lot of influence at the ILD and effect his future. Either way, he would miss the children. Other than Joss being his son, he'd come to love all the children. The younger ones didn't look at him as the home help. They still valued his efforts.

Gardt rode his hover disc to the venue and slipped quietly into the back of the theatre. Now he crept into the back of the auditorium to stand in the shadows. The theatre staff knew him. He'd been to most of the rehearsals. The play was halfway through and Gardt realised the audience was engrossed in the story. The drama and fight scenes were well performed for a school production. He'd ensured Mr B had passed on his suggestions to improve the backdrop and scenes, and this had really set each act superbly. He'd been told theatre critics would be in the audience. They would have a big influence on the future of *'Captivated'* being taken up with regular theatres.

The finale came and everyone stood up with the cast and sang the Pirates war chant. Gardt found himself singing with gusto. The audience sang the strange words without knowing what they meant. Gardt was glad that only he knew their true translation, for if the crowd had known, they would be fearful. Memories of Vashla, the intimidating sadistic space pirate, standing among decapitated heads with blood dripping from her weapons, sprang to mind. People here had no idea of the danger. The audience clapped and cheered. The performance was a total success.

He slipped out of the theatre as the lights dimmed. The family he loved and cared for were unaware he'd been to the show.

CHAPTER THREE

# Rakal's World - Earth

## Late 2001

On another planet at the other end of the galaxy, at a different time, a family of dual gender, alien derived inhabitants were integrating themselves into the local population.

An archaeology lecturer was piling his books into his car to leave the University for the weekend.

'Wait up Davidson,' a lanky man called out, 'I've been, wanting to catch up with you.'

'Hi Guy,' Tam replied, 'I hear you've been offered an overseas teaching position, Harvard, is it? Congratulations.'

'Yeah, I worked for it,' the tall man smiled back. 'Congratulations to you too, family life and all that. Will you be going to the Egypt or Arizona digs this year? Or is that not on the cards now?'

'I haven't really decided yet Guy. I have to admit I've been on my own, or just with me and Kat, you know, my child, so long that having a partner in Rakal is taking a little getting used to.' He slid into the car behind the wheel, 'it sure is different, and, now I can travel more easily using my skip flying mode, I can get home more often, it's working out well. Naturally, I'd love to go to work on the digs overseas, it'll just take time working out the where and when.'

'Yeah,' Guy nodded scrutinising the skip, 'looks like an ordinary car, I saw you arrive this morning and you were really flying.'

'Yep,' Tam patted the dash, 'now I must be off. My new partner has a relative visiting from the other end of the galaxy. Apparently, we can't keep this Vashla woman waiting.'

'Man, oh man, I can't compete with that,' Guy waved.

Tam closed the door and set off, first along the road, then into the early evening sky. He flew the skip away from the University campus higher over several cities and towns until he approached his hometown, then he dropped to a lower altitude skimming over the treetops. The property opposite the family home was now a building site where the burnt out remains of what he'd always known as the Old Farmhouse were being reconstructed. The journey had taken minutes when formerly, using conventional transport, it would have taken a couple of hours. The Davidson family had been careful not to alert suspicion so had stuck to conventional means, but now the world knew of their existence, it freed them to use this method of travel.

Tam smiled at the welcoming sight of the long drive beyond the entrance of the wrought iron gate. Road level now he'd put his skip down on the bitumen. The old English circular garden near the entrance to the house was in full bloom. The many extensions enhanced the country farmhouse ambience and gave it the appearance of a grand country manor. In the field, adjacent to the home, behind the clay tennis courts, Tam could see the spaceship Rakal had made famous the world over during his recent global media jaunt. Beside it was a larger elliptical craft with imposing leg-like appendages. It resembled a large black spider rearing up ready to strike. An involuntary shiver ran down Tam's spine. What would this Vashla be like?

Tam rushed inside and was greeted by Davrew, the tall blond dual gender head of the household.

'I'm so glad to be one of your children,' Tam smiled and hugged his bearer tightly.

'I love my fifth born just as much as my first,' Davrew smiled and spun Tam around. 'Your boys are in the Rakal's spaceship with the guests. Dinner is at six.'

'I'll get over there then and be back soon. Will everyone be home?'

'Mostly, your father is just taking a stroll around the garden. He's getting stronger every day.'

'Great news, I'll catch up with everyone soon, I'd best get out there and meet his Vashla.'

'You'd better,' Davrew nodded.

Walking up the rampart to Rakal's craft he couldn't help but feel both vehicles were imposing. Kat, their fifteen-year-old gangly son sat with a younger boy, both engrossed in handheld computer games in the recreation room.

'Hi Kat, how are you?' Tam smiled at their son.

'Good, this is Agai, we're playing Mario Brothers,' Kat replied without looking up.

'Hi Agai,' Tam smiled at the boy. He looked up for briefly and nodded a greeting. There was a competitive spark in his large dark blue eyes as he held up the game and returned to it. 'Okay, I'll go to meet your mother Agai, and Kat I'll let your father know we're having dinner in the house at six.'

Tam strolled into the control room and found Rakal there with his guest. Rakal immediately stood and hugged Tam, planting a warm firm kiss on happily accommodating lips.

'Vashla, this is my partner Tam.'

The woman was athletic. Her eyes dark a marked contrast to the boy's crystal-clear blue eyes. She was as imposing as her craft, fit and battle ready. Her smart practical attire, pants covered by a tunic top, accentuated her curvaceous figure. Tam kept looking from Rakal to the visitor, clinging to his arm, glad of Rakal's' nearness.

'We've been invited to dinner at six,' Tam said. 'If we leave now, we can introduce you to the rest of the family.'

The woman simply nodded as they walked into the room the boys were in.

'Agai, we go now,' Vashla said.

The boy immediately put the game down and stood at her side. Kat seeing this, reluctantly rose to stand beside Tam who sensed that Vashla was accustomed to being obeyed. As they left the spaceship via the rampart with the homestead and grounds before them, Tam smiled.

'What do you think of our home?'

The woman seemed surprised by the question. Awkwardly she looked more carefully at her surroundings.

'Different,' she grunted.

'They prepare their own food, grown on the property, Vashla,' Rakal explained.

The woman shook her head, allowing the shining black cascade to blow about her face. She said nothing. The child walked obediently beside her.

Kat walked comfortably at Tams' side.

'We grow all kinds of fruit and vegetables,' Kat remarked, 'and we all take it in turns to work in the garden and to cook.'

'Ours is a large family and working together is how we get things done,' Tam smiled, 'you are about to have a fine vegetarian meal.'

'No meat,' Rakal added.

Tam stopped and looked up into Rakal's eyes.

'What do you mean?'

'Vashla likes fresh meat.'

The woman simply raised her eyebrows.

'Vashla has changed since meeting Agai's father.'

'Kat go ahead with Agai will you, let the family know we're nearly there please,' Tam stammered.

'I didn't kill him. I even returned him to his people,' Vashla shrugged. She'd stopped beside them.

'Why would you kill him?' Tam couldn't help but ask, curiosity overcoming apprehension.

'I always did before, but the people on VaLinta showed me other ways. They would work together,' Vashla shrugged, 'I went there when Agai was to be born. They helped until they all died.'

'How did they die?' Tam continued to probe.

'There was a sickness. They would become hot and have spots all over the skin, then, they would sleep, and finally stop living. They would not let me restore them. They said the sickness was their punishment. I did not know why they would not let me help them.'

'That must have been incredibly sad for you to lose many friends,' Tam continued. 'How many died?'

'Many, there is no one left living on Linta. The last was Schishila. She helped me birth Agai,' Vashla solemnly replied. 'It is now my world, I call it VaLinta.'

They were nearly at the house, the freshly cut grass smelt fresh and was damp underfoot. The garden gate at the side of the house creaked as they went though and walked along a path between a vegetable and herb patch beside the house. Inside, the house was warm, the kitchen filled with the aroma of food roasting. The long table in the dining room that adjoined the kitchen was being laid.

Vashla stopped on entering the busy room, so did the chatter in the room. She scanned the many faces and the table laden with food. 'This reminds me of the Linta people,' she spoke to Agai, 'listen well son.'

The guest was introduced to her hosts the head of the household Davrew, and partner Richard, then the many children.

'I've been unwell,' Richard explained, 'but I'm recovering now.'

The meal began with the younger children staring at the giant woman. Tam wondered how much this alien and Rakal had in common. There would be much to discuss when they were finally alone.

CHAPTER FOUR

# Rakal's World - Earth

The next morning, Tam walked back into the home, having slept on board the ship with Rakal. Kat had stayed in the dormitory with the younger children and Tam was anxious to catch up with the child before he left.

'The children are all growing up too quickly. Even though I come home most weekends now, I am surprised at how much the youngest kids have grown, Ness and Gill, especially,' Tam remarked to his parents at the kitchen table.

'Well they're not babies now at nine and ten. Wait till you catch up with Sal's twins Saz and Sam, even Raz the seven-year-old acts like a teenager! They can't wait to get back into their own home,' Richard rolled his eyes.

'Your Kat is fifteen now and heading towards his sixteenth,' Davrew said, 'we'll need to start planning for that party.'

'He's taller than the others,' Richard added, 'and being all boy in nature, he seems tougher.'

'He is all boy,' Tam agreed. The back door swung open.

'Hi Tris,' Tam greeted a gangly youth with jeans and t-shirt, as he entered the kitchen. He was fond of his siblings' third born child. 'How are you today?'

'Good Tam, I'm going out. Tod is taking me to see the portrait he did of Bon, the one he painted for the Archibald competition. It hangs proudly among the other entrants this year, even though it didn't win.'

'Good on him entering, it's a great portrait.' Richard nodded.

'Will Rakal and his guest be joining us?' Davrew asked.

'I don't think so. They were in a heated discussion when I left. They seem to enjoy the banter.'

Having gulped down some cereal and jangling his keys, Tris waved goodbye. The door slammed shut behind him.

'Tris is not yet partnered,' Tam commented, 'perhaps Tod is the one?'

'Tod? Painter and artist Tod? I doubt it, he's a bit long in the tooth,' Richard scoffed.

'I wouldn't be so sure of that. Tris has been visiting his workshop a lot lately,' Davrew countered. 'Tod thought the world of Bon.'

'Everyone did,' Tam said getting up.

'Your Kat is old enough to have a partner too, but he has to find the right girl,' Richard got up and put the dishes in the sink.

'Kat isn't in any hurry,' Tam sighed. 'He's been with most of the eligible girls about town, from what I can tell.'

'A chip of his grandfathers' block,' Davrew grinned impishly while swiping Richards arm.

'I noticed that the rebuilding of the old home opposite is coming along nicely,' Tam took a mug from the cupboard and poured a black tea. 'Kar and Lar are doing well in their construction business from what I hear.'

'Sure are,' Richard replied, 'the house is taking longer to rebuild because they've got so much other work on.' Richard poured more tea and handed a mug to Davrew as he sat down.

'Ness and Kat have been helping too,' Davrew added, 'they've become builder's labourers.'

'I need to wake up Kat,' Tam drained the last of his tea, 'I wonder if Agai enjoyed his stay over with the youngsters in the dorm?'

'I guess you'll find out soon,' Richard grinned. 'As you can see, we spend a lot of time in this kitchen Tam. It's the best place to catch up with all our children and grandchildren. Early on the great grandchildren were being fed, then you and Tris, and soon the older ones will be down.'

'I only hope the other children didn't keep Agai awake, that child seems to have a short temper, a bit like his mother.'

'Speak of the devil,' Richard grinned as the twins Saz and Sam, came running into the room with Shea and Ness at their heels. 'The twins can't wait for the new house to be built so they can get away from the dormitory. Sal really had made Aunt Nancy's place a haven for his family.'

The children had the distinctive blond flax hair and blue eyes, except for Shea, who was darker in hair colour and skin tone and had a much more solid build. With a clatter of dishes and cutlery being set out on the table Tam took the opportunity to run up the stairs to the dormitory. It was difficult not to laugh at the dishevelled look of the youth hunkered down with the blankets wrapped like a cocoon around him.

'Didn't get much sleep Agai?'

'I'm not used to noise,' the youth replied.

'Doesn't seem to have bothered Kat,' Tam grinned at the youth sleeping soundly in the adjacent bunk. 'Wake up, sleepy head, we've got to make a move,' Tam shook the boy. He yawned and stretched.

'The littlest ones cried and were taken away. Do they always cry like that?'

'They are babies, newborn to toddlers. This house is ever expanding in number. Their parents would have taken them to their rooms so as not to disturb the older children,' Tam explained.

'Well it didn't work,' Agai grumbled.

'Never mind, you can catch up with your sleep later,' Tam tousled Kat's hair affectionately.

'I've got to go across the road and help on the house. Can Agai come over too?'

'I'm not the one to ask,' Tam let Kat sit up. 'Kar or Lar would be the ones. Remember Agai is a guest and may not want to lug bricks or dig ditches while he's here.'

'There's always someone to help on the weekends, I like to join in, seeing something built from nothing is great,' Kat explained to the other boy.

'What sort of work do you do? I mean do you help Vashla, clean up or do stuff with getting meals?'

'No,' he shook his head. 'I do sometimes help put heads in the Library after Mamma returns from a raid.'

'Heads,' Tam squeaked.

'Uh ha, that's the only sure way to kill someone. Otherwise someone like Mamma can restore them, and some of the ships Mamma raids, she wants to keep.'

Tam gulped. Kat looked bug eyed and shook his head. 'Are you for real?'

Tam stood up and walked to the window opening it to the fresh air, 'perhaps Agai would like to find out what plans Vashla has for today.'

'I'll just get cleaned up and head over to the old house to see what help they need,' Kat muttered while stumbling out of bed and heading for the bathroom.

'What, don't you want me to go with you?' Agai looked perplexed, 'what is wrong with having a library?'

'Here a library is for books, not heads, Agai. There are some things you take as normal that we don't,' Tam felt a headache coming on. 'I'm just going back to Rakal and your mother. Will you join me now Agai?'

The boy, although confused nodded, pulled on some clothes quickly and followed.

Tam walked back into the recreation room aboard Rakal's craft with the boy in tow. Rakal and Vashla were still in deep conversation.

'So, Zorn wants to partner you Vashla? He has a mean disposition,' Rakal was saying as they entered.

'I have not said yes or no,' Vashla replied.

'But Mamma you said he can't be trusted,' Agai said.

'I was promised to him at birth, and, although my father is now dead and I don't have to honour the agreement, it is customary to do so,' Vashla explained.

'I thought he took your fathers head!'
'He did,' she replied.

'More talk of decapitation. Rakal, I need to talk to you,' Tam felt stern words were in order. Rakal gulped knowing the what the tone in Tam's voice meant.

## CHAPTER FIVE

# Rakal's World - Earth

'There is no threat,' Rakal stated. 'Vashla knows I'm sworn to protect this world and its people.'

'The boy said she goes on raids and brings back heads, clearly he knows nothing about living a communal lifestyle.'

'How could he?' Rakal was standing beside a window in the recreation room looking out at the farmhouse. 'This world is nothing like they have dealt with before. Vashla has known nothing but her normal solitary life. Her only dealing with a social community was with the Linta people on the world she now calls VaLinta, when Agai was born.'

Tam stopped pacing and joined Rakal at the window. 'How much of that life did she and the boy experience?'

'I wasn't there, Tam. From what Vashla has said, he was young, maybe five, when the disease killed all the people. She described what happened months later, then only briefly, as it distressed her so much. I think the association with the child's father had changed her outlook too.'

'She is your ally?' Tam stood on the opposite side of the window leaning on the wall.

'Yes, and I've asked her to also vow to protect your world. Vashla is my Mothers niece, so we are related. Many of the ones you would see as *space pirates* are. We know nothing else. Survival is our only goal. We have no home world as our parents send us *off world* as soon as we can fly. They choose to live on the different planets they take over. My parents did not stay together to raise many children, as your family have done. My mother had many children and they were left to grow on their own on different worlds. Zorn is also related to me. He is a threat. I am trying to ensure we have protection.'

'Protection! These space pirates, with no concept of our lives, or our way of living, or how they can affect our lives, are a threat?'

Rakal took two steps to close the gap between them. He touched Tams face gently.

'This world, and the way you live, is a new way of being for me, and my solitary relatives. They are powerful but very alone. It took me many years to understand how much I needed to be with you, and your family,' Rakal moved forward and gently kissed Tam.

'Vashla loves the boy but her only concept of rearing the child was from the Linta, they were a nurturing community. She had no example as her family simply left her in space with two older siblings in her teens. She knows nothing else. They only stayed together long enough to capture their own ships and go their own ways.'

'She must be a lonely woman,' Tam snuggled into Rakal's arms, 'that's so sad.'

'Sad, but we can change. You've taught me that,' Rakal smiled and they kissed with passion. 'Do you have to go soon?'

Tam grinned and cuddled close.

'Ouch,' Tam muttered, 'my breasts are sore, they have been for a few days. I'll catch up with Tris later to have a medical checkup.'

'We can go now,' Rakal said concerned.

'Tris isn't home right now. He went out with Tod Longmire.'

'Your family need more than one medic.'

'We know that, since what happened to Bon, our most skilled physician. It was all too devastating to lose such a vital member of the family. Tris isn't the only one training in that field. Izzy, Miri and Peter's youngest is too, and now it seems Rill and Raz are too.'

'Your siblings have so many children, and now there are more babies from their babies.'

'We're a growing species, we dual gender race,' Tam commented before taking Rakal by the hand and leading him to their bed. 'I've got other things on my mind now Rakal.'

Rakal smiled and followed.


Later that day Tam and Rakal went into the clinic Bon had used as a base for all his medical diagnosis and treatment. Tris was there pouring over his studies. Although he had the same blond hair and blue eyes distinguishing him as a Davidson, he carried his lanky frame proudly in the mannerism of his fully human father. He also had a strong resemblance to his father Peter, with a high brow and dimple on the chin.

'Hi, Tam, Rakal, how are you and our house guests?'

'Good. I just want a quick checkup thanks Tris,' Tam smiled. 'Our house guest is taking her boy Agai into town, with our parents, to buy some clothes. Davrew mentioned shopping and Vashla thought this was such a foreign concept she wanted to see what it was. They'll also meet up with Aunty Pat and Uncle Bill.'

'That'll be an interesting trip then,' Tris grinned.

'Vashla is used to taking what she wants, not paying for it,' Rakal winked, then changed the subject. 'Tam may be unwell, that's why we're here.'

'Okay, we'll do some checks,' Tris pointed to a chair, 'don't worry Rakal, Tam looks well.'

A short while later they left the clinic in a subdued silence.

'It's good to hear Miri and Peter are enjoying their trip overseas,' Tam offered diverting the conversation from what they'd just discovered. 'Tris said they sent a post card, quaint and old fashioned though that is.'

'Kat is fifteen, and now you are going to have another child,' Rakal bought the conversation back to the matter at hand.

'Looks like it,' Tam smiled, 'I'm happy about it Rakal. What about you?'

'Happy?' Rakal replied, 'we are just getting time alone together, and now there will be a little one.'

'Rakal, I do have a large family to draw on as baby sisters, and a child together now would be a great event to share. You do want the baby?'

Rakal looked at Tam carefully. The mousy brown hair slicked back, the broad shoulders, the purposeful poise, the reason he'd returned from the extremities of the universe. 'You want this child?'

Tam nodded.

Rakal pulled Tam towards him. 'Then of course I want the child too.'

'It will be a new experience for you, I know. I had planned to go on a dig over the summer, being pregnant could make it difficult. Maybe if you came with me to help, we could manage,' Tam smiled delighted at the prospect. 'Now that our transport and communication can be openly used, the world is a smaller place. If I need medical assistance, it is always close at hand.'

CHAPTER SIX

# Rakal's World - Earth

Ash greeted his parents with a warm hug.

'Ah, the smell of fresh baked bread, there's not a smell more comforting or homely.'

'Cass put it in the oven over an hour ago, the loaves should be nearly ready,' Davrew replied.

'Cass took our two kids, Ness and Rill to town,' Ash smiled. 'They are looking for new clothes to travel with. Ness has gone all out to become a designer, loves those reality TV shows on 'Next Top Model, and 'Next Top Designer'. Rill is into the production of crafts and is more interested in creating macrame wall hangings. By the stars, they could end up working together. They argue less than they used to but still have a dynamic relationship.'

'Funny how we worry about how our own children get on,' Richard grinned. 'Cass is well, and the children are always a delight.'

'Cass is a wonderful partner, I'm lucky to have her,' Ash smiled while downing the dregs of his mug of coffee.

'Well, I'm off to town to meet Gem. You know we're starting up a business together? Branching into the mobile phone and computer market, it's really exciting.'

'Gem seems happy with Jake and Amber,' Davrew nodded and put some fresh toast on the table for Richard.

'Yes, and their growing family,' Ash nodded, 'Maya is a great sibling to the babies. He doesn't seem in any hurry to partner and start a family.' Ash gave Davrew and Richard a quick hug, 'I must be going, we're all meeting at the lakeside gardens in town.'

Not long after Davrew and Richard were alone in the kitchen again.

'Maya is more interested in travel, space travel.'

'So is Shea,' Richard added with a shake of his head. 'Maya is twenty-two and can handle the dangers that may wait, but our other grandchild is only ten.'

'Shea seems to be the driving force in starting up a barter business with our interplanetary cousins,' Davrew stretched and stood. 'It's time we made a move too my love.'

'That's what worries me, Shea is too young to see the dangers,' Richard replied as he too stood. 'Having Rakal and his guest Vashla here only reminds me how dangerous space can be.'

'They will find their own way, Richard. And really, have they ever been so young?' Davrew hugged Richard.

'They've always been more advanced than I can cope with, but I'm only a bloke from the bush. I never dreamed I would have such a big family. Much less so talented and diverse a family, it's kind of nice.'

'Nice,' Davrew agreed while they lingered in the embrace.

CHAPTER SEVEN

# Rakal's World - Earth

In the spring of 2005, with a three-year-old in tow, Tam and Rakal were in central Australia, at an archaeological dig, where ancient marsupial fossils were being uncovered.

Tam stood up and took the broad rim hat off his head to fan his face. The sweat made his blue t-shirt stick uncomfortably to his skin. His khaki shorts were covered in red dust.

'We've got a bit of a routine going now, haven't we love?' Tam smiled at Rakal.

'You mean you figuring out where you want to dig and me digging?' Rakal had cleared a large trench and the small team of archaeologists were busily scraping the soil with little spatulas and brushes. 'We've been on a few of these trips now, Tam my love. I told you before I can learn and adapt.'

'I know,' Tam grinned. 'Our Mata is such a curious child.'

'Into everything, that's for sure,' Rakal agreed.

'Kat is much more interested in working with young Melody Smart than looking after Mata,' Tam squatted back down beside Rakal and brushed away soil from a newly discovered fossil. 'She came with the other students to help, and Kat is besotted with her. It's just as well I asked Mata's cousins Raz and Rill to join us to supervise, Kat being an older brother can be protective but also blind to the child's wayward wanderings.'

'Raz is still doing medical studies?' Rakal scratched his nose. 'I lose track of all your family preoccupations and at twelve, I noticed his parent Sal is keen for the child to find a partner.'

'Raz and Rill still play with Mata like children here. The pressure of studies isn't so intense, and they can enjoy themselves.'

'How old is Rill?' Rakal looked towards the younger children playing a card game in the tent nearby.

'Eleven,' Tam glanced up at him, 'we'll have to be careful with this one, I'll block around it and pull it out in one piece if I can.'

Rakal handed Tam a plastic box. He watched as Tam carefully worked the soil around the fossil, preparing to excavate it. He nudged Tam's shoulder and pointed towards Kat and Melody who were working nearby. Tam nodded aware they were listening.

'Did you see Sal last night on TV Melody?' Kat asked.

'I did, he's your brother?' Melody was enthusiastically scrapping the ground clearing away soil from some small animal bones.

'My sibling yes, and all that talk about global gardens and climate change is interesting stuff. Sal is a botanist and gardening guru.'

'I liked that the show is about meeting people from all over the world and showing their gardens and Eco-friendly ways.' Melody replied, wiping sweat from her chin with her gloved hand.

'We're getting some good results here. This could be a bird's wing. I'll follow the formation along this ridge,' Kat pointed his brush at the dirt and smiled at the pretty brunette beside him.

'That could be a Pterosauradon, a winged reptile from the Megafauna period about 10,000 years ago,' Tam suggested. 'We may even be lucky enough to have the leg bone of a Phascolonus gigas here. They're the original wombats only much bigger than our present-day animals.'

Just then Raz and Rill came running up with Mata in tow.

'Can we go to the river with the local kids?'

Tam noticed a group of dark-skinned children giggling. Standing a short distance away, wearing little and swatting at flies, waiting eagerly.

'That sounds like a fine idea for us all. What do you think, Rakal, my love?'

'We have been working for several hours and it's hot,' Rakal fanned his face. 'I can go on if you wish.'

'Melody, how about it? A dip in the river I mean?' Kat stumbled over his words.

'It's nearly lunch break,' she smiled at Kat. 'I guess we could have a quick swim, eat, then come back to work. We've only got a few weeks to work in this area.

The Tribal Elders of this Aboriginal Community have been generous, but we do have a deadline.'

'We have a deadline too, Melody,' Tam stood and rotated his shoulders to ease tired muscles, 'we have a partnering ceremony, like a wedding, to go to next week. Tris is partnering Todd and we all have to be home for that.'

'Tris and Todd are close family?' Melody started brushing sand from her hands.

'Yes, Tris is my sibling's child, as both Bon and Imi are no longer with us, we all plan to support Tris on this special day.'

'Bon. Was that the one that?' Melody put her hand over her mouth.

'Yes,' Kat nodded. 'Bon was the one murdered by that insane surgeon. Imi died in childbirth years earlier.'

'Oh, I see,' Melody stood up accepting Kat's hand to help her rise.

'Perhaps you could come to our home down south to witness this too, it'll be a great party,' Kat still held her hand.

'Goodness, thank you, but I couldn't,' Melody blushed. 'I would love to cool off in the river now.'

'Come on then.'

Kat and Melody led the way. Tam pulled Rakal up and brushed the sand off his massive arms. 'We can keep digging later in the cooler part of the day.'

As they approached the river, they could hear and see the children running and jumping into the river from tree branches, giggling and screaming all the while.

'Mata is big for a three-year-old, but I can't forget that our white blood and susceptibility to infection is still there. We must be diligent,' Tam smiled as they walked hand in hand.

'I spoke to Vashla last night,' Rakal spoke slowly, whispering so that only Tam could hear.

'Is she planning another visit?'

'No, not to us, she is concerned about Zorn and the Xambans. She tells me she's been 'hearing' her war cry sung.'

'Hearing?'

'She has an intuition or sense of it being sung. This is something she taught Agai's father and she believes it is being sung there.'

'So, she will go to investigate?'

'Yes,' Rakal nodded. 'If she can hear the chant, so can Zorn.'

'Oh, and that could lead to trouble.'

'Yes.'

The river was a welcoming relief. The children splashed and tormented the adults who happily sprayed water at their attackers.

Tam laughed at Rakal, who was no longer the lumbering great monster he had been, the first time he'd visited their home world. Now he played with their child, lifting Mata, high above his head then dipping the youngster into the water. There was now a gentle protectiveness about Rakal, and a gracefulness in his movements, even though the gravity on this planet was foreign to him, he had adapted. Tam had changed too. They were Dual gender and the future was always uncertain.

## CHAPTER EIGHT

# Gardt's World - Ghaur

'Gardt, are you home?' a stout bald man knocked on the door. He walked outside into the yard. 'Hello, anyone home?'

Gardt walked out from behind the shed. 'Mr B, how good to see you.'

'There's been a few changes here recently, I see.'

'Sure have. You know the family moved out. After sixteen moon turns looking after the kids, getting meals, washing, and cleaning, it's a bit of a change to say the least.'

'The floodlights are down,' Mr B pointed to the lights sitting at the back of the shed.

'The authorities say I have no rights. When the family moved out, they cut the power and water. I can cope with the lanterns and I get water from the creek. It's turned out not to be as difficult a transition as I thought it might be,' Gardt smiled nodding towards a box beside the door. 'What's in the box?'

'Some things I hope you can use. I can purchase things for you without the authorities knowing. I'm happy to help my star script writer,' Mr B shook Gardt's hand.

'Come inside. I don't sleep out here now. I've cleaned up inside. It was empty anyway the family took every stick of furniture.' Gardt walked to the door, 'I've managed to find some old furniture. A neighbour threw out a table and I found a couple of chairs at the tip. The best find was an old lounge that was left out for street collection. With time well spent cleaning out the fireplace, I can keep warm, cook, and boil the kettle.

'Good, then the soap and shaving gear, shoes and old clothes will come in handy. I bought a blanket too. Will you need that?'

Gard nodded. 'That's great! Come in.'

'It's been hard for you since you've been left alone?'

'To be honest I didn't think being a non-citizen would mean so much. When I tried to buy furniture, clothes or even a newspaper, I was refused because it wasn't for the family. The vegetable garden is my sustenance now. I can keep up with the news by getting papers thrown out by my neighbours, but I miss simple things like meat and turning on a light. I have the old wood barbeque for baking but nothing much to cook.'

'I can help there, no one will question me buying a few extra portions with my food each week,' Mr B smiled and handed the box to Gardt. They entered an the almost empty house, sat on miss matched chairs beside a garden table, to relax by the fire. 'I see you have the old cot from the shed in here. Perhaps I can get a new bed for you?'

'No, Mr B that would be too much. I'm still on the watch list and I couldn't let you risk your own safety. I'll keep checking the tip, I'm sure something a little better will turn up, after all it's what I slept on since returning from space, it isn't so bad.' Gardt put another log on the fire and the crackle was a backdrop to their conversation.

'Anything you need I can help with,' Mr B added. 'The new play starts next week at the Grand theatre, it's already in rehearsal at the school theatre. I'm sure it will be a hit.'

'Thanks for letting me know. They can't stop me going to a public building. I'll come and see the rehearsals,' Gardt poured hot water from a pot into two mugs and the aroma of leaves steeping filled the room.

'Is something else bothering you?'

'A little,' Gardt nodded. 'It's just a crazy feeling I get,' Gardt set the mugs on the table, 'apart from missing the kids, and by the stars I even miss her ladyship and the husband. There's something else that's keeping me awake at night.'

'What's that?'

'A kind of yearning to be back in space. I wake up wishing I could feel the propulsion of huge engines vibrating the spacecraft and to see stars flitting by. I've always missed it but since the family have left the longing has grown stronger. After so long planet bound, you'd think I'd just forget it.'

'Can't help you there,' the portly man smiled. 'This is good Gardt,' Mr B had drained his mug. 'I best go now though, rehearsals start shortly.'

Gardt walked his guest to the door and watched his benefactor leave.

Many moons turns later, on a cold and wet afternoon. Gardt sat by the roaring fire on his reclaimed sofa, reading scavenged newspapers from the previous week. There was knock on the door. His heart skipped a beat. No one came here. No one ever spoke to him, other than Mr B. His palms became sweaty as he walked to the front door. His lantern illuminated a hand drawn picture, a mural he'd lovingly sketched, of the family he missed so much. The knocking louder and faster made him rush.

'I'm here, and on my way,' he opened the door to be greeted by a drenched and dishevelled pair, Ria and Bru. 'By the stars! Get in here you two, you look wet through.'

'Thanks,' Ria muttered. Bru just nodded and followed Ria through the door. They took off their raincoats and hung them on a coat hook, one of the few original pieces that remained from their time in the house.

'Come through to the fire,' Gardt held the lantern high and led them through. Pausing in the hall briefly for them to see the portrait he'd done of the family.

'That's well done,' Ria muttered.

'The house looks so different,' Bru commented.

Ria rubbed her hands together and held them over the fire. 'This is lovely and warm.'

'Okay, tell me what's wrong. Why you are here? And why your wet trough? Why didn't you drive here? Is it your father? Is it the children?'

Ria and Bru exchanged anxious glances.

'This is insane,' Ria said.

Bru sat on the old sofa leaning forward, clasping, and unclasping his hand. This nervous body language made Gardt very uneasy.

'Well?'

'We caught the train. We didn't want anyone to see we'd been here,' Bru began, 'as you know the station is three blocks away and we walked that in the rain.'

'I'm a non-citizen, but surely there's nothing wrong with you coming here. It is your former home.'

'It's not that,' Ria looked directly at Gardt. 'You know how my father, has always been the dominant figure in our lives, and the children's?'

'Of course, Dreece is the head of the family and the children's grandfather,' Gardt replied. 'Please, just tell me what's going on!'

'It's Joss and Sam. You know Joss has always been determined to be one of the first colonists to the new worlds. Well, he and Sam took the last ship, without our permission. The first ship should be there and have arrived at the new planet,' Bru explained. 'There's been no communication with the ships since they got past our orbiting space station.'

'They are just children, Gardt! Joss is only nineteen, and Sam seventeen. They are just babies, my babies,' Ria began to sob. Bru put a comforting arm around her shoulder.

'We went to the ILD, you know the Immigration Launch Department,' Bru continued.

'I know, I worked there,' Gardt couldn't help saying.

'We've been there every day for the last week. They let us into a control room viewing deck. We see dials and machines but hear nothing,' Bru clasped Ria's hand tightly.

'Father keeps telling us that it's Okay, we'll hear something soon,' Ria whispered. 'Many other parents and relatives go too. The whole group of colonist ships are full of young, eager people.'

'Dreece won't allow any bad publicity and the people from the I.S.C.C., you know Interplanetary Space Colonisation Corp, are everywhere at the ILD,' Bru continued. 'Many other parents and relatives of the colonists have become concerned.'

'The newspapers say the I.S.C.C. is financially backing the whole thing, in an extravagant way. This project is to bring new colonists to worlds that will allow trade and offer a great future for those who go. I can hardly believe these stories, but I can understand kids like Joss and Sam thinking it would be an adventure,' Gardt stood at the fire looking at his guests. 'I've not been to the ILD in years. I'm not allowed. They didn't believe anything I told them when I returned, they disgraced me and called me a liar. So, what do you want me to do?'

'Well,' Ria began, 'some of the people who've been going every day have whole families aboard, several generations depending on their qualifications and status.'

'They were to go ahead and prepare for the next set of colony ships,' Bru continued.

Gardt listened with growing trepidation. 'Have there been any reports back to the ILD headquarters?'

'Not that we know of,' Ria whined. 'Please go and see what you can find out. You might remember some security bypass or way into the computers. They're simply not telling us anything.'

Gardt thought for a moment. He sensed that Ria and Bru had been lied to. He didn't know how he could live if he didn't try to help.

'They won't let me in as Gardt Ness, but,' he paused and turned back to the fire, 'they might allow the famous play writer Mr G G Ridgeway in. It's been years since I returned from space, I don't look the same. Are you both warm and dry now?'

'Yes, but we came by train,' Ria wailed.

'You have your communicator?' Gardt asked.

'Of course,' Bru added. 'We'll call a commuter car and get in the same way many of the other families are doing.'

Gardt looked at his former wife and second husband then asked the question that had been burning his lips. 'You've never once asked me, either of you, what happened out there. Give me one good reason why I should help you now?'

Ria stood up and took two steps towards him. 'You love those boys, Gardt, as we do. Aren't they, reason enough?'

Gardt nodded. 'We'll go then.'

CHAPTER NINE

# Gardt's World - Ghaur

'I can't believe I'm here,' Gardt whispered as the commuter sped away.

'I'm glad it's stopped raining,' Ria patted down her hair and walked briskly beside Bru up to the guard. Gardt walked behind them. His is heart pounding wildly as they went through the security check. The meaty guard turned his steel eyes towards him.

'This is Mr Ridgeway, he's a friend of the family,' Ria explained. 'He's also the guy who wrote those plays, you know, those space action adventures.'

'Yes, I know. I went to one my niece was in. It was good too. You can go in, but go straight to Com Station One, do not deviate,' the guard pointed to the path.

'We know the way Guard. We've been here every day this week,' Ria snapped.

'Don't fret Mrs, I'm sure it's just a communications glitch, everything will be fine,' the guard replied.

'I hope you're right,' Ria nodded and marched along the path.

To the average person entering this base, they would only be aware of a series of building scattered along a winding dimly lit road. It was early evening and the place had an eerie feel.

'Is it as you remembered?' Bru asked fidgeting with his collar.

'Not really,' he replied. 'In each of these buildings I was trained in different skills. I made friends and built my life and dreams around one objective. Getting into space.' They continued along the path. 'The Guard will call ahead to make sure I'm clear to go in.'

'Probably, it's usual procedure,' Ria agreed.

'Don't worry Gardt, even the old man has no objections to you coming here tonight,' Bru added.

'Why?' Gardt became uneasy.

'Seems he's in the dark about a lot that's been going on too,' Bru explained.

The side entrance to the building had one down light over a khaki painted door. 'They've asked us not to use the front entrance. They don't want to arouse the interest of the local press.'

Gardt didn't care about the press, or anything else, he was walking through time into an exciting past. The guard at the entrance handed them each a tag that served as a pass. It was plastic with their names hastily printed in bold black type. He read his badge and clipped it on his jacket, 'G G Ridgeway, Playwright.' Gardt smothered a smile, this was a serious situation.

They proceeded into a large room beyond the small entrance. A small crowd of people were turned to a large glass window which ran that full length of the room, watching what was happening on the other side of the

glass patrician. There were no seats and as it was a viewing post. Ria walked ahead through the milling people,
with Bru and Gardt following. Ria met and hugged a
small wiry looking woman of mature years. She was
smartly dressed in designer clothes. Her grace and ele-
gance had not diminished with age.

'There seems to be something happening dear,' Ria's
mother nodded towards the window.

'Thanks for waiting and taking care of the children,'
Ria gazed over to Bru and Gardt. 'We managed to bring
some help.'

'Good I hope you can make some sense of it all.
Now my feet are killing me, I'll go home.'

'Can we go with Grandma mum, it's dead boring
here,' the eldest of the children begged.

'Mum, would you?'

'Of course, dear, I'll take them with me.'

'Thanks mother that would be great,' Ria hugged
each of the children then watched as they filed out behind their grandmother.

'Your mother looks well, being divorced must suit
her,' Gardt couldn't help but comment. 'The children
have grown so much. I don't think they recognised me.'

'Well, it has been a while and with all this going on,'
Ria shook her head and pointed at the window, 'this is as
far as they'll let us go.'

'It takes a short while for your eyes to adjust to the
lights,' Bru pointed to the view screen, 'there are Control
Room Staff behind that window.'

Gardt had already begun to make out shapes behind
the view screen wall. The whole room was filled with
faces milling close to the window to see the array of

people and control panels on the other side. Most were watching for some change in the screen's opposite with space view to change. There were several other screens that were blank. Gardt recognised that the communications array seemed oddly inactive. With ten spaceships, having departed with colonists and support vehicles, this should be the hub of the project.

'It's too quiet,' Gardt pointed out, 'there should be more activity.'

'There is something happening,' Ria cut in excitedly, 'those centre terminals over there weren't manned yesterday.'

'And that middle image has dots on it,' Bru added, 'so we'll have to be told something soon.'

'The dots are in a V formation. Can you see?' the pitch of Gardt's voice had risen. 'There are ten yellow dots and one large red one at the peak.'

'You don't like the look of this?' Ria stammered seeing his reaction.

'Surely not that much had changed since I worked for the ILD,' Gardt shook his head. 'Where's your father?'

'He's over there,' Ria pointed to the side of the control room, 'he's coming out.'

'Those dots are in local space, they haven't gone anywhere,' Gardt told Ria and Bru.

'That's impossible, father said they'd left local space three days ago,' Ria countered.

'They're having a meeting. Your father and the two heavies in suits, a shorter guy in a white coat, and that tall guy in the indigo blue suit,' Gardt watched as the group appeared to be in deep discussion. 'Can they see us through here?'

'No, this is a one-way view. They have a blank wall so as not to distract from their work.'

'Good,' Gardt ground his teeth.

The grumbling in the room ceased for a short time while they all watched the discussion.

'Hey, mister.' A short round-faced man rounded on Bru. 'What's happening?'

'Beats me buddy, I know as much as you do.'

'What about you?' the short man turned to face Gardt. He only reached Gardt's his chest.

'Nothing, same as you,' Gardt replied surprised at the other man's affront. 'I'm glad Ria, that people here don't know who I am.'

The hubbub in the room subsided as all eyes turned to the Control room. The suits and Ria's father had finished their discussion. Suddenly, the atmosphere changed, the room became a hive of activity with people rushing to workstations.

'Dreece is coming out now,' Bru dragged them towards the door. The crowd around them turned towards the opening too.

'Who are those two goons with him?' Gardt was struggling with Ria and Bru to get closer through the milling crowd.

'I.S.C.C. men,' Bru answered.

'The money men,' Gardt replied, 'they look intimidating. Big men in smart suits with bulging muscles.'

'They are,' Ria agreed. 'I don't like them much.'

'Nor do I,' Gardt crossed his arms across his chest and stood silently watching.

Dreece saw Ria and Bru he started towards them. The heavies pushed him through the other spectators to their side. Gardt realised his former father-in-law looked uncomfortable.

'Now we'll find out what's happening! That's the messenger boy,' a voice from the crowd yelled.

'Ladies and Gentlemen, may I have your attention?' The room fell silent. Dreece held his arms up and spoke clearly with all the authority his position afforded. 'There have been some promising developments in the last two hours. We have located our complete fleet. The condition of our proud colonists is yet to be ascertained. We'll call you immediately any further developments occur. Right now, however, we ask that you leave by the exit on your left. The Guard will take your names and contact details as you leave.'

'Hold on,' someone behind Gardt yelled, 'we've been waiting here all day. Many of us have been here every day for the last week. Now something is happening, you want us to leave?'

'We can make no further statements until more information is gathered. Thank you for your attendance.' The muscle man announced and pointed towards the door. With military precision, the crowd was ushered out with names being taken as they departed.

'Well, I haven't been much help,' Gardt sighed as he joined Ria and Bru in the queue.

'Name and contact number?' The Soldier at the door demanded with pen poised over notepad.

'Ness, 763042' he replied absently.

'Ness', the guard queried, 'that's not what your badge says'.

'Of course, not Sergeant, Ridgeway is my pen name, I apologise for any confusion. I'm here with Ria and Bru Ryland at their request. It will be their contact number you need, as they are the immediate relatives involved.' He pushed Ria forward and tried to side swipe any further questions by moving to the exit. The door was immediately blocked by another soldier.

'I don't think we have all the details we need from you, Sir.'

They watched everyone else leave and were the only ones remaining in the room, other than, the two burly soldiers.

'My father, Commander Dreece Corma, will sort this out,' Ria looked around but couldn't see her father. 'This is a simple misunderstanding. Mr Ridgeway, the Playwright, is our guest. I'm sure you've heard of his plays mostly being performed in schools?'

'Yes, yes, my daughter performed in one. Commander Dreece Corma you say is your father?'

'Of course,' Ria replied.

The clipboard holding soldier sent his companion into the control room. Shortly after Dreece and two suited big men came into the observation room.

'Ness,' Dreece hissed with unmistakable antagonism, 'what the blazes are you doing here?'

'Father,' Ria interrupted, 'he's here because I, or, should I say, we, Bru and I, asked him to come.'

'He's grounded. He's scum. Not fit, or even permitted, to step inside these gates. Now, if you can get your ugly face out of here, we might be able to rescue our people.'

'Rescue,' Ria squealed.

'Now, Commander, let's not rush into any hasty expulsions here,' the huge dark suited man beside Dreece stepped in. His deep sharp tone held an unmistakable authority. He looked as crisp and sharp and his well-tailored suit. 'After all, this person could assist us in this matter.'

The second business suit nodded agreement while his thin lips and bulbous nose turned towards Gardt. His scrutiny was unnerving.

'You are Gardt Ness, former ambassador and soldier Gardt Ness, of the failed Milliner Mission, eighteen moon turns ago?'

'Yes,' Gardt returned the cool gaze.

'Good,' smoothly replied, 'we have need of your services.'

CHAPTER TEN

# Gardt's World - Ghaur

In the debriefing room star maps and pictures of space-ships surrounded them as they were seated.

The I.S.C.C. men spoke, in an intense huddle for a few minutes with the Commander.

'Ness is about to go on a little trip,' Commander Dreece announced when they ended the discussion. 'Ria and Bru, you can go now, there's no need to wait around.'

'No father,' Ria stood up. 'Joss and Sam are out there, believing they are going on some great adventure to be colonists on some wonderful planet. We've heard nothing for days. Now something is happening, and you want Gardt to be involved, not us? We have the right as parents, to at least know what's going on.'

Bru hit his fist on the table, 'we've been waiting for days and heard nothing. If Gardt is going somewhere, we should go along for the ride to find out where our boys are and be there when they return.'

The indigo suit I.S.C.C. man looked them over. 'So long as our organisation is not liable for your safety, I see no reason why we should delay any longer. The journey could be dangerous. Are you prepared to accept this?'

'In other words,' Gardt grunted, 'if the I.S.C.C. don't have to fork out any money, it's worth the risk.'

'Exactly! We've wasted too much time discussing what needs to be done, now, it's time for action,' the indigo suit concluded and ushered them through the door.

'Let's go then,' Bru held Ria's hand and followed Gardt.

'What are we letting ourselves in for?' she whispered.

They were scrubbed as clean as the day they were born during the decontamination process. They were poked and prodded, hooked up to heart monitor machines as they sweated through round after round of fitness testing. Finally, dressed in starch white overalls, they shuffled down a long corridor and into a huge elevator.

'Where're we going?' Ria said puffing, trying to keep up with their escort's long strides.

'Beats me,' Gardt was grinning, 'I believe its space.'

'You're excited!' Bru shook his head in disbelief.

'I guess that means I'm not grounded.'

Dreece fixed him with a cold glare. 'This way,' he turned glancing through a Spaceport window and led the group into a room with a huge screen on one wall. 'I shall be in command of this operation. Ria and Bru are officially designated civilian observers, and you, Gardt Ness, will assist in the successful outcome of this mission.'

'How, Commander, do you expect me to do that?'

'Please sit down, all of you. I am about to show you a transmission we received a few hours ago.'

Everyone turned to face the screen as it lit up. 'Transmission replay' an automated voice seeped into the room.

An impressive figure filled the screen. Large sparkling black jewel eyes peered out from the screen, darting from one person to another in her audience. High cheek bones on a long light skinned face crowned by a huge mass of black hair that cascaded from a solid gold hair band. Below the bare shoulders, a mass of golden chains with inlaid black jewels, leading to a plunging black top that barely secured large breasts. Her powerful arms were as lavishly adorned with golden arm bands, and her hands clustered in rings. Her eyes were as hard as the stones in her jewellery. Gardt held his breath and listened to her deep resonant voice as it filled every corner of the chamber.

'I am Vashla, born of Marela and Antalasa. I bring with me ships and people within them. They are mine to do with as I please. They came into my territory without my permission. They came without weapons to fight me. They are weak, as weak as you are. I should wipe them away now. See how weak they are!' The image immediately changed to a scruffy looking youth with wild hair and eyes to match. They watched him on the control deck of one of the colony ships. They could see the fear in the eyes of those around him. He grabbed the nearest person, a young ensign, and threw him easily to the floor. He fired at the ensign who with an agonising scream, died before their eyes.

'You see, weak ones from this worthless little planet, I have them for me.'

'Why don't they fight back?' Bru shouted, 'there's only one of him and many of them.'

'They can't,' Gardt explained, 'she has pinned them, paralysed them to the spot.'

'Quiet everyone, listen to the rest of the transmission,' Dreece ordered.

She held her head high puffing her chest out gloating at the obvious discomfort she could see in those watching. 'I may allow them to go free,' she leaned forward in a conciliatory manner. 'I may even allow them to go to Xamba, if you still wish them to go to their original destination, and their death.'

'What can you do to prevent this?' She smiled and touched the chain on her chest. 'If you give me what I want, I may release them to you.'

'What do I want? That is, who do I want?' Her eyes scanned the room. She was silent for an agonisingly long moment, all eyes riveted to the magnetic dark eyes.

'I want my Ness, your hero, Ness. I hear the Victory chant and I know my Ness sings it. My Ness must have shown you how to win, and to sing the Victory song when you do,' she paused and smashed her fist on the bench. 'I want my Ness, now!'

The screen went blank.

'This was the first of three similar demanding communications,' Dreece announced. 'The Vashla creature has manoeuvred the fleet into a V formation behind her own craft, holding them there.

'Have her threats become more violent?' Gardt barely whispered.

'Yes,' Dreece admitted.

'Gee thanks Dreece. I finally get a chance to get off this planet into space and find out immediately it's my final journey. You are so kind.'

'What threat?' Ria turned to face her father.

Gardt regarded his former wife. Her face was now flushed with anger. 'My guess Ria,' he decided to be honest, 'is that Vashla said she could destroy all the ships in one hit.'

'That's impossible!' Dreece spat.

'I'm sorry to break the bad news to you commander, she could do it,' Gardt couldn't help but enjoy his former father-in-law's predicament.

'Father,' Ria continued with a glare in Gardt's direction, 'I don't understand why we would be heading out into space to meet this person. Surely, negotiation from a safe position is the best option.'

'Safe,' Gardt grunted, 'that's rich. Do you really think anyone on this planet is safe with that sadistic, murdering marauder hovering overhead?'

'I can't believe this!' Bru erupted. 'What-ever-she-is could be a threat to the whole planet, not to mention our colony fleet. What's going on?'

'We have had several transmissions from the woman with nothing more that verbal threats,' Dreece tried to sound convincing.

'I can tell you all that Vashla is more than capable of killing every living thing on our planet. I've seen her do it. She's a pirate, murderer, and destroyer of worlds. She had me captive with her for nearly over two moon turns before she inexplicably returned me here.'

'We have no evidence...' Dreece started, Gardt interrupted.

'You didn't listen to me when I told you the dangers of space travel. 'No one listened. Vashla is someone I really don't wish to meet again. I can tell you one thing,' he paused to be sure they were really understood, 'she doesn't kill unless she's really angry.'

'She looks pretty upset to me,' Ria said.

'Commander,' Gardt leaned forward and glared, 'Commander, Dreece, Father. What's the plan? Are you hoping I will be a sacrificial offering and she'll let ten spaceships with everybody aboard go, just like that?'

Bru was standing beside Ria, watching the older man.

'That was the general idea,' the Commander replied.

Gardt started to laugh, softly at first, then stronger and longer until tears welled up in his eyes.

'I am off planet now. Do you feel the engines and the movement?'

'This is a runabout, we plan to meet the fleet and dock, transporting passengers, then leave,' the indigo suit stated.

'Funny thing is, I really don't mind. I was starting to feel stuck to the ground. Being in space is where I want to be,' Gardt said as he started towards the door. 'This condemned man is going to eat a hearty meal. I believe the Galley is this way.'

'You're going to eat!' Ria shook her head.

'Yep,' Gardt reached the door and put a hand up to the entry light that flickered as the door opened.

'We should all take some refreshments. It will be about an hour before we make the rendezvous point. It could be the last good meal we have for a while,' Dreece suggested. Then walked towards the door that had shut behind Gardt.

'I've lost my appetite,' Ria was shaking her head again but followed.

'One other thing bothers me, Father,' Bru said while taking Ria by the hand and leading her to the Galley. 'What did this Vashla mean when she said we were sending the Colonists to Xamba and death?'

'There is no need to listen to that creatures' ravings, the I.S.C.C. know exactly what they are doing,' Dreece replied.

Gardt heard that comment as they entered.

'Hmph, Commander Dreece,' Gardt spat, greeting his companions as he loaded his tray with food. 'That could be the main problem. Had you thought of that? They are the money men, aren't they?

## CHAPTER ELEVEN

# Above Gardt's World Ghaur

They ate then returned to the shuttle craft's main control room. They watched as the view before them displayed what had been dots on a console now appeared as the spaceships with a huge and foreboding craft at the apex of the V formation.

'It's a bit different close up, isn't it?' Gardt pointed out.

The view screen lit up.

'My Ness, you are here!' Vashla exclaimed in delight.

'We did not initiate communications,' Dreece yelled as he ran to the controls to see what had happened.

'Vashla has been known to kill from a distance. What makes you think she can't see we are here and contact us?' Gardt shrugged at the older man. He stepped up to the control panel.

'I see you haven't forgotten me Vashla.'

'No,' the woman glowed as she licked her lips provocatively.

'She seems to remember you very well,' Ria remarked.

Gardt laughed. 'You're not going to tell me you're jealous, are you Ria?'

'Don't be ridiculous,' Bru countered hotly.

'My, my, we do still bristle, don't we Bru?' Gardt continued the banter.

'Agai, get them, bring them here,' Vashla commanded. In an instant a brilliant white light flashed in front of the control room and before them stood a muscle-bound youth carrying a large weapon, he pointed it at them menace.

'Move,' the youth demanded.

The four reluctantly stood to go with their host.

'I will return with the shuttle when required,' the indigo suit nodded. Gladly allowing the departure of Commander Dreece, his daughter and son-in-law, and Gardt. He stood poised at the control to make a quick return trip to Ghaur.

A white light enveloped the small group.

CHAPTER TWELVE

# Above Gardt's World Ghaur

Gardt didn't dare to breathe as the white light engulfed them. The rest of the shuttle crew remained behind. Only he, Ria, Bru and Dreece reappeared on another spaceship deck. They were now with her.

'My Ness,' she hissed possessively while stepping closer to her prize.

'Agai, you may take these and ask what you will of their culture, I know it intrigues you.'

'Where?' The youth asked.

Vashla turned and gave the youth an encouraging smile. 'Where you wish,' she nodded towards the other spaceships on the view screen before them, 'with the others to play with. I will be some time.' She moved her hand dismissively.

Agai pointed the gun at the trio and summoned them to leave through the door. 'You don't want me to stay?'

'No,' was the swift and chill reply.

Vashla walked to Gardt and began circling him. He felt like shark bait.

'You lied to me, my Ness,' she began slowly, softly.

'How,' Gardt replied swallowing the lump in his throat.

'You said you would be a hero. You said you would return to your woman. You said your people would stay on your home world and not come again into my SPACE!' Her voice grew louder with each word. It was almost hypnotic. Gardt knew the danger, he'd been there before.

'You're right Vashla, I did lie,' he stared bravely back into her charcoal black eyes. He noticed she had a fuller figure, but no other signs of ageing. Indeed, the thick mass of hair seemed darker than he remembered.

She wrapped her right arm around his waist, while tracing the fingers of her free hand over his chest. He tensed, fearing what was to come. Slowly Vashla worked her way over every part of his body, inspecting every muscle, his teeth, and ears, then hair she tugged and ruffled. He stood as still as possible while his heartbeat faster.

'You remember what I like, my Ness?'

He felt her penetrating eyes delve deep into his being. With deceptive speed and strength, she pulled him forward by the hair and began to tear his clothes off his torso. The fabric tore like tissue paper and his body was now exposed. Held in a kneeling position, Gardt could only grimace as her razor-sharp nails began drawing lines in his back. She laughed and slashed his face. Quickly she was on top of him stripping what fabric remained from his body. He turned and struck her with a powerful blow, temporarily stopping her assault. She retaliated with venom. He soon felt blood flowing from his mouth as well as the other parts of his body. The final indignity came as she rubbed his maleness then held her-self above him. He was barely conscious and yet still aware of her sexual arousal. The pain would not stop until she had her gratification.

'Vashla, no, I can't.'

She chortled. 'Oh, yes you can, my Ness.'

In delirious agony, he writhed while she continued until the climax. Gardt lay trembling and spent beside his exultant conqueror. He didn't move for fear of what would come next.

She lay beside him, looking him over carefully.

'You are not the same my Ness, but I think I like the way you are.'

'I'd never have guessed,' he uttered before surrendering to an exhausted unconsciousness.

## CHAPTER THIRTEEN

# Above Gardt's World Ghaur

Agai had led the trio of Ria, Bru and Dreece into the adjacent control room. The youth was pacing about, waving the gun erratically and frowning.

'Are you going to ask us questions lad?' Dreece snarled at his captor.

'No,' The youth shouted. 'I should be with Vashla, you, stay still. Quiet.'

'What is he doing now?' Ria whispered to Bru.

'I've no idea. He seems to be deciding if he should do something with the controls on the panel there.'

They watched standing silently as requested while the youth walked to towards the array of switches.

'I should help interrogate this Ness person,' he yelled again.

Then he moved again waving the gun in their direction before turning to flip some switches. The view screen filled with the image of Vashla abusing her Ness.

'No sound so she can't hear,' the youth explained watching as though this were an everyday occurrence.

'Oh, my God,' Ria stood stunned and held her hand over her mouth to stop from screaming.

'Silence,' the youth commanded.

Dreece stood with his fists clenched and an expression of sheer disgust. Bru was gagging and trying not to look. He stood in front of Ria and took her in his arms. The youth looked quizzically at them.

'Silence,' he demanded again. 'Vashla has interrogated before, she likes men.'

'We can tell,' Bru snorted.

'This one is different,' the lad grunted.

'I knew Gardt Ness was disgusting, allowing this creature to use him,' Dreece sneered.

'Oh, for the love of the stars Dreece,' Bru retorted, 'a blind man can see she just raped him. He certainly hasn't allowed her to do anything. He did punch her.'

'This is so bad. Father, Bru, have you forgotten that we are here to save the children and the colonists?' Ria asked tearfully.

The view screen image showed Gardt slip into unconsciousness. Vashla then lifted him like a rag doll and paced him on a table in a chamber nearby.

'Restoration chamber,' Agai stated unemotionally.

They all watched as Vashla set dials and gauges, as though she was preparing to cook a meal. With that the youth flipped off the switch.

'Move,' he yelled getting them all into the next room where comfortable chairs grouped around small tables were found.

'Sit.'

'Ria, sit here,' Bru suggested holding her hand.

Dreece was seething but sat in the chair opposite.

Meanwhile Agai slung the gun over his arms and opened a panel in the wall of the room. He flipped a control panel out and pressed a button, the machine dispensed a large bowl of stew that smelled very appetising. He took a seat, put the gun on the table pointed in their direction, and began to eat with gusto.

CHAPTER FOURTEEN

# Above Gardt's World Ghaur

In a nearby room, Vashla was humming happily to herself while washing. She carefully chose a gown. It had to be dramatic and alluring. She dressed and admired her reflection, her black eyes shone like jewels. That's enough of Ness for a time. Now, it's time to deal with the others. She swept out of the room and moved purposefully to the main control room.

A short while later Gardt woke and stretched. He got up off the bed.

'Didn't want to change me hey, but, you do, Vashla,' he said staring at his reflection, 'don't know why you don't just bloody well leave me dead.'

'No fun in that,' Vashla's voice erupted from the walls. 'Come to the Control room when you are dressed,' she demanded.

Gardt grunted and mimicked 'no fun in that.' Then he took his time, washing thoroughly. He put on the clothes Vashla had left out for him. His own were gone.

Smart, comfortable, practical in that it covered him completely. There was no sign of the marks, or scars from his captor's talon-like nails. The injuries were all healed. He knew where to go. This was the ship she'd held him prisoner on many years earlier. Even though he was curious to find out the fate of the Colonists fleet, he savoured the solitude and silence.

'I've been too long on my own,' he muttered while running his hand through his hair and inspecting the emerald green body suit with padding on the chest. 'Time to go, I guess I'll be back,' he spoke to his reflection.

'Ah, my Ness,' Vashla welcomed him with a possessive kiss. 'As you can see, I've rearranged the little fleet, and released the Pinners as you suggested.'

The view screen showed the colonist ships were now sitting in a group with their largest ship in the centre.

'I didn't say a thing,' Gardt retorted pulling away from her grasp and moving a short distance away. He noticed the youth Agai was still brandishing a weapon menacingly.

'Ah, but I hear the talk in your head, I hear a great deal,' Vashla paused to smile wickedly at her captives. 'I have learnt a lot about these people the same way.'

'So, that's how you knew when I woke up.'

'Yes, it's something new I've been working on. An acquired skill you would call it.'

'Same as, I acquired the skill to navigate for you on this ship, so many years ago, I've not forgotten. I was a skilled pilot and best student at the academy. Having to survive is a great incentive to learn.'

'What do you mean Pinners? Are our boys safe?' Ria couldn't hold back.

'They can move, but they are still trapped,' Gardt explained, 'it leaves you fairly immobilised for some hours after being released. They won't be moving much but they will be fine.'

'Temporarily pinned for only one cycle of your planet's rotation, and they will stay in my control until I find out why you were sending them to their death.'

'What do you mean?' Dreece shouted, 'the people on those ships were highly trained and skilled colonists, ready to explore and inhabit our new planet.'

Vashla was swift to slap Dreece across the face, sending him helplessly flying across the room.

'Father,' Ria squealed and ran to his side.

'Why bother with them Mamma,' Agai spat, 'they are stupid enough to send these creatures to the Xambans to die working in their mines.'

'I do not think Agai, that they are aware of their destiny,' Vashla moved towards the youth and relieved him of the weapon.

'You felt that in my mind; my suspicions, didn't you?' Gardt swallowed hard, feeling uneasy and vulnerable.

'Certainly,' Vashla replied.

'How old are you boy?' Ria asked.

'Never mind that Ria,' Bru was helping Dreece sit comfortably at the side of the room.

'Now you can destroy our fleet quickly, they are sitting ducks,' Dreece groaned. 'All our work, all our planning and training, they are sitting in a circle ready to be picked off.'

Gardt rushed to the control panel and started working the controls. Agai moved to pull him away but Vashla stopped him.

'There are other ships coming this way,' Gardt pointed. 'Who are they Vashla?' His fingers sped over the controls. 'I've rearranged the colonist's fleet into a formation for protection.'

They watched the view screen as a set of distant lights appeared to be getting nearer.

'That's the Xambans of course,' Vashla said. 'They are coming for their slaves. They have a good bargain with the ones on your world called I.S.C.C.'

'Slaves,' Dreece exploded. 'You must be insane woman, the I.S.C.C. funds the colonisation, and they want it to be a success.'

'Silence,' Agai shouted moving towards the older man. 'Sit! Vashla knows her space, and the Xambans. You know nothing,' Agai sneered.

'Agai, move back, I'll deal with this.' Vashla calmly walked over to the controls, fiercely struck Gardt twice across the face. He swayed but held onto the panel, unblinking he wiped away a small drop of blood trickling from the corner of his mouth.

'What bargain? These people are private citizens, highly trained and paying for their journey to settle a new colony on a new planet. Is it all a lie?' Gardt looked Vashla in the eye, standing his ground.

'What about our boys,' Ria wailed.

Bru stood up beside his wife, drawing her close. 'This is unbelievable.'

'The planet is real, the probes and preparations have all been carried out,' Dreece continued to defend his colleagues. 'The colony is vital to our survival. How can there be a bargain with these Xambans? The I.S.C.C. came in after the initial plans were made to help finance the mission.'

'They have their own ships?' Gardt queried.

'Yes,' Dreece replied, 'they had to oversee the operation'.

'By the stars,' Bru exploded, 'there are hundreds of people on those ships, many hundreds more training to go on the next set of colony ships. You are expecting us to believe that our authorities have been negotiating with their lives?'

'How could they possibly get away with it?' Ria finished Bru's query.

'Getting away would be the least of their problems, if your people walked into the trap,' Vashla retorted. 'I tell you these people were sold, and the ones who sold them gained free passage to the Newton sector.'

'Sold,' Dreece sneered, 'you don't know anything.'

'Now look at that.' Gardt pointed at the image on the smaller screen to the left of the main view panel. 'These are the colony ships, and there are a group of other vehicles coming here from deep space.'

'The Xambans,' Vashla nodded.

'And here,' Gardt continued, 'from our world, there is another craft taking off. My guess is the I.S.C.C. want to seal the deal.'

'There is no deal,' Dreece yelled.

Vashla pushed the older man again, leaving him slouched against the wall. Ria and Bru went to help him.

'There is no evidence that any of this is real,' Dreece grunted as he rose painfully to his feet. 'The I.S.C.C. have simply financed the operation and ensured the whole program runs smoothly.'

Gardt looked over at the older man feeling some sympathy for his situation. 'You really don't get it Dreece, you are as much a pawn in this game as the colonists on those ships are. They are all being led to their death!'

'The ship from the planet is not coming this way,' Agai brought their attention back to the screens.

'They will not get away,' Vashla added, 'but, they are too far away to pin.'

'We need to set a trap ourselves,' Gardt said as he turned again to the control panel.

'How?' Agai was being drawn into events.

'You will see. We can move the colony ships.'

'He is so clever, my Ness. You people are so foolish, not to realise his potential,' Vashla stood right beside Gardt, flashing him a flirtatious smile, and giving him a quick pat on the butt. 'Do let me have fun with them when you've got them close enough to play with.' She laughed wickedly.

The whole circular formation of colony ships moved like a cartwheel through space towards the fleeing I.S.C.C. ship. The fleet were slower than their prey, however, with Gardt expertly handling the controls, he manoeuvred the spaceships into position. Each colony ship sent a beam at the target ship on his command. Slowly the forward momentum of the I.S.C.C. craft dwindled until it eventually came to a halt.

'They are trying to pull against it,' Agai was now engrossed in events. 'Will it work?'

'Watch,' Gardt replied. 'As surely as the stars radiate heat, they will come to us.'

The I.S.C.C. craft was now slowly being dragged towards the fleet and Vashla's ship had now became centre of the circle, waiting for the craft to be drawn further into its trap.

'You will learn much from my Ness, Agai,' Vashla smiled warmly at the youth. 'I will go and play now and...' she turned towards Dreece. 'I will get your evidence.'

'They are in position now, Vashla,' Gardt advised.

Vashla kissed Gardt passionately. 'You are a little slower my Ness, but you've still got it.' She laughed and took two paces and winked as a glowing light surrounded her. Vashla had gone.

'You are helping her,' Dreece spat out.

'I'm helping our colonists. I don't expect you to understand or condone my actions. I gave up on hoping you would believe and support me a long time ago.'

'How did you know how to do that?' Bru asked with his arm wrapped around Ria.

'I was well trained, wasn't I Dreece?' Gardt offered. 'Besides, I've been living Planet-bound too long, and now I'm back in space where I should be, it's all still there inside me.'

'She loves you, Gardt,' Ria suggested, 'and, by the stars, I do believe this boy Agai is your son.'

'So, it would seem,' Gardt agreed while looking over the gangly youth brandishing a gun. The boy said nothing. 'Agai, do you have any friends?'

The boy shrugged.

'Friends, what are friends?'

'People you can talk to and be with, just to be yourself with,' Gardt replied

'Friends,' Agai shook his head, 'not here, on a distant world, we have visited.'

'Well, Agai, I hope we can be friends, but to be honest, I was thinking someone a little closer to your own age.'

'Why?'

'Friends are special because you can talk to them. Tell them things about yourself. They tell you things about their lives. Mostly Agai, they help you not to feel that hollow empty feeling you get inside when you're on your own too much.'

'Friends,' the youth repeated. 'Maybe Kat, on the planet Earth, when we were visiting Rakal. He's a relative of Mamma's.'

Gardt stepped towards the boy and put a hand on his shoulder. He took the gun the boy had picked up and put it on the table. Then he held out his hand to the youth, taking the boys hand and gripping it tightly.

'This is a custom we have, a greeting,' Gardt explained. 'Friends?'

Agai nodded as they shook hands.

'Now, let's go to the colony ships and let them know what's happening. We may even find some young friends for you there.'

They took two steps away from the controls and disappeared into a shimmering white light. Ria, Bru and Dreece were left alone in the control room.

CHAPTER FIFTEEN

# Above Gardt's World Ghaur

'We've been sitting here ages Bru,' Ria sighed.

'I think we should look around, stretch our legs,' Bru nodded towards the door.

'I'll stay here. I'll see if I can do something to release the colony ships. There has to be a way on this control panel.'

'Father,' Ria was following Bru to the door, 'you've been looking at that panel since they left. Don't you think you should just admit you don't know how to do anything and come for a walk?'

Dreece glared at his daughter, Ria shrugged and followed Bru out of the control room.

'We daren't go too far or we'll never make our way back,' Bru muttered.

'This looks like sleeping pods,' Ria ran her fingers across the polished surface of the wall. They investigated the next few rooms before finding the room they'd eaten in earlier.

'The storage room didn't offer anything we could use as a weapon,' Bru sighed.

'We may as well go back to father,' Ria squeezed Bru's hand.

They walked back into the control room to see Dreece slumped in a chair beside the control panel.

'No luck then,' Bru remarked.

'I can see where the colonist's ships are, and the huge Xambans ships. They're three times the size of any of our vehicles. Their weaponry could be equally large.' He thumped the panel, 'I can't even get the control panel to perform basic scan functions. It seems like I'm locked out.'

'So, what can we do now?' Ria asked.

'Wait,' Dreece grunted.

'We can get a drink and something to eat,' Ria added.

'Just as well Agai showed us how to use that food machine,' Bru was beside Ria.

They didn't wait long before the bright light glowed again. Vashla had returned. At the sight of her hand luggage, Ria screamed then fainted. Bru started gagging then ran to the corner of the room to be sick. Dreece felt the blood drain from his face. He stayed as if paralysed to the spot in the chair he sat in.

With one hand Vashla poured jewels and coins from a bag onto the table before Dreece.

'Some evidence,' she announced with a broad satisfied smile. 'These,' she dangled two heads, that she held in the other hand by the hair, close to his face, 'memories with proof of their plans.'

The blood still dripped from the skulls. Dreece backed away, his skin ashen as he tried to flick at the spots of blood off his clothes.

'That,' he pointed, 'was an I.S.C.C. Executive.' Dreece held his chest, his heart was thumping like thunder, pain stabbed him, and he slumped into the chair. Vashla laughed as she strode away, the heads swaying.
'I'm going to my Library,' she announced, 'a little hobby of mine, reading.' She grinned wickedly at her captive audience. 'My reading is something my Ness does not approve of,' she laughed and left the room.

CHAPTER SIXTEEN

# Above Gardt's World Ghaur

Minutes later Agai returned with Joss and Sam. Ria rushed to her boys hugging them tightly. She sobbed.

'Are you alright?'

'Yes mother,' Joss gently turned his mother aside. 'What's wrong with Pa?'

Bru was holding the slumped older man in his arms.

'Agai,' Gardt snapped at the youth, 'find your mother. We'll need to restore this man. We need him to complete the negotiations.'

'She said she was going to the library, he had heads with her,' Ria wailed. 'My boys, you're alive, thank the stars,' tears streamed down Ria's face. She wiped her tears away and went to her fathers' side.

'What's wrong with him?' she asked.

'Looks like he's had a heart attack, but I've other things to worry about now,' Gardt was looking at the control panel. 'The Xambans are hailing us.'

Agai was quick at his task. He returned within minutes with his mother. He was talking excitedly to Vashla as they re-entered the control room.

'We went to every ship, Mamma. They were all full of people.'

'And who are these two?' Vashla pointed a talon-like nail at the boys.

'They are my new friends Joss and Sam. I met many more on the different ships. They play games and talk to each other. They learn together. I could see in their minds that they belong with those two Ria and Bru, so bought them here.'

'I see,' Vashla sneered, 'you take these two with you now Agai. We will speak later about these friends.'

'Yes Mamma,' Agai obeyed.

'And take these two with you too. This female's snivelling is more than I can bear.'

Agai nodded and led the small group away, Ria clinging to Bru, with Joss and Sam in tow.

Gardt waited till the door closed behind them. Vashla slapped him forcefully. Again, he swayed but held his ground.

'The boy needs friends,' Gardt stated.

'Perhaps,' Vashla replied. 'You've already made an impression on him.'

'He is my son, is he not?'

'He is.'

'We'll take this old man to the restoration chamber, as you suggested. We need a negotiator, one that is known to these people.'

Gardt carried Dreece down to the next level and placed him in the room he knew too well. Vashla walked beside him and was ready to set the dials when the chamber was sealed.

They left Dreece there and returned to the control room.

'Vashla, I should kill you for the pain you've caused me,' Gardt spoke boldly.

'You could try,' she replied flashing her dark coal eyes venomously at him.

'I will begin negotiations,' she announced while punching some switches on the control panel. The screen sparked to life and the image they saw sent a shiver through Gardt.

'Zorn,' Vashla hissed, 'what do you want with these insignificant weaklings?'

'My dear Vashla, they are our slaves. What do you have to do with them?' his deep voice rumbled. His flashing charcoal eyes glistened, and a mass of dark wavy hair, so much like Vashla's, he could have been a male version of her.

'Zorn, I have nothing to do with them. I don't want them. I don't need them. There is a question about them being your slaves that must be resolved.'

'The deal was sealed. No intrusion into your space. We were to be handed slaves for work in the mines. The I.S.C.C. were paid well for this delivery.'

'That, we can see,' Gardt lifted a handful of precious metals and sparkling jewels and waved about for Zorn to see.

'Zorn, much has changed. You have intruded on my space. You made a deal with people who had no right to deal with. These I.S.C.C. had no agreement with the authorities on Ghaur to sell you slaves. The people on these ships believe they are starting a new colony on a new world.'

'They are my slaves. We did not violate your space. We took care not to. I want my slaves and I will have them, and our payment,' Zorn lent forward, and his face filled the view screen, his piercing black, green eyes shone menacingly. 'I will have them for the mines on Xamba. I will have them, or you will die.'

The view screen went blank.

'Zorn has an advantage. I have only this ship, the ten colonist's ships and the I.S.C.C. vehicle pinned and immobile. My resources are limited,' Vashla pondered her options.

'What if we can give them slaves?' Gardt replied.

'How?'

'I have an idea that might solve a problem on Ghaur and deliver Zorn and the Xambans their labourers.'

'Do tell, my Ness. You have become useful to me once again.'

'We will need Dreece to help with the process. My plan is to use prisoners. Criminals sentenced to death on Ghaur, to be conveyed to the Xambans as slaves. The I.S.C.C. have betrayed the trust of our people, Ghaur has become overpopulated, perhaps the I.S.C.C. who did this could swell the numbers, we could get rid of these unwanted people'

'We would need to transport them quickly,' Vashla considered the proposition.

'Do you still have the fleet of transporters you captured at Ranagahhn years ago?'

'Yes, my Ness, I do.'

'Good, then we've no time to waste. We must get Dreece onto the task.'

'Very well.' Vashla returned to the restoration chamber and to the task of restoring the old man to life.

## CHAPTER SEVENTEEN

# Above Gardt's World Ghaur

'This is crazy,' Dreece yelled. 'You're telling me that if all the governments agree to release all their death row prisoners and we give them to this Zorn of the Xambans, in return all the colonists will be released!'

'Zorn wants slaves. He doesn't care which ones,' Gardt replied calmly.

'My Ness is right old man,' Vashla stared icily at the restored man before her. 'We do not have time to argue. My transporters can do the transfer. These people must be collected into containment areas that I nominate for dispatch. They will be on the Xambans carrier ships and your colony ships will be released.'

'I still have trouble believing the I.S.C.C. could do this,' Dreece stood, his shoulders slouched. 'What you want to do is impossible.'

'They even intended to sell the colony ships Dreece,' Gardt held a large jewel up to the older man. 'These were just a down payment. They were set to make a fortune at our colonist's expense.'

'I will do what I can to persuade the authorities that we have no alternative course of action,' Dreece shook his head miserably.

'Don't waste time, old man. Zorn is not a patient man. I know, I've kept him waiting,' Vashla chortled.

'Mamma, you wouldn't consider accepting Zorn now would you?' Agai asked anxiously.

Vashla just smiled at her son and shook her head.

'Now I have Ness,' she linked her arm through his as they all returned to the control room, leaving the restoration chamber behind.

'So, the colonists will return to Ghaur?' Bru asked.

'Possibly,' Gardt rotated his shoulders to release the tension in his muscles, 'I've been thinking about that.'

'Father,' Ria was relieved to see her father walk back into the room. 'I thought you were dead. Are you alright?'

'I'm fine daughter,' Dreece took hold of his daughter's hands. 'You look pale Ria, I am alive, although I don't know how. I'm sure I did die.' He sighed and looked at the others, 'I need to communicate immediately with authorities to get things moving. This sort of thing can take years to set in place.'

'How archaic. You will take them evidence. Agai, take the one without hair on the face and squinting eyes,' Vashla turned and grabbed a bagful of jewels.

'Can these Government authorities on Ghaur be trusted?' She turned to Gardt. He nodded.

'Take these as well,' she threw the bag at Dreece who caught them clumsily.

'The others can wait here for your return.'

'Please, can you tell me is Agai going?' Joss asked drawing a surprised look from the imposing woman.

'Why do you ask?'

'It may be a good idea, if someone who was on the ships when the Xambans attacked could give an account of what happened,' Joss replied.

'It may,' Vashla agreed. She ushered Joss to join Dreece away from the rest of the group. Agai returned from the Library with a decapitated head in a transparent box, he then stood beside the negotiators.

'You have limited time. I will have the transporters ready in one of your moon turns. Go,' she shouted as the trio were instantly shrouded in the white light.

## CHAPTER EIGHTEEN

# Above Gardt's World Ghaur

'You have a planet Vashla, Agai was telling me about it.'

'A planet, my planet, and you want to know where it is and what it's like?' Vashla growled and moved close to Gardt.

'Oh my,' Bru took Ria's hand, 'I think we should go for a walk, Sam, come with us, before things turn nasty.'

'Wait,' Gardt demanded, 'this is something you should know.'

'It is far enough away from my family to be safe,' Vashla's black eyes glared at the view screen, 'Zorn is my cousin.'

'Agai said it had beautiful plant life, clean air, expansive seas and river systems. He also said it was lonely with just the two of you.'

'What right have you to ask?' her nostrils flared.

'The right of a man you held captive for twenty-two months. The right of a man you raped and killed and restored again, and again, for sport,' Gardt held his ground as Vashla leered at him. 'The right of a man you returned to my home world, only to be humiliated. I have the right of a man, who, could grow to love you, but for your cruelty. Vashla, it's a simple question.'

Vashla lashed out but Gardt ducked and grabbed her arm twisting it behind her.

'The right of a man who has been rejected by the people I thought were mine. The right of a man who is now witnessing the foolishness of my people that has led them into this trap.'

Gardt held firm while Vashla glared at him full of rage. Once she stilled, he pushed her away forcefully, she almost fell over but recovered as Gardt walked to the other side of the control panel.

'Don't hit me and listen,' he spoke steadily. 'I have the right of a man, who has fathered your child, the right of a man, who wants to be a father to him, and to all my family. Joss is the son of my marriage to Ria, and Agai is the child of our union, albeit violation of my body. If you want a future and a place for us to be a family, or if you don't want this, decide now. If you don't want to trust me as a partner and father of your child, then, kill me now, only, do it properly, take my head and put it in the library. I've had enough bitter disappointment in my life. The choice is yours.'

Gardt looked Vashla in the eye. 'What will it be?'

A white light flashed on the other side of the room. All eyes turned towards it.

'They've agreed', Dreece announced as the light disappeared.

'Mamma, what's happening?' Agai stood beside Joss.

'This,' Vashla replied pulling her arms free from Gardt and wrapping them around his neck.

Ria, Bru and Sam all let out a gasp in unison. Vashla didn't strike Gardt or tear him limb from limb, instead she planted a firm passionate kiss on his lips. They embraced till Gardt pulled away.

'Let me breathe woman,' he smiled at Vashla and then kissed her with equal vigour.

'Can we get all these details seen to? Agai here impressed the officialdom very much, with our evidence, accompanied by Josh's account of what happened, they accepted.' Dreece pointed at the decapitated head. 'We've flitted about five continents with this instant transport, all day. I really don't want to stand about, watching you two like this.'

Vashla and Gardt both laughed.

'That seals it then,' Gardt said softly.

'Can we eat now, I'm starving?' Agai said while putting his load down on the table.

'That's our boy,' Gardt smiled.

CHAPTER NINETEEN

# Above Gardt's World Ghaur

The Xambans wasted no time in preparing their carrier craft to rendezvous with Vashla's ship for the transfer of prisoners. While these preparations were made, death row convicts were being assembled.

Everyone on board Vashla's craft had eaten and rested while all the activity took place. Agai and his half-brother Joss, had been with Sam in the games room. They were getting to know each other while playing games, the computer panels lit up as the competition was fierce, the banter flowed. Agai smiled when he won.

At the control panel, Dreece spoke to the President of the United Alliance, the largest government body on the planet Ghaur.

'Lobby groups have already sprung up in defence of these condemned men,' the tall striking looking man in a silver suit was saying. 'There's going to be hell to pay. I'm glad we'll be saving taxpayers credits but, man oh man, some media crazies are saying this is a stunt.'

'This is no stunt, Mr President,' Dreece found himself explaining, 'the threat is very real.'

'We only have your word, and, that creature's evidence on that.'

'Perhaps I could arrange a small demonstration of strength,' Vashla returned to her menacing demeanour.

'Vashla,' Gardt interrupted, 'I don't think that will be necessary.'

She smiled broadly as she touched the control panel. The desk the President sat at began to shake, the papers on it slid about and the lamp fell over with a clatter.

'What's going on?' The President held on to his desk, his knuckles turned white with the strain.

'This is just a little of what I can do to your people from this point in space,' Vashla pointed out. 'Do I have your attention? A well projected aim at a target, any target, can cause immense damage to your world.'

'By the stars, woman, you'd do that?' The President asked.

'I could, but I wouldn't. Zorn and The Xambans are capable of inflicting much more devastation on your world. Zorn has six ships here with a more powerful range of weapons. He's not above destroying his enemy to get what he wants. I believe however, they do not wish to waste their resources, but want slaves to work in their mines.'

'Very well, I'll see that the final arrangements are completed as soon as possible,' the President replied regaining his composure when the shaking ceased.

'My transporters are ready to commence the moment your prisoners are gathered,' Vashla nodded then flipped the switch and the view screen was blank.

'Thank you, Madame Vashla, he needed some pushing,' Dreece concluded with a short bow to the dark exotic beauty.

'Now, to Zorn,' Vashla remained at the control panel as the screen image changed to show the imposing face of the warrior.

'Vashla,' the guttural greeting seemed to fill the room.

'Zorn,' she replied coolly.

CHAPTER TWENTY

# Above Gardt's World Ghaur

'The prisoners will fill your carrier ships before the next cycle of the planet below is complete.'

'Good, my need to move soon is great,' Zorn tugged at the tuft of hair on his chin before adding, 'what of our other outstanding business?'

Vashla paused and walked with a slow taunting sway around the room. A low throaty growl began from the on-screen aliens' loins, culminating in a shout, 'Vashla!'

A white light engulfed the figure on the screen. Within a blink the onlookers were confronted by the tall swarthy creature in the control room, only an arm length from his tormentor.

Vashla laughed. 'I do think you are foolish Zorn. You will have your captive workers. Be pleased with your efforts. Go now and forget the rest.'

'You promised me Vashla,' the words rolled out like a thunderous drum-roll.

'I promised you nothing,' Vashla replied sternly waving her had as though remonstrating with a small child.

Zorn moved two steps closer to the woman.

'Why? You said Agai needed to have a family and someone to learn from. You said you wanted more than the aimless life you've been living. I have everything you need to satisfy those requirements,' he stepped closer and grabbed her arm. 'You are beautiful and would please me.'

Vashla pulled herself away from his grip and looked fiercely at him.

'I have Agai's father and a future with many people for company. These colonists, my Ness's people need a home. I need people to fill my world. Agai needs friends and his father,' she flipped back her hair and stepped away from the intruder. 'I tire of killing your runaway slaves Zorn. Your life is not for me.'

Zorn glared at her and growled again. 'Who is this weakling, that I might tear him limb from limb.'

'That would be me,' Gardt stepped beside Vashla and put his arm around her waist. 'You would be a bit late tearing me limb from limb, Vashla has already done that to me. Then she restored me, several times if truth be known.'

Zorn became more menacing and his eyes flashed with hatred.

'You cannot change the fact that I am Agai's father,' Gardt said with a crack in his voice.

'You will do nothing Zorn. The planet VaLinta is mine. I have earned the right to do as I wish. You have your cargo being loaded now,' she pointed at the activity on the ships opposite, 'so go and oversea their boarding and departure to your mines. Leave now!'

'These people,' Vashla nodded at Ria, Bru, Joss, Sam and Dreece, 'are small players in your game Zorn. Take the players you have and go.'

'The prisoners will die slowly working hard,' Zorn grunted.

'That may be so,' Dreece nodded his reply, 'they were all waiting for death to greet them, as criminals they will not be missed.'

Vashla steely eyes glared at Zorn. 'Leave now Zorn, you cannot claim what is not yours.'

'You have your planet and your people Vashla, but you will not travel freely in space from this moment on. I will see to that.'

'Our people, our colonists will still need to travel,' Dreece whined.

'Silence,' Vashla shouted. 'There will only be need to travel from this world to mine,' Vashla pointed at the tall man, 'I will keep peace with you, cousin, that is all I will do! You travel where you will.'

The alien stroked his beard again. 'Very well, you may travel in this sector to your world, beyond that you will be in danger. You will tire of that life Vashla and beg to be mine.'

'Not unless I lose my sanity. I doubt I will ever be bored with my Ness. We will be busy overseeing our new world. You will not be visiting, Zorn, unless you improve your manners.'

Zorn's eyes flashed like freshly fanned flames. The white engulfed the alien, and he was gone.

'Gardt,' Vashla turned to gently embrace him.

'That's the first time I've ever heard you use my first name Vashla.'

'You will not be bored,' Vashla stroked his face then pulled him into a deep kiss.

'Hang on,' Gardt pulled away briefly, 'I'll be grounded planet side again, just on a different world.'

# Rakal's World Earth 2005

On the way home from the dig in their skip Tam noticed that Rakal looked tired. Mata had fallen asleep the moment they headed off, and Kat was moody.

'What did you think about camping out, Rakal? Not quite as comfortable as the motel or the spaceship, is it?' The last couple of trips were much more comfortable.'

'No.' Rakal said simply. 'You do this normally when going to a dig?

'Yes.'

'Melody is staying at the dig for three more days. Do you really think she'll fly to Victoria to come to the farm?' Kat asked.

'She said she would, Kat,' Tam turned backwards to answer. Rakal was driving and Tam was in the passenger seat.

'Yeah, I just wish she'd come with us.'

'She had commitments Kat. You know that. It was good of her to change her plans and take a few days out of her schedule to come to Victoria before heading back to Uni in Perth.'

Kat nodded sullenly and stared out the window. They were flying low over the treetops. The journey that would normally take days by conventional transport, only took hours.

'Central Australia is a beautiful place,' Tam smiled at Rakal. 'The fossils are delivering great insight into the prehistoric animals from this continent's ancient past.'

'It is a hot place,' Rakal replied, 'the water was cool.'

'When you get near home, could you land? I'd like to catch up with Mica and Ash at the new house,' Tam smiled.

'Ah, Mica is still in the news on television,' Rakal commented, 'I did kick start a career there, did I not?'

'Certainly, Rakal, my love, Mica is a diplomat now,' Tam nodded, 'meeting foreign dignitaries, discussing climate change, sustainable energy supplies, the political result of changing from traditional coal and oil based products to the entirely green energy source we use, while retaining many of the benefits by augmenting both sources of power generation. It's heavy duty activity.'

'You see your siblings often, why do you want to see Ash and Mica now? We'll see them tomorrow anyway.'

'There will be too much going on with preparations for the partnership,' Tam squeezed Rakal's leg gently. 'I know you are tired, it's been a big fortnight, but Ash is doing the mechanical miracle thing in the press shortly, with Mica doing his diplomat thing too. I just want to say hi before they head off on a whirlwind journey around the world.'

'They'll have to lobby pretty hard, I think,' Kat joined in. 'Is this world really ready for us and our free fuel source?'

'Good question,' Tam smiled back at their oldest child, 'we'll have to wait and see.'

Rakal had dropped the car to the road surface.

'I really like how the new farmhouse has been built with a dormitory upstairs for the little ones mirroring the one in my parent's property,' Tam smiled glancing across to Rakal. 'I know, I've said that before.'

'Shea and Maya have really set up a good trade with our cousins in space,' Tam pointed to a pile of spaceship parts in the yard beside the house. 'There will be much more in future. I wonder that the Governments on Earth haven't figured a way to tax that yet.'

'Our car registration and licence has become a hot topic already,' Kat added, 'my skip costs me twice what my friends in town are paying to put a car on the road, or should I say, in the air.'

'I am tired, Tam, will we be long?' Rakal asked.

'I can go in, and you can take the children home, if you like. I'll walk back after I've caught up with the globe trekkers.'

Rakal shrugged his shoulders with relief and nodded.

'I'm not a child,' Kat said indignantly. 'I could have partnered years ago!'

'You could have,' Tam nodded, quickly kissed Rakal before getting out of the skip. 'I won't be long.'

Rakal and Kat waved.

Tam trudged with loud footfalls on the gravel pathway to the house, which roused the dog inside, who greeted him with yapping at the entrance.

'Hello there, anyone home?' Tam called over the din.

Walking into the warm welcoming lounge room Tam shook off the chill from the cool night air.

'Ash, Mica,' Tam hugged his siblings briefly, 'it's good to see you.'

'You too, how long have you been home?'

'Just now, I wanted to see you before all the hustle and bustle tomorrow,' Tam explained.

'You've seen the results of Shea and Maya's labours outside?' Ash said cheerily.

'Sure, heaps of stuff there, can you make something out of it?'

'Naturally, I'm the tech gadget whizz you know,' Ash smiled broadly. 'Great junk out there to make lots of useful innovative tech stuff and machinery, my aim is to enhance the world and solve energy problems.'

'So just minor miracles then,' Tam grinned back. 'Now don't get on your hobby horse Ash, I just wanted to have a chat about some of the other imports they've been bringing back.'

'Our cousins from Orthama, have been travelling here for a while,' Mica nodded. 'They're just coming more often now. Some are staying and taking partners. You know Sal's twins, Saz and Sam, both have partners now.'

'Yes, I was away at Uni when I found out. Rakal and I took a quick trip to visit Vashla on her planet. That boy Agai seems lonely, he needs company. Then we went to the dig with Kat and Mata, so I missed all that excitement last month.'

'They are both sixteen and overdue to partner,' Ash commented while handing Tam a hot coffee.

'This is just what I needed,' Tam wrapped chilled fingers around the cup as the next eldest sibling Sal walked into the room.

'Hi Tam, you look bushed, if you'll pardon the pun,' Sal grinned.

'Bushed I am,' Tam chortled, 'poor Rakal, I think camping is not something he'll want to do again. The bed, he just couldn't get used to it, not his usual comfort level. Having to do rostered chores, especially the dishes, oh no.'

'We do chores, on a roster, I guess that's a Davidson necessity,' Mica beamed, 'can't imagine Rakal liking it though.'

'Where's everyone else? Over at our parents across the road?'

'Raz is upstairs rehearsing a solo flute piece for tomorrow,' Sal stood near the fire looking at Tam, enjoying his own hot coffee. 'The children under eight are in the dorm at our parents' house and the older ones are upstairs with Raz.'

'There will be a lot of raw hormones bouncing around up there,' Ash grinned, 'I remember being almost twelve and sexually mature, it was one emotional roller coaster.'

'Raz doesn't seem interested in partnering yet,' Sal smiled and sat down beside Tam.

'Kat doesn't seem to want to partner either. He is more interested in chasing girls, or he has been until now,' Tam sighed. 'We don't have many women in our family, other than Amber.' He put his cup down and got up to stretch. 'Gem seems really content with Jake and Amber, that's good to see. Now it looks like my child has got his heart set on Melody, a girl I know through work on the digs, she'll be arriving for a short stay for Tris and Todd's union.'

'Whatever happens, we'll all manage,' Sal sipped the refreshing liquid. 'Jod and Weet are the same age my twins were when we moved to the old farmhouse here after Grandma Nance died.'

'And now it's a bigger home, and we are a much larger family,' Tam bear hugged his sibling. 'I've got to head off, said I wouldn't be long.'

'Here, use this,' Ash handed Tam a bracelet, 'it'll save you getting a chill and transport you direct to the rec room on the ship.'

'Thanks,' Tam smiled, 'I'll surprise Rakal.' Smiling he pressed the bracelet control and disappeared into a white light.

## CHAPTER TWENTY-TWO

# Rakal's World Earth 2005

The next couple of days were typical of a Davidson family get together. There was organised chaos, rosters, and routines for everyone to help the event run smoothly. This wasn't quite a Royal wedding but in the Davidson stronghold, Tris, being Richard and Davrew's grandchild, partnering their long-time friend and creator of artistic works that adorn the furniture and walls of their home, Tod Longmire, it was a special event.

Melody was one of the visitors from around the globe. There were others arriving too, from the extremities of space.

Tam walked with Rakal, together from his spaceship across the field at the back of the farmhouse towards Vashla and her son Agai.

'The boy looks wild,' Tam whispered to Rakal.

'He is.'

'And she looks,' Tam tried to find the right word, 'fidgety.'

'She is finding her way,' Rakal nodded. 'Since she was last here, from what she's told me, she has remained on her world, not plundered at all. The father of the boy calls to her from his world with her war cry being sung on that planet. It is driving her crazy.'

'Why doesn't she go and find out why?'

'Vashla has been creating a safe place for the boy on her world, perhaps for the boy's father too,' Rakal smiled at Tam. 'She was so impressed with your family and its communal living, that she's planted her own vegetable garden, and orchard. She has showed me images of them, like your happy snaps. She even built a dwelling on her planet.'

Tam let out a soft whistle.

'The tables are being set up for the feast. With so much activity going on, will Vashla and Agai find this a bit overwhelming?'

'Perhaps my love,' Rakal replied, 'she can retreat into her spaceship when she likes.'

'Kat's found Melody,' Tam nodded towards the activity nearby. 'The work roster we were sent includes Kat. He's helping put up the trestle tables. She seems happy to be with him.'

'Our job is simply to keep Vashla and Agai entertained,' Rakal grinned.

'Along with our other interplanetary and international guests,' Tam pointed towards the other three spaceships in the field nearby.

'More relatives from the original breeding programme?'

'Yes, mostly dual gender clones and those humans who brought them here,' Tam nodded. 'The French family, with Andre as the patriarch arrived yesterday. He's so happy that Zena partnered and produced five children, now he's a proud grandfather of six.'

'Will those children, take partners from your parent's grand children?'

'Now, there are more to go around, who knows? We original colonists did a lot of mixing there. Andre saw both his eldest offspring partner with my siblings, Bon with Imi, and Sal with Sim. Zena partnered an off-world cousin.' Tam turned to Rakal, 'Andre is happily chatting to my parents, we can concentrate on Vashla and Agai.'

'Vashla, Agai, we welcome your return,' Rakal let go of Tams hand and moved towards the new arrivals. 'You have a different spaceship today.'

'I have several,' the exotic dark-haired beauty replied. She looked uneasily around the gathering crowd.

'Vashla, Agai,' Tam greeted the visitors, 'this will be another new experience for you, there will be ceremony, feasting and you will meet all the extended family.'

'There are many people,' Vashla looked anxiously about.

'Many more to come, the proceedings really begin about four o'clock and its only two now,' Tam explained. 'Perhaps Agai would like to go and help Kat and Melody set up the tables.'

The boy nodded to his mother and took off.

'We have other interplanetary guests. If you come with us, we'll introduce you.'

Just then a group of young children with Mata in the lead ran up to them. 'Can we eat soon?'

'We'll all eat soon Mata darling,' Tam grinned with adoration at the child, 'perhaps at the kitchen you'll find some snack to keep you all going. What task have you little ones been asked to do?'

'We must clear an area in front of the stage and sit there quietly,' the child replied.

'Quickly get a snack and then go to your task,' Tam instructed.

The giggling group of toddlers set off after their child.

Two hours later the crowd had gathered in the late summer evening. There were large screens hanging at both ends of the field, everyone at the event would see the proceedings clearly. Also, the partnership was being telecast, one channel dedicated to showing the whole ceremony. Highlights would be on other channels in news spots. The Davidson's no longer hid from the world. This was one way the general community could see their integration in action.

Tam watched his parents Richard and Davrew stand on a small purpose-built stage. Richard, now with mostly white grey hair and a slightly tubby stature, raised his arms to hail the audience. Davrew, still tall and flaxen haired, the dual gender head of the household, stood proudly at his side.

'Welcome all, family, friends, and companions from every corner of this world and space. Today I will pass you over to Sal our fourth born offspring to host this event, with experience in the media, producing television documentaries. I think you'll agree, he is clearly more suited to the role. Before I do that, I would like to say just a few words,' Richard cleared his throat then began. 'Tris no longer has parents alive to say how proud they are to see this day arrive. As Grandfather of this remarkable person, I've seen grow since Bon's tragic demise, into a fine family medic and person we can all rely on. Todd Longmire has been a family friend for many years, more my love Davrew's friend initially, but a friend who has been loyal and true to us, throughout good times and bad. I'm proud indeed to be here to see them partnered.'

Richard then stepped aside and allowed Davrew to take the microphone. 'I'm also extremely proud of Tris and delighted to see our good friend and artisan, Todd Longmire, join his life to our family,' Davrew beckoned Sal to stand at the microphone. 'Sal will now continue.'

Sal was a younger version of Davrew, with long blond hair tied back in a neat ponytail, smart dark suit, and a blue polo roll neck under this to add colour.

'This is a significant day for us all. This is our first legally recognised partnership. The local authorities now understand who we are, and, why we are here, so they have asked us to pay taxes, as regular citizens, which we have always done.' He paused for a moment to let the crowd noise settle.

'We now also have amongst us in our extended family, architects, artists, cabinet makers, cleaners, designers, dressmakers, electricians and documentary makers,' Sal smiled and bowed. 'We've always been small farmers, gardeners, historians, musicians, medical practitioners, and now painters, plumbers and photographers, roof repairers, singers, tutors and so many more trades and skills.'

'And now, to add to these diverse occupations, as you can all see, ladies and gentlemen, people of Earth, our star born relatives and friends. I introduce our own marriage celebrant, Pip, third born of Bon and Imi, who will perform the ritual required by law and combine our own celebration of star union.'

## CHAPTER TWENTY-THREE

# Rakal's World Earth 2010

Tam got up and checked the decorations and preparations for Mata's eighth birthday were well underway. A broad smile lit Tams face when thinking about how Kat had become the great protector of his little sister, like the time she's fallen into a blackberry bush and got tangled, he'd patiently got her out then unceremoniously dumped her in a bath to clean her up. Mata had always been a feisty child, curious about everything and she bought a lot of laughter to their lives.

A lot had happened since Tris and Tod partnered. His parents had been to England twice to greet the arrival of their two children.

At home, Tam was glad Melody had continued to visit the Davidson's farm, but surprised Kat was not who she spent time with. Instead she became his half sibling Shea's shadow. Now married, they had and presented him with two beautiful children, a nephew and niece. Kat had not been perturbed. On his overseas travels, he found, an exotic Greek girl, who captured his heart. They married and presented Tam with two beautiful granddaughters. So, the family moved on in single and dual gender families and spread out to other countries.

Tam was deep in thought when Rakal barged into the room.

'What's wrong?'

'Vashla has just contacted me, there is big trouble brewing with Zorn.'

'You've been saying that for the last few years, Rakal, calm down now and tell me what has happened.'

'Vashla went back to the world Agai's father came from, she has taken him back with her to her own world. Zorn has declared that she may never leave that world or trade again.'

'So, how did Vashla react to that?'

'You can guess. She told him he can't tell her what to do.'

'That's no surprise.'

'Zorn has declared war on her and Agai, and anyone she is ally with.'

'Oh, you mean us!'

'Yes.'

'Surely, Zorn would not be interested in Earth, at the other end of the galaxy?'

'Apparently, he is.'

Tam ran long fingers through his hair. 'This could be devastating. Who knows what effect this might have on Earth? Could we be in danger?' Tam gasped. 'What are we going to do?'

'You know I will defend this planet and protect it. Vashla has sworn to do the same. Her world is a long way from ours though and we must protect them both. Zorn has a fleet of ships and many hundreds of warriors.'

Tam quickly put aside the notebook with half prepared list for the upcoming birthday party and jumped up out of the control room chair.

'Tam, you go and tell your parents,' Rakal walked to the control panel and started the view screen, 'go now and alert Sal that we may need a worldwide broadcast on the situation soon. Mica is now a diplomat as well as a linguist, let Mica deal with contacting the world authorities. I have a planetary defence in place.'

'The small satellites,' Tam murmured, 'I thought they were just a warning array so that incoming asteroids could be detected.'

'They also have an attack function,' Rakal was busy bringing up screens and working, 'I must go and see what the danger is. Go to Mata and the family. Be safe.'

Tam felt the prickly sense of unease now turned to alarm.

'Rakal, I don't want you to go, not without me.'

Rakal turned to Tam and planted a passionate kiss on willing lips.

'I will be back,' Rakal stated emphatically when he pulled away.

Tam almost laughed. 'Like in the movie, you'll be back.'

'Please go now Tam, I need to discuss tactics with Vashla.'

'Tactics, two former space pirates, a great distance apart. Even through the grid by the most direct line, we're still isolated. By the stars Rakal, do we have the odds greatly against us?'

Rakal simply nodded. 'Go now Tam my love,' Rakal pushed Tam towards the exit, 'tell the family that there is great danger. I will determine how much and return quickly.'

Tam stumbled away calling back. 'Make sure you do come back Rakal.'

Outside the spacecraft, the warmth of the sun hit Tam. He dashed across the field, while the chill news seeped into his bones. He rushed to the farmhouse through the vegetable and herb garden. The gate creaked as he went through. Tam felt worried about who would be home to tell, it was a weekday. Then he remembered, Richard and Davrew were home, just back from an overseas trip. Yes, it would be best to speak to his parents first. Calming his pounding heart, he went inside.

## CHAPTER TWENTY-FOUR

# Vashla's World VaLinta

Vashla had sent Agai on an errand, one Gardt suggested. To collect a rare fruit off a tree from the other side of her world. This planet seemed almost too small for her to share with her son.

Vashla shook her long black hair and rubbed her eyes, it was time to focus on the task at hand. She needed allies, ones she could rely on. She waited for Rakal to contact her.

Tracing back through the family tree, all the different branches of the known grid links, Rakal was one not too distant relative willing to help. Her motley little fleet of twenty different craft were no match for Zorn and his fleet. She knew she could not trust her cousin to keep his word. They would not be left alone to live in peace.

Gardt entered the room laden with chopped firewood and stacked it by the newly built chimney. The house Vashla had built originally had only three rooms, a control room, recreational room, and bedroom. They had extended the rudimentary building after their last trip. Agai had used some of the skills he'd learnt on his trips to Earth.

Zorn now restricted their travel so much, even the opportunity to meet their companions, without any trade was limited. It was more than a disruption. Vashla did not tolerate fools, and she considered Zorn one. He was a bully though, and one to be wary of. She didn't take his threats as idle whims.

The Davidson family on Earth had provided another valuable link. Maya and Shea were interplanetary traders with their cousins from the planet of origin. They had many cousins who had many friends. These too were willing to assist Vashla in maintaining a peaceful resolution to the conflict that could become brutal. She smiled and whistled at the report showing these non-violent people were capable of repelling Zorn when the need came. They were likely to become her best defence.

There were many good pilots and navigators among this branch of the galactic clan. They also had skills enough to repair and build new spaceships. That was a resource she was lacking. Now Vashla pondered her need for an army. She had always relied on her own strength and cunning to survive. Now she was building a colony on her planet of people from Gardt's overcrowded home world. They needed to be sure of their safety and freedom to travel, trade and live.

Gardt was whistling as he stacked the firewood in the tinderboxes. She smiled and glanced up at him, drawing her eyes away from the grid pattern on the screen, and her preparations for battle. He was her Ness, now she was his. This was a new experience for her. Vashla had become part of a pair, inseparable in many ways, yet, so very independent of the other. He saw her glance and winked. She could not help but smile at his impish grin.

'There's more wood chopped stacked by the wall. Plenty to keep this cottage cosy and warm for a while,' Gardt dusted of his hands and walked over to the control panel. He put his arms around her waist. 'You're still preparing for battle?'

'I must.'

Gardt lifted her hair gently. The shiny black mass of ringlets fell back down her back.

'Take a moment to come outside and see my handy work in the garden. The fresh air will clear your mind.'

'Very well,' Vashla reluctantly agreed to allow Gardt to lead her away from her planning.

'This is really an incredibly beautiful and diverse planet,' Gardt said. Then he showed Vashla the newly turned soil and named the vegetables recently planted, showing her the shoots. He smiled seeing she was feigning interest. 'We'll be able to feed ourselves from the result of my labour.'

'I do know this is good, Gardt,' she breathed deeply, the fresh air was crisp and refreshing. 'It is good to be outside for a moment.'

'Agai will be back soon,' he smiled, 'I'll be able to propagate the seeds from the fruit he brings when he returns.'

'I see your new colonists are finding the old VaLinta village a good base. The buildings are still solid.'

'Yes,' Gardt wiped the dirt from his hands after discarding some weeds.

'I didn't expect the many cylindrical constructions there to be homes that offer shelter. The previous occupants must have had a large community. My home world is so over-crowded, the new colonists are enjoying making them their own. They are able to set up home and start afresh in these old foundations.'

'Free from fear at present,' Vashla commented.

'Yes,' Gardt took her hand in his, 'it is a burden for you, I know.'

'It's my World. I won it fairly. I intend to keep it safe, along with the families that are now living here.'

He drew her towards him and planted a kiss on her lips. When he pulled away, he led her to a garden seat. They sat down to enjoy the view.

'You picked a good spot to build a house Vashla,' Gardt pointed at the greenery of the scenery around them. They were high with a view of a vast valley sur-rounded by mountains. 'I love going down the steep slope to the river it's so peaceful. The trees in the forest are so tall and strong. Perhaps one day I'll build you tree house so you can escape the new settlers.'

'We're a good distance away from the VaLinta vil-lage, there's room for more people.' Vashla raised an eyebrow, 'they may need to defend themselves though. I expect Zorn will attack and not restrict his battle to space. I've known him to be ruthless in acquiring people on other worlds. I rescued the Linta people and this world from one such attack. He always wants slaves as workers for his mines because his disregards the workers he has. When they die, he simply looks for others.'

'Surely, if he encouraged a peaceful settlement on these mining planets, he could get willing workers for a share in the rewards.'

'Zorn doesn't like to share anything.'

They could see Agai approach on his single mini-skip and watched as he landed the vehicle nearby. He unloaded a box and carried it to where they sat.

'I picked the fruit you wanted Gardt, and some other plants that looked interesting. They are quite different to the plants here.'

'I was just saying to your mother that this planet is so diverse, the jungles, lakes, deserts, are vast. I really enjoy the open space.'

'Where do you want these?' Agai held up the box.

'Put them on the garden table,' Gardt replied, the boy gladly left the box and headed inside.

'Agai is enjoying the technology gained from the people on Earth, the planet Rakal lives on. They have a large population there too, yet they also have unpopulated regions.'

'I would like to visit that world one day,' Gardt said wistfully.

'When Zorn is no longer a threat, we can travel safely. Your people can come in more numbers and journey along the grid to other planets will be frequent,' Vashla patted Gardt's leg.

'I hope that won't be far away, Vashla, or, that the road there is not difficult.'

'Difficult,' Vashla sighed, 'we'll soon see how difficult it will be.'

## CHAPTER TWENTY-FIVE

# Vashla's World VaLinta

Later that day, Gardt took Agai on his mini-skip over to the VaLinta village, on the pretext of seeing how the colonists were getting on.

'I see there's been more work done in the village, the paths have been resealed,' Gardt said to Agai as they landed.

'There's still much to do,' Agai pointed to the dilapidated buildings. 'The VaLinta had power and water sources, these are still being reconnected to all the homes. Soon the new colonists will have their basic needs provided.'

Dreece greeted them. He'd been like a caged animal since arriving. On the liberation of the colonist's spaceships and safe arrival on VaLinta, Zorn had prevented them returning to their home world. He looked up at Gardt and Agai from the tree stump he was sitting on. Dreece had been forced to join his grandsons adventure, along with his daughter Ria and son-in-law Bru.

Although he could communicate with the authorities on Ghaur, he was powerless to change his position.

Gardt had no pity for the old man. Dreece had been the instrument of his own confinement on Ghaur after his return from space.

'Gardt,' Dreece grunted, 'when can I communicate again with our home world leaders? We must make plans to bring more colonists here, and to arrange for those who don't want to stay to return.'

'Why Dreece,' Gardt feigned surprise, 'hadn't you realised you're not a world leader here?'

'I need to get back,' Dreece shook his fist.

'To an overbuilt and overpopulated world? Your work was to arrange for colonists to forge a new life here, you can help them do that,' Gardt pointed out.

'This world has many places for you to live in. This village is only one the Linta people created, I can show you others,' Agai suggested.

'You did help put together a good founding team Dreece,' Gardt admitted. 'The gardeners have already planted vegetables and prepared the way for the colony's independent living. The agricultural scientists have been exploring ways to start growing crops. Agai has shown them natural sources of food, how to hunt and forage for wild animals and edible plants, and he's taken them to the best places to fish. All the colonists came here knowing they wouldn't return to Ghaur, of all those I've spoken to, none of them have any regrets.'

'They did Gardt,' the grey-haired man started to raise his voice, 'but, as you well know, I was never intended to be part of this expedition.'

'No, but you are now, so why not make the best of it?'

'I never had a home until we came here, old man,' Agai snarled at Dreece. 'I'll go and find my half-brother Joss, and Sam. We've a game to finish.'

Gardt slapped Agai on the back. The boy was more comfortable in his company now, accepting his new status as son. Gardt smiled as Agai strolled away, his golden hair bouncing as he moved. Joss had also come to realise, that the former gardener and housekeeper of his childhood, was really his own father.

'I'm so glad the boys get on together,' Gardt said to Dreece.

'Hmph,' Dreece replied.

'I'll go find Ria and Bru, I've bought some seeds for propagation.'

The old man pointed the way and continued to stare up at the sky, then back to the adjacent paddock where the spaceships were parked. Gardt realised the old man was bitter at the changes in his life. He shrugged and walked away. It was up to Dreece to either get used to it or go mad.

Ten ships, with five hundred colonists on board, left their home-world Ghaur. Their perilous journey through captivity to freedom ensured a happy group of arrivals on Vashla's world. Not the planet they had originally planned to settle on, but, as they prepared to colonise another planet, they'd taken with them, all they thought they needed to start afresh. The planet itself provided a rich bounty to supplement their supplies.

The activity around the craft had ceased since they'd unloaded their necessities, only occasionally did the colonists go back to retrieve something they could use. Now there were preparations to sow crops, wildlife to study, plant life to be foraged and catalogued, and new homes to settle in. The governing body was autonomous. The nature of the group was determined to be peaceful and harmonious. The weapons they used were for capturing prey and feeding the colony. Gardt hoped that Vashla's predictions would not come true.

Gardt smiled at Sergeant Rymus as he strode along the path in the opposite direction.

'Doing the rounds Rymus?'

'Of course, every day, just to ensure everyone is safe in their new homes,' the tall solidly built man replied. He was their security chief and presently his duties were light. Everyone knew each other and any sign of disruption to the running of the fledgling community quickly quelled.

'Does Vashla have any news of Zorn and his henchmen?'

Gardt shook his head and waved farewell. He walked on thinking of the differences between Vashla's world and his previous home, Ghaur. Wild aromas filled his senses from the fragrant flowers along the path. Dust stirred up as he walked adding a cloud at his feet, while the sky above was a fine and clear expanse of blue. He savoured the warmth of the sun that seeped into his bones. On his home world, the buildings smothered the skyline while a continuous haze caused the sunlight to struggle to reach the soil. The military regime ruling every facet of life sucked individuality and free thought out of its citizens. Now these people had an opportunity to forge a free new world.

His mind turned back to the task at hand. He wanted to take the seeds to Ria and Bru and return quickly to Vashla. That woman was wild and unpredictable, at times frightening, even now. He'd come to enjoy her company, and fret over her obsession with a war she was certain was coming.

CHAPTER TWENTY-SIX

# Zorn's Mining World Xamba

Zorn strutted about on the platform. Surveying the assembly below. There was no need for long winded speeches. They knew why they were there, each soldier and warrior in the mass below. He raised his arms and shouted, 'WE PREPARE FOR BATTLE!'

The troops below shouted, 'Zorn, Zorn, Zorn!'

He smiled and soaked in their fervour.

He left the podium with a wave and marched back to the space port centre. A little man scuttled along beside him at one side and a burly soldier strode step for stride on the other.

'Lord Zorn, the mines are most profitable, the trade with our new neighbours showing great reward, better than we imagined. Here is the proof in the figures,' the little man squeaked while pointing to a board in his hand.

'The planet is stale. The air thick with dust, and, it smells,' Zorn replied. 'It's putrid. I long for a new world to conquer.'

'Commander Zorn,' the other man drew his Leader's attention, 'the recent rebellion by workers has been suppressed.'

Zorn nodded.

'The reduction in their food rations has further enhanced our profit, my Lord,' the little man added.

'Do we have enough to quell the nerves of our newly acquired army?'

'Yes, my Lord,' the little man replied.

'My mercenary army have travelled from all corners of the grid and given me the opportunity to take what I want.'

'They are prepared to go to war for you Commander,' the soldier replied, 'they will do your bidding, they've been training in earnest. The enemy annihilated.'

'Excellent.'

Zorn had no plans to settle anywhere, his mines made him rich. He ate the finest food, slept where he could be pampered, took females to his bed then moved on, and, feasted on his foes. He wanted no one to control him. He had to have the power.

His concern was that Vashla used the grid too. Her planet was on his path of his territories. He wanted that planet. He wanted her. The grid was invisible to those who did not know the Ancients' ways. The family Zorn and Vashla had come from knew many secrets. Now he knew Rakal, another distant cousin, had been using the grid and finding another home world to settle, his thirst for dominance needed to be quenched, and soon.

## CHAPTER TWENTY-SEVEN

# Rakal's World Earth 2010

'Maya, get a move on, everyone will be at our grandparent's farmhouse in half an hour. You're still not dressed. I know it's late in the year, but twenty ten will be over before you're ready.'

'I'm dressed, just not in a shirt and tie,' Maya walked towards his cousin while combing his hair, the tight curls were always falling over his eyes in an untidy mop. 'Just because your Melody likes to see you dress for the family, doesn't mean I have to.'

Shea rolled his eyes, 'torn jeans and a long-sleeved tee, hardly business attire.'

'Is this a business meeting? I thought we were going to dinner with the family. The usual browse and eat and chat,' Maya tucked his comb in his pocket. 'I know we'll talk about what's happening, with our trade business with our cousins in space, nothing big. It's all going great.'

'You are kidding right,' Shea replied. 'This is going to be like setting off a time bomb.'

Maya looked his younger cousin up and down. 'You do look sharp.'

'Thanks, Melody bought this leather jacket for me, in a London High street shop, and it's so comfortable,' Shea held out the jacket front to show off.

'You do take the bait so well,' Maya smiled.

'Cousin, you're a torment,' Shea grinned back and thumped Maya on the shoulder. 'Melody took the children to the city to see 'The Lion King'.'

'So, we can do the boring stuff without being interrupted,' Maya grinned as they walked out the door. 'You know, the pollution in the city would be nonexistent if our free clean fuel was used.'

'Don't preach to the converted buddy.'

They jumped in the skip and sped off.

'How are we going to break this news, Maya?'

'We tell the truth.'

The business partners arrived and parked beside the farmhouse surrounded by an assortment of other vehicles.

'Thank the stars we don't have to hide our transport skips in the attic as we had to when we led our secret lives.'

'Sure,' Maya grinned, 'I bet the extra space came in handy for more dormitory beds, our family seems to be growing every day.'

'How many of the children are with Melody in the city?' Shea asked as they walked through the gate at the side of the house and through the vegetable patch.

'She has her hands full, Amber and Cass are with her to keep the youngsters in line. Basically, all the children are under eleven in that group.'

'So, we should be free to discuss all the gory details,' Maya opened the back door and let Shea walk through first.

'Should we mention your fear fart?' Shea smiled impishly as he passed through the door.

'I don't think so,' Maya shook his head, and shoved Shea playfully, 'it wasn't funny.'

'I thought it was at the time.'

Inside a banquet had been prepared giving off an appetising invitation to eat. The plates and cutlery between terrines of soup, platters of fish, bowls filled with baked vegetables, rice, pastas, and breads were laid out.

Richard and Davrew welcomed them first, Sal had returned from filming a documentary in Europe, Ash had returned from the garage, Miri and Peter were back from a trip to India, even the family linguist Mica was there. Gem had arrived for the home cooked meal with Jake.

'Tam will be here soon,' Richard hugged his grandchildren.

'The whole gang,' Shea smiled.

Tam walked in moments later, carrying a tray of fresh baked bread rolls. After finding a space for it on the table he hugged his siblings and their teenage children.

'Everyone, please eat.' Davrew ushered the gathering to the table. After eating the family moved to the communal living areas to soak up the warmth of the fire and relax. Maya and Shea asked Richard and Davrew to be close at hand an important discussion was about to take place.

Richard used his wine glass as a chime tapped it with a spoon. Silence fell as all eyes turned to the patriarch of the family.

'That was a lovely meal, I hope you all enjoyed it as much as I did,' Richard smiled at the familiar faces of his family. 'We have Maya and Shea here tonight wanting to share some important news of recent events, while our youngest children and great grand-children are away enjoying a show, we can have a healthy discussion.'

All eyes were on Maya and Shea. 'As you know we recently went on a trading trip, with our cousins in space, Rinra and Colu. We are gaining valuable technology and resources for our projects here on Earth,' Maya began. He stood beside the warm fire and spread his hands to soak up the heat.

'It's important that we all know what it is like out there,' Shea added. He stood beside Maya and addressed everyone in the room, 'and, more importantly, what action we suggest is taken.'

'We'll take you back about ten days to our last trip,' Maya added.

## CHAPTER TWENTY-EIGHT

# Rakal's World Earth 2010

Ten days earlier, Shea and Maya had left Earth behind them and sped off to the Grid to meet up with cousins on the other side of the galaxy. Their ship was a small carrier, the front control room compact. The rear cargo storage area was spacious. The craft had been built to their design by Ash the family mechanic, inventor, and all-round whizz with anything mechanical. Designed for speed and maneuverability, with the capacity to carry whatever cargo they could trade. It was ideal for the task.

Shea opened communication as soon as they were in the grid, slipping effortlessly from one side of the galaxy to the other, in the Ancients high speed access line. Like a giant escalator speeding from one point in space to another.

'Hi Colu, are you ready for our trading trip?'

'Sure. Rinra is here too, and looking forward to going to trade, it's a wild planet we're heading to.'

'How wild?' Maya asked, while looking at Shea, who was touching a panel in front of him.

'Nothing we can't handle,' Colu replied.

'I have everything we need within reach, Maya, we'll be fine.'

'We are not fighters Shea,' Maya sighed, 'I hope we don't have to be.'

'We knew there were dangers doing this job,' Shea replied wearily, 'we've been over this before.'

'I know, we Davidson's do too much debating.'

'I'm almost at our rendezvous point, Colu. See you shortly.'

They slipped out of the grid and swung into orbit above Orthama, near the giant space station. This was the home, created and extended over the years, to house the survivors of the dead planet below. Expertly, Shea docked, and the two travellers left to meet their cousins.

'Rinra, Colu, great to see you,' Maya and Shea warmly greeted their cousins with boisterous hugs and firm handshakes. Then they headed off to inspect their produce for trade.

'Well, here you have it,' Shea showed Colu and Rinra the vegetables and nuts in the edible bins aboard Maya and Shea's carrier.

'All fresh,' Maya added.

'And these are a bonus,' Colu walked slowly around the mini skips.

'They sure are beautiful machines,' Rinra agreed.

'They can travel pretty fast, the space station is really too small to use these mini skips,' Shea moved towards another section. 'I believe your traders might be interested in them.'

'They sure will,' Colu rubbed his hand gently over the sparkling metal, 'they don't have anything quite like this.'

'What about this?' Maya pulled out what appeared to be little metal boxes. 'They're iPods with music already loaded. Don't know if this lot will sell, but thought it was worth bringing them to see what would happen.'

'Music?'

'You bet.' Maya held up a small box the size of his hand, flipped on a screen, pressed the icon on the pad and gritty pop music rang out. 'Touch screen, it's all the rage back on Earth.'

'What about weapons?' Rinra asked while fiddling with the music icons on the box in his hand.

'Now, Rinra, you know we are pacifists.'

'We are too, but weapons sell,' Colu added.

'What about these?' Shea went to a bin full of balls of all shapes and sizes. He picked up a round soccer ball and threw it at Maya who caught it easily.

'Sport is big on our world,' Maya shook his head and tossed the ball full pelt at Rinra, 'they must play games.'

'We don't go socialising with them Maya, they're a rough lot.'

'But they have what we want?' Shea looked about the cargo hold, 'and we should be able to trade?'

'My contact says we'll get all the old junk technology we want,' Colu smiled and nodded.

'Good, Ash is a whizz at turning junk into something amazing,' Shea added as he touched an icon on the iPod. A fast fiddle melody filled the room and Shea did a few quick dance steps.

They all laughed.

'Okay, we'll follow you,' Rinra swung his cousin around in dance fashion, then headed for the door with Colu.

Back in their small cockpit, Shea and Maya watched the view screen. They travelled close behind their cousins' larger spaceship.

'I still can't get over how much Rinra looks like old man Cal,' Maya linked his fingers and stretched his arms out to relieve the tension in his shoulders.

'Well, you know old man Cal was one pro-duc-tive sperm giver,' Shea tried to imitate the slow drawl of the Texan, not very successfully. Maya laughed.

'We're coming up to the Traders home world, Colu will put into orbit shortly. We'll just take up position nearby.'

They dropped speed and settled in a stationary orbit above the planet.

'Meet you both, planet side,' Colu chirruped a brief message.

'Got the co-ordinates partner,' Shea drawled again.

A short time later, on the planet, the four family members met up and headed for the local town centre to meet their prospective buyers.

'Did you notice there were a heap of other ships in orbit too?' Rinra asked.

'Always are on this planet,' Maya nodded.

'Don't know about you, but we're tall most places we go, but here we're not,' Shea walked stride for stride beside Maya, Colu and Rinra, along a well-worn cobble stone path that led to a town square.

'It can be a bit intimidating,' Colu agreed.

'There are our Traders,' Rinra nodded towards three huge creatures' shrouded in capes and hoods.

'By the stars, Shea, I feel like we've stepped into the pages of a Charles Dickens novel. It's only the brilliant orange sky that gives away we're on another planet.'

'There is lots of technology for sale in the stalls,' Maya had picked up a trinket on the way to their rendezvous.

'Let's get this done. They can come to the ship to see the merchandise,' Rinra held out his hand to one of the three Traders who shook it enthusiastically.

'Guhamp, meet my family, Shea and Maya are here with goods for you to look at.'

The tall dark man with purple skin stretched over scrawny limbs nodded. His hand stuck out from the heavy cape and took Shea's hand with a vice like grip. Then the group were led to a tent behind a stall that had stacks of bits and pieces for them to scavenge through.

'This is awesome,' Maya smiled as he rummaged through the scrap metal.

After that meeting concluded the four cousins chatted.

'Funny, the way that guy was acting, he seemed to be a bit anxious about something,' Shea nodded towards their trading partners.

'We struck a good deal,' Maya mused, 'they did seem a little agitated. Perhaps there is something here we're not seeing?'

'Colu and I will do another stroll around the market,' Rinra replied, 'perhaps we'll find out why they're nervous.'

'We'll meet you back on our ship,' Shea was looking around the stalls and could see nothing but a busy marketplace.

'We'll be there shortly. The goods exchange is set. We don't want to be late,' Colu added before heading off in the other direction.

Back on the ship, Maya and Shea were busy in the cargo hold.

'That was a good deal we struck,' Maya smiled.

'Yes, most of the stock here in exchange for heaps of old gadgetry, Ash will be in Heaven when we get that stuff to him,' Shea lifted the crates with hover platforms near to the hatch.

'What a great reaction to the iPods? Man, I thought that big guy was going to flip out he was so excited.'

'I loved his little dance,' Shea agreed. 'they couldn't have been happier with that simple technology.'

'They are coming alongside,' Maya watched the docking spacecraft manoeuvre.

Guhamp announced his arrival. Maya opened their cargo hold, and with little discussion, the transfer took place with the help of levitation platforms. Quickly the transfer was done.

'Let's have a drink to celebrate,' Shea offered a shot from a bottle of spirits.

Bowing low and muttering, the purple men backed away.

'They made a quick getaway,' Maya shook his head. He accepted and downed the colourless liquid in one fluid motion.

'Colu, I think we should head off too,' Rinra said, 'there are a few more ships outside than I like to see.'

With that Shea and Maya headed for the control room as their cousins made a quick transport to their own vehicle. The Traders had already closed the hatch and disengaged from their dock.

'The big ship is the one to watch,' Colu was now speaking to them from the other ship.

'Why?'

'It's Zorn,' Colu replied.

'Zorn?'

'Zorn. I've heard that name, some relative of Vashla or Rakal, or both, I think,' Shea offered.

'That's the one,' Colu continued, 'he is kind of a tyrant in many different places.'

'He's a bully,' Rinra added, 'and I think we should head off. Word on the planet, with our traders in the market, was that Zorn wants a cut of any deal taking place there. Naturally, they were none too happy about him muscling in on their trade.'

'That's explains why they were nervous,' Maya glanced at Shea. His hands flashed over the touchscreen panel. 'We'll be off then, catch up with you soon.'

'Sure will,' Colu saluted and the view screen went blank.

'We're being hailed by the big ship now,' Shea looked at Maya. 'Shall we chat?'

'Why not, we are heading off now anyway.'

The image on the screen was a huge man with masses of dark hair, a beard to match, and with his dark penetrating eyes and scowling face that made Shea shiver.

'I am Zorn, Lord of this planet. That planet is mine and you will only trade there if I permit it.'

'Well howdy do Lord Zorn,' Maya replied. 'We didn't see your name written on the planet, and the people there seemed happy to trade with us. As far as Universal Law is concerned, we can trade with anyone who wants to, of their own free will, trade on their own planet. We'll be heading off now.'

Maya cut the connection.

'We'll be in the grid in a jiff. Colu and Rinra are already heading off?'

'That goon growls,' Shea shook his head, 'he can't follow us both since we're travelling in opposite directions.'

'He's firing up!' Maya quickly manoeuvred their craft around the incoming fire and slid into the grid at speed.

'By the stars, Maya, Zorn is following Colu and Rinra.'

In the lounge of the old farmhouse, the room was silent as all eyes in the room anxiously watched Maya and Shea.

'Colu and Rinra got back to base with Zorn on their tail,' Maya continued, 'the growling creep actually claimed Orthama as his own planet.'

'Our family members sent him packing, he left quickly enough with their encouragement,' Shea went on. 'It was a close thing. The point is, they are armed, and they knew how to handle him.'

'Being one ship against a well-armed space station that had weapons he didn't know about, aimed at him, Zorn left,' Maya explained, and shivered at the thought.

He rubbed his hands together above the fire, to banish his fear.

'The point is, Grandfather, Davrew, family, we feel there is a need for us to arm ourselves. We are pacifists. Zorn doesn't know this, when he comes along the grid to our world, he will want to take control of the planet,' Shea scanned the room to judge the reaction. He saw a room full of stunned faces. 'I suggest we learn some things about defence and offence from our human colleagues,' Maya waited for the assembled family members to digest the information.

CHAPTER TWENTY-NINE

# Orthama Space Station

Colu and Rinra rushed down the ramp of the space dock.

'Nayiri, alert the control room that we are on our way. We're being followed by Zorn and he's ready for a fight,' Colu shouted as they ran out the door.

They continued through the outer maze of deck dock links. Through the extensions to the original space station into the older main corridor.

'I only hope we get to the control room before Zorn gets through the grid,' Rinra panted as they ran along the wall of heritage. The long corridor that led to the centre of the space station now adorned by images of the original inhabitants and their descendants. The results of the propagation programme that had been created to have their species survive.

'Do you think the security plan that our ancestor Anthony Cassurina put in place will be enough to repel Zorn?' Colu puffed as they skidded along the final curve of the passage.

'Hope so, Colu, it's over fifty Earth years since it was set up,' Rinra pointed to the next exit. 'Shea said it's hard to believe there was no defence system put in place before his grandfather and the other founding sperm donors arrived.'

'Well, we know that the old man, the original citizen of the dead planet below us, said that the sperm programme was a success. Who's to say the defence system won't work?' Colu pushed the control door entry pad.

'We are living proof that we've been seeded, there are thousands on this space station now.'

Bursting into the main control room they saw the communication view screen light up. There before them was the menacing face of the outraged space pirate Zorn. Glaring black eyes shone with venom, dark hair about a rugged bearded face, filled the screen.

'I claim the planet as mine,' Zorn bellowed.

'It is not yours to claim,' Vini of the elders calmly replied.

'There is no sign of life on the planet below, so it is mine to claim,' Zorn sneered.

'I believe you will find our claim is that of linage, we are direct descendants of the people who originally populated the planet. Our forebears managed to make the planet uninhabitable. It is quite barren of vegetation, or life, of any form. In time to come it may regenerate, we hope to be the colonists to re-inhabit it.'

Zorn let out a low rumbling growl that ended in a gut-wrenching pitch. Moments later, his ship turned, and his weapons flashed across the perimeter of the space station.

'Next one will hit.'

'I believe that would be unwise,' Vini replied totally unperturbed, 'we do still have the technology that caused the devastation on the planet below, we could demonstrate on a little planet not far from the grid. I believe you have workers mining there. They would all be lost, and the planet would be lay waste. Shall I show you?' Vini bought the image of Zorn's mining planet to the screen an orb beside it swivelled and pointed an arm that extended out from it.

At the same time an identical orb left the space station and took position halfway between Zorn's craft and the extreme edge of the space station.

Colu and Rinra held their breath.

The long silence was intense. Vini remained calm and stayed waiting for Zorn's reply. This came when Zorn simply turned the vehicle and slid back into the grid, disappearing and shortly after re-appearing near the orb above the mining planet. They watched him quickly fire at the orb and destroy it. Their view screen then went black. Vini turned around and greeted Colu and Rinra.

'It's good to see you back,' Vini continued speaking curtly, 'will all these trading trips bring danger back to our home?'

Colu, avoided looking into the Elders' eyes.

'We tried to lose Zorn before entering the grid,' Rinra offered lamely in defence.

'Will the Elders be meeting about this?' Colu asked nervously.

'Of course,' Vini replied. 'You will both need to come before the Elders to explain the situation. You will be advised when.'

With a wave of the Elders hand they were dismissed.

'That was close,' Rinra wheezed.

On the return to their living quarters they walked along the corridor of linage. Colu stopped in front of the images and reached for the touch pad. Bringing down under the Elders' Vini picture, the image of Callum Bennett the human, he studied the features of the man.

'Do you think I look like Cal?' Colu asked Rinra, 'Maya and Shea are always saying I do.'

'Look Colu, you do have similar features, the best way to see is to judge for yourself. Here, bring up your image, put it beside the human.'

They compared the two pictures, and they did have strong similarities they both had the same jaw line, high cheek bones.

'Cal is what Shea says is a carrot top, or redhead,' Rinra pointed out, 'you have the same fair hair, in some lights it does have an orange tinge.'

They stood silent for several minutes, each considering the implications of the events that had taken place.

'That was a close call,' Colu looked along the images, 'we can thank the stars that Antony Cassurina stayed here when the other humans went back to Earth.'

'I share his DNA so I must be his descendant offspring,' Rinra bought up the image, 'I guess we look a bit alike too.'

'It's a good thing he said he had nothing to go back to. Had it not been for his insistence that we should build a defence system, we'd be in real trouble today. We would have had nothing to repel Zorn with.'

'True, and we wouldn't be speaking the languages of the humans either,' Rinra was studying the image.

'They were about the age we are now when these pictures were made,' Colu compared Rinra to Anthony with eyes wide set above a large nose.

'One of tales he used to tell us as youngsters was how he had lost his parents at an early age, he'd lived with friends on the street,' Rinra explained what he'd be told. 'He said it was tough, but they were like a family. When he came here, he had a new family, there was only the Old Man left of the Orthama originals then. He didn't leave the Old Mans' side until he died.'

'We better get back to our quarters, and let Shea and Maya know we're alright,' Colu nudged Rinra.

'Soon the Elders will call us to explain what happened,' Rinra whispered.

## CHAPTER THIRTY

# Rakal's World Earth

Just after sunrise on a crisp clear winter morning. Sunlight reached into every crevice in the farmhouse. Peter and Miri made their way to the purpose-built hall, at the end of the property. It was still too cold to exercise outside. They took up position at the front of the room, other family members started coming in. Standing side-by-side Peter and Miri began their graceful Tai Chi dance, absorbed in the precision of each movement, focused and relaxed, totally in sync. The hall filled within a short time and each Davidson family member joined them in the exercise routine.

Richard and Davrew rarely made it to this first Tai Chi session of the day, but today, about thirty minutes after Peter and Miri had started, they joined the group for the stretching and warm down part of the session.

'Chilly morning,' Richard greeted their eldest child Miri and her human partner Peter.

'Not too bad in here,' Peter replied, 'the frost will soon clear and it should give us a beautiful day.'

'We wanted to talk to you both,' Davrew got straight to the point.

'Of course,' Miri handed a towel to Peter, 'about our proposals for self defence classes being taken a step further?'

'We are pacifists,' Davrew ran long fingers through his hair, mimicking Richards' mannerism. It made Miri smile. 'I don't like active aggression.'

'Nor do we,' Peter dabbed his face and put the towel around his neck. 'As you can see, the Tai Chi is popular. The martial arts are simply an extension of that, and Aikido is controlled retaliation, like Judo.'

'The kick boxing is proving popular too,' Miri added.

'We were thinking of bringing in help from outside, like a military adviser,' Peter held his breath.

'Ash is able to develop weaponry for our skips and spaceships. Previously only defence has been the priority, but with what Rakal is telling us is really happening, we need more,' Miri looked nervously at her parents. 'We have the safety of our children, grandchildren and great grandchildren to consider.'

'You don't have to remind us,' Richard straightened up his aching back. 'We're catching up with Ash and Cass for lunch across the road. Would you be able to meet us there about eleven?'

'Sure,' Miri nodded.

'I don't like naturally aggressive people around my family,' Davrew sighed.

'We've had Rakal and Vashla around for many years, and they are hardly pacifists,' Miri reminded them as she hugged Davrew then pulled away. She looked into the crisp blue eyes filled with concern. 'We'll head off to change and meet you for lunch then.'

'Okay,' Richard smiled and took Davrew by the arm, 'we'll see you there.'

'We've a catch up with Pat and Bill before then,' Davrew added.

'Yeah, I wonder what that's about,' Richard shrugged.

'I guess we'll soon find out.'

Richard and Davrew, arm-in-arm, strode in step, through their large wrought iron gates and across the road. It would be a good fifteen-minute walk to Pat and Bill's entrance, and a further ten to their door.

'We could have taken the skip,' Richard mumbled trying not to puff.

'We both need the exercise, and this is a good warm down from the Tai Chi,' Davrew grinned and hugged Richards arm.

They crunched along the gravel drive to the house and knocked on the door.

'Hi there,' Pat answered. Pat held her finger to her lips, and they tiptoed inside.

Pat peeked around the corner from the kitchen with a smile as she beckoned them into the warm kitchen. They soon shared the joke, seeing Bill in his wheelchair with their two cats comfortably cradled on his lap. Bill was sound asleep, with his glasses barely on his nose. They sidled past as quietly as possible and sat out in the conservatory barely containing their amusement. Pat signed T with her fingers in front of her and they both nodded. Pat's movements and the kettle boiling woke the big man.

'Bloody cats! What are you doing there?'

'I can't imagine why they climb up on your lap,' Pat feigned surprise.

Richard and Davrew both burst out laughing.

'When did you lot arrive?'

'Just now cousin, I don't think the beauty sleep worked for you,' Richard grinned while making his way back into the kitchen with Davrew close behind.

'I never was an oil painting,' Bill spluttered.

'You can say that again,' Richard nudged Bill's shoulder with his fist.

Pat quickly set down mugs of hot tea on the table, shortly after a plate of breakfast muffins. Retrieving one for herself, she slathered it with butter, pointing to the others to indulge.

'To think you two were at each other's throats when you were growing up, and even when you first settled at the old farmhouse place. It's hard to believe that now,' Pat smiled as she sipped her tea.

'Times do change,' Davrew grinned.

'What have you on your mind cousin? You have something important to say, you said,' Richard warmed his hands on the mug.

'Yeah, well, it's like this,' Bill began, 'we're on our own now, both the girls live away, and they have families of their own.'

'We noticed,' Richard replied, 'so?'

'So, we're moving to the coast to a little cottage in a retirement complex,' Pat replied for Bill who suddenly appeared to be tongue tied.

'I am 73, and this place is too big for us now,' Bill muttered as he stuffed a piece of hot buttered muffin into his mouth. He seemed to be avoiding eye contact with his cousin.

'We don't want to sell the house,' Pat was now strumming her fingers on the side of her mug, 'we thought long and hard about it.'

'We want you to have it,' Bill cleared his throat, 'our girls may want some part of this place, in the future. But, with one interstate and the other overseas, there's not much point hanging around here.'

'You have an ever-expanding family, we want to see this house lived in,' Pat smiled at Richard who was rubbing his big hand through his mop of unruly hair. 'Your grandchildren and great grandchildren can make a place here for themselves.'

'I know it's a bit of a jaunt in the old station-wagon for you guys,' Richard was leaning forward in his chair, 'you've been living on the coast half the year and here the other half. Why don't you just keep things the way they are?'

'It's like this. Pat has been a rock all these years, looking after me since the accident. Your kids have really helped us run the farm, keeping the garden and grounds up to scratch. Damn it they are more part of our lives than our own girls. Sal and those two Saz and Skye, the impish twins, they helped keep me sane after that darn tractor pinned me down. Now I see their kids and I'm chuffed. It comes down to the fact that Pat needs a break from all the work. Where we're going now is set up to help if I can't do something. Pat can take time out for herself.'

'Pat, you certainly deserve it,' Davrew nodded.

'Is money a problem?' Richard bit his lip as he asked this question.

'You've always been a cheeky bugger,' Bill leaned back in his chair. 'We don't need the money from the sale of this house if that's what you're thinking. We've been making good money over the years, off the land. We'd never have managed without Sal and the kids. Things are tight but nothing we can't manage.'

Pat reached out and held Bill's hand. 'It's time for our sea change, that's all.'

'We do need to say that we've been worried about what's happening in the space thing. Shea and Maya have been trading and gathering what looks like junk to me. Where's all this heading?'

'From what Rakal tells us with news from Vashla, down a dangerous road,' Richard winced.

'We are pacifists, the thought of what they are saying becoming real is very frightening,' Davrew said with a sigh.

'Could this really mean a war? An interplanetary war?' Pat put down her cup, added some more muffins to the plate and pushed them to the centre of the table.

'Whatever happens, it's gonna affect everyone on Earth, right?' Bill was now clasping Pat's hand tightly.

'If it escalates as Vashla predicts, there could be five planets involved, and, it seems greed and envy is the cause. This Zorn is a madman with a mining planet and an urge to dominate Vashla and her world. Naturally, our trade with our cousins on Orthama space station is at risk. It's all very scary,' Davrew summed up. 'We'll have to protect Earth, Orthama is a dead world but our space station origins are a vital link, and Vashla has a consort from another planet that is tangled up in all this, his name is Gardt. His planet of origin is like ours. We're not geared to fight. Rakal and Vashla are.'

'This planet has had battles raging for centuries, we have armies on every continent,' Richard stood up, 'maybe it'll all come to nothing.'

'It may not,' Bill added. 'I'll tell you what I think. You know I don't just sit about stewin'.' He rubbed the stubble on his chin with thick fingers. 'I reckon it's like I saw on one of those reality TV shows. There was a group trying to get from one place to another with obstacles in their way, the one guy who'd made himself leader got them to this gorge crossing. They were given ropes and pulleys and winches to help them get across. The leader guy said, 'I can't do this, I don't know anything about pulleys and ropes.' Another guy in the group said, 'No you don't, but I do. I work with these and this is what we need to do.' Next thing the whole group were working together to get across and won the day.'

'So, you think we need help from experts in the defence and offence arena?' Davrew got up too and pushed his chair back in.

Bill nodded. Pat smiled.

'I think that's what Peter has in mind, we're going to the new house now for a chat,' Richard held out his hand to his cousin. They shook hands with vigour. 'Let us know when you're planning to move, and we'll come and help.'

'Sure.' Pat smiled, with a quick kiss farewell.

## CHAPTER THIRTY-ONE

# Vashla's World VaLinta and above Orthama

Rakal slid his spaceship into orbit after travelling through the grid to Vashla's World. His ship was small but fast. The gravity was comfortably set to suit his body at much less than the heavy downward force he experienced on Earth. Since Tam was not with him, he felt free to set it that way.

This spacecraft wasn't the only one he'd obtained, as Vashla had her own fleet, through plunder and death, so had he. That was a life he no longer practiced. His own fleet was now hidden in stationary orbit on the black side of Earth's moon. He knew that his own presence on Earth was creating interest in the planet by others like Zorn. This was dangerous.

His view screen image displayed his voluptuous cousin. He nodded his greeting.

'Where shall I park?' Rakal noticed the planet Va-Linta looked a lot like Earth from this vantage point.

'Stay there. I'll join you. We need to discuss our plans with our allies. Will you take us to Orthama station?'

'Of course,' Rakal replied, 'Zorn is restricting your travel?'

'You have only just arrived. He'll not notice your quick departure if we go now. We'll be with you shortly.' A small craft the size of an escape pod docked within minutes of him closing the view screen.

'Rakal, it's good to see you cousin,' Vashla raised her hand waist high as was the traditional salute among her family. 'You have met my son Agai, this is his father Gardt. They need to see the plans we're making. Like others on our home worlds they do not realise the full danger we are in.'

Rakal nodded and pressed the controls.

The craft slipped quickly into the grid and exited at the Orthama co-ordinate. The space station before them was large and majestic. Its three-rotating triangular shaped extensions were joined by tubular corridors.

Vini, representing the Elders of Orthama, greeted them. They walked along the corridor of linage, before entering the Great Meeting Room. The surviving Elders were seated in a semi-circle facing an audience of workers, still filing into the auditorium.

'We were only expecting Rakal and Vashla,' Vini pointed towards the vacant seats in the semi-circle.

'We can sit here,' Gardt suggested towards the front of the audience.

Vini nodded and quickly reallocated two seats at the end of the front row. Rinra and Colu having been comfortably placed now were standing at the side of the hall. The Elder then stood at the front of the room and the murmurs from the audience subsided to silence.

'I represent all our Elders,' Vini pointed out their leaders to the assembly. 'We have important guests, Vashla and her cousin Rakal are with us, to discuss how we can move forward. The discussion is to be how we can develop self defence systems for our planet and their worlds.'

'Our experiments have resulted in a steady population increase. Primarily, we are working to regenerate Orthama, and make it habitable once more, so we can live on our free world again. Zorn is a threat we must repel. If he attacks now, and in force, we have a limited defence system, and no weapons to fight him with. Please listen carefully everyone, and feel free to contribute. Vashla and Rakal, please speak now.'

'I am Rakal,' he stood to allow the full effect of his and imposing statue and dress to hit home. He wore his raiding clothes without the weaponry. 'As you all have learnt the languages of your sperm donors, and adapted your own unique culture, this will be another step in your development.'

'If we need it,' a dissenting voice from the audience called out.

'We're here to show you the wisdom of our suggestions,' Rakal looked about the auditorium. Many of the pale faces looking back resembled his own Tam. 'On Earth, where I now live, with my beloved Tam, we live a peaceful life. Tam is one of your own descendants, born from the family Richard the human, and Davrew, one like yourselves from Orthama. They are pacifists and don't look for a battle, or they haven't until now.' His dark eyes were mesmerising to the onlookers who were silent. Vashla joined him in front of the audience.

'I am Vashla, a former predator, known on Earth as a space pirate. 'Pirates', this is an interesting term, I have discovered that on Earth, Pirates are those on Earth who take advantage of others who are vulnerable. They take their victims' possessions, often kill their prey, leaving no trace of their actions behind. I have plundered and murdered for my own gain. I've captured and taken all that I felt I needed.'

'You are both a threat to us,' one of the Elders stood to voice dissent.

'I no longer do this,' Vashla continued. 'I have changed because of the family I live with. This does not mean I cannot draw on my experience to defend all our worlds including Earth, Orthama, Gardt's home world Ghaur and of course my own world VaLinta.'

'Why should we believe you?' the Elder rose again.

Vashla flipped back her hair allowing the lush ringlets to cascade down her back while motioning the man to sit.

'Rakal is my relative, our kind have always been taught to take what we want. I am more recently tamed by love. My beloved, as Rakal described his Tam, is Gardt. Zorn is our relative also, he has no calming love to change his ways. All our worlds need protecting from him.' She looked at the faces before her. They were all pale, all scientists, who. had lived their lives aboard this space station. Taking a deep breath, she continued. She needed to show them how important her planet was and why they needed mutual protection. She wondered if these people were able to fight for themselves.

'My planet is a lush word with potential to support a growing population. I will allow some people to settle there, but not too many. Gardt's home world is very overpopulated, and I have offered to be a new colony world for their adventurers. I welcome those of you who would like to breathe fresh air, to learn to grow plants, harvest new crops and develop this world, to join them. The original inhabitants the Linta, now known as Va-Linta, died of an illness. Apparently, on Earth, when indigenous cultures have been met by other peoples, the spread of diseases that have wiped out or decimated the original populations. This is something I wish to avoid at all cost. I don't know the origins of Gardt's people, although, I suspect they may have the Ancients in them, they are bipeds, like yourselves. I will ask Gardt to speak shortly, and our son Agai also has some interesting suggestions.'

'Gardt does seem to share many of the attributes of the people from Earth, I live with now,' Rakal spoke projecting his voice, as he had learnt to do from touring Earth. Public speaking, slowly and clearly, throwing his voice into the room so it reached every ear. 'The people of Earth are diverse, there are many who live ordinary lives, work to provide food for their families, and strive to be healthy. There are many fighters too. These people will attack for their own gain and use people for their own benefit. They have police to combat these thieves and abusers. They make laws, or, rules that must be obeyed, and the police enforce the rules. They also have a world army run by an international governing body, and most countries have their own armies, with soldiers to defend their boundaries. Soldiers are trained combatants with weapons of destruction, large and small, for individual defence and attack. It is an interesting world.'

Vashla beckoned Gardt to join her. He stood, his body, tanned, toned and strong. He took his place at her side.

'My world Ghaur, it is full of government controls. We must obey many rules. The population has increased so much we are not able to cope with the needs of the people. Our leaders planned an escape, immigration and colonisation to other worlds,' Gardt cleared his throat with a cough. 'My people live on every part of the world. It has limited resources and our technology has been developed, beyond the understanding of the normal citizen. We also have police and armies that are run by one dominating government. From what Rakal has told me of Earth, the people are more independent, control their own lives, yet they are more willing to start battles. My home world Ghaur, is full of fear, control and obedience.'

Vini stood beside the guests, standing on a hovering platform to add height and look them in the eye. 'We are pacifists. However, we are not a people without defences. Orthama was once a beautiful planet with a large and diverse population. The Ancients, we believe, settled all our worlds. They made the grid for travel between these worlds. As on Earth, most of the population were peaceful, living to provide for their families, only the few, who wanted power, sought to fight. They were eventually the cause of our destruction. Our battle with one group against the other was damaging and finally the reason the planet below is now uninhabitable.'

Lowering the hover disc, Vini looked to the side of the hall.

'I will ask Rinra and Colu to come and speak about their encounter with Zorn, who followed our two young traders home recently,' Vini paused, allowing the murmur from the audience rose, as the two youths walked to centre stage. Vini held hands high to silence the gathering and allow the youngsters to speak. Unlike the Elder, who wore a ceremonial robe, they wore simple coveralls. Nervously they stood and addressed the assembly.

'We have seen many cultures, on many worlds, since embarking on our interplanetary trade missions,' Colu began shakily.

'Our family on Earth have two explorers like ourselves, Shea and Maya,' Rinra continued more boldly. 'They are gathering equipment to build new devices for travel and to help people on Earth combat disease, starvation and generally advance the people's living standards.'

'We are doing this for the same reasons, and to explore other worlds and their people,' Colu added then stepped back to let Rinra finish.

'We met our trading partners from Earth, Shea and Maya. Our spaceships travelled together to the planet Ozer, to meet our contact Guhamp, and complete our trade,' Rinra explained.

'Everything went well, our business concluded quickly. The people on Ozer were nervous and we soon discovered Zorn was the reason,' Colu added.

'They didn't wait around after completing the transfer of goods,' Rinra continued, 'they were in a hurry to get away. Zorn's huge battleship was nearby, and he contacted us demanding that any trade on the planet Ozer was his to control. We made it clear we were independent and would trade where we were welcome.'

'We decided to leave quickly, Shea and Maya went through the grid towards Earth and we went the opposite direction slipping into the grid towards Orthama,' Colu concluded. 'Zorn followed us, firing at us while we evaded. Zorn wants to be in control of every planet he encounters, many traders are fearful of his reprisals.'

The audience murmur began again.

'Zorn took a shot at Shea and Maya. They slipped away from him easily and slipped into the grid. Then he followed us here. He claimed Orthama as his own world. Vini deployed the defence orbs and sent him away, with a threat ringing in his ears. He was left in no doubt, we could lay waste his world, with one the press of a button. It worked.'

'We made our position clear,' Vini now took over the address. 'Zorn was sent away with a threat. It was not an idle threat. We are scientists who have utilised technology to bring our population numbers back from the brink of extinction. Our sperm donors from Earth provided strength of will. Self defence skills were provided by Anthony Casuarina, one originally bought here from Earth, was particularly influential in ensuring we had a defence mechanism in place for this station and our planet. Many of the humans who remained, helped us create facilities to keep fit and ensure our survival. We do need to make plans to defend our worlds, now more than ever, and to

find peaceful ways to live our lives through our connec-
tions.'

One of the other Elders rose to speak.

'I see no great threat in this Zorn. He came here following our traders and claimed Orthama, we quickly
turned him away making it clear this world is ours. Why
should we be dragged into the defence of these other
worlds over our Orthama?'

Vini replied, 'that's exactly what we have come here
to discuss. Thank you for raising it Asahm.'

Again, Vini raised the platform.

'We are here today to discuss our future and how we
can protect all our worlds from this foe. Zorn is a cousin
of Rakal and Vashla. We must learn to defend ourselves
but also to keep our way of life free from hatred.'

The heated debate began in earnest and continued
for many hours.

## CHAPTER THIRTY-TWO

# Vashla's World VaLinta and above Orthama

Back on board Rakal's spacecraft, Gardt took Vashla in his arms.

'That was exhausting and intense.'

Rakal nodded and sat in the control chair.

'We'll travel quickly to your planet Vashla,' he caressed the control panel like a long-lost friend. 'We are being hailed.'

'Did we not make ourselves clear?' Vashla pushed away from Gardt, venting some frustration on her partner.

'We did invite discussion, Mother,' Agai reminded his mother whose black eyes flashed with anger.

'Rinra, greetings,' Rakal answered the screen image. 'Do you have further questions?'

'Well, not so much a question a request. Does the invitation to come and see VaLinta still stand? I'd like to take it up, so would Colu and two of our friends. Is that alright? We can follow you now, hugging your slip stream, to conceal our presence. Just in case Zorn is watching.'

Vashla nodded and Rakal relayed her approval.

'Agreed. We go now.'

'We are right behind you, Rakal,' Rinra confirmed.

The view screen went blank and their journey began with a small pod from the space station following in their wake.


'I'm surprised Zorn hadn't claimed this planet years ago,' Rakal commented as they entered orbit.

'He didn't dare. My father took me there as a child, Zorn was there with his family. I was promised to him then. Our parents made an agreement to never challenge one another for it and, they agreed to leave its people free and under protection from other invaders.'

'That sort of agreement has never stopped Zorn before,' Rakal retorted as he manoeuvred his ship through the atmosphere towards the parking area on the surface.

'When he killed my father, he took over many of my father's possessions. I swore he would pay. Zorn attempted to woo me,' Vashla barked briefly with laughter. 'Before going back to Gardt, I did consider it, mainly for the benefit of my son, Agai. I know this would never have been a good choice. He is a fool. He only took control of one of my father's planets, a mining world. He works his miners on that planet to death and needs to renew his workforce often. Recently, from Gardt's home world, Ghaur, we gave him death row prisoners to meet his needs. It was a necessary arrangement to save the lives of innocent people who believed they would be colonists on a new world.'

'This planet VaLinta, it's so much better than living on a stuffy old space station,' Agai stretched as he stood to leave.

'Where I live on Earth is good too. The people there are different. Some are very gentle and kind, while others are mean and vicious. Somehow, we need to draw on both these traits to increase our chances of survival, here, on Earth and on Gardt's home world.

'So, you think we are all descendants of the Ancients, and good and evil is in us all?' Vashla looked directly into her cousin's eyes.

'By the stars,' Gardt shivered, 'that's deep. Not something I'd expect you to say.'

Vashla smiled, turned to Gardt, and pulled him towards her. 'There is much about me that you have yet to learn,' she planted a passionate kiss on his willing lips.

'I'm gone,' Agai rolled his eyes and ran to the exit.

Rakal laughed and followed the boy out. Rinra and the group from Orthama were just coming out of their vehicles as they departed the space craft.

'I'd like to take a good look around, Agai,' Rakal squinted into the early morning sunlight. 'Can you show me around? I'll join your visitors tour. If that's acceptable?'

Agai just nodded, they walked stride for stride towards the visitors.

'Hi, thanks for allowing us to come to VaLinta. We didn't get to meet properly back there. I'm Rinra, this is Colu, Ty and Arda. As you heard in the meeting, Colu and I are traders with Maya and Shea from Earth.'

'I've heard Shea and Maya speak of you,' Rakal held out his hand in greeting.

Rinra shook his hand, being familiar with Maya and Shea's Earth greeting.

'Ty is a botanist, trying to develop means of reintroducing plant life on Orthama, while Arda is with our food production team. We're interested in how we can help learn from the developments on this planet. How you grow or produce food, how the planet is managed. If we can help in any way to contribute to this, it will be mutually beneficial.'

'I can show you around,' Agai offered, 'but, I don't know about you, I can't go on without food.'

'Agai is always hungry,' Rakal laughed, 'just like the young people on Earth.'

Back at Vashla's cottage they ate fresh bread heaped with cheese.

'On Earth, they have all kinds of meats, here because the colony is so new, we eat mostly vegetables. There is wild fruit as well. I do fish and hunt for small animals to supplement our diet,' Agai demolished his meal spitting crumbs as he talked.

'What is meat?' Arda asked.

'Is it bit like the fungi we grow in the hydroponics lab?' Ty queried.

'Meat is from animals,' Colu added, 'sounds horrible to me.'

'You didn't say that when Maya gave you that hamburger to try,' Rinra added with a grin.

'It was tasty,' Colu shrugged.

'I do hunt some of the wild creatures on this planet some of them are like the pigs on Earth,' Agai said as he stuffed more bread into his mouth. 'Very tasty.'

'A hunt,' Rakal sighed, 'I'd like to try that.'

'After you look around the village, we can hunt if you want to. I just need to get my skip,' Agai replied.

Vashla looked sternly at her son.

'We don't know if Zorn noticed our journey, or that we can be safe. I'd prefer our guests stay close to the village. There is much to see with the early stage of the colony developing food production, distribution and settling in other former Linta villages,' she said suppressing a yawn.

'We are all weary from the long debate,' Gardt put his arm around Vashla's waist, 'perhaps after a rest we can explore more. The sunshine is warm and the seating outside the cottage is comfortable.'

The group retired to the garden and sipped fresh fruit juices while lazing in the sun.


Later that day, Agai and Rinra were the only ones to venture away from the village.

'There are wild animals in the forest. If we fly towards the lake, we'll see some,' Agai pointed ahead. 'I hope we can bag a good beast to feast on tonight'.

They were on a two-seater skip, skimming the treetops. Rinra clung tightly to the crossbar, knuckles almost turning white.

'There!' Agai shouted.

They watched a heard of animals emerge from the trees to go down to the water. Rinra's jaw dropped.

'I've never seen anything like them. What are they?'

'They are Limnash, like the deer on Earth, although you've never seen them either. They eat grasses and run fast. They are fun to hunt because of their speed, and they have good tasting meat.'

'How do you hunt them?'

'I've tried from on the skip, but the sound frightens them off. We have hunt on the ground.'

Agai expertly landed their small craft a good distance from the animals. He handed Rinra a weapon and took his own with him. They walked along the tree line out of view. Putting his finger to his lips Agai indicated they should be silent and urged Rinra forward with a nod of his head. They moved closer, stepping with care.

Rinra watched the animals intently and became distracted by the way the sunlight made Agai's dappled fair hair glint different hues, so unlike his family members. At that moment, he didn't notice a tree stump and stumbled. The animals nearby heard the crash and scattered.

'I told you to be quiet,' Agai turned on Rinra and, not bothering to help his guest up, he strode off.

A little shaken Rinra stood and brushed off the leaves and dust.

Again, Agai turned around and raised a finger to his lips. Rinra glared at him and carefully followed.

There was a huge crashing from the forest behind them and Agai pulled Rinra quickly behind a tree. 'Ludbous', Agai warned, 'like the wild pigs on Earth, big and fierce with tusks, and heading for the water.'

Agai lifted his gun and aimed in the direction of the crashing undergrowth. Shortly after a huge wild creature came stamping through the threes, three swift shots flew out from Agai's gun. The beast seemed to barely feel the impact and kept charging towards them.

'Shoot Rinra, this will take more than one gun can deliver. Shoot.'

Rinra, beside Agai and almost crouched to the ground, followed Agai's lead. They both fired again several times and the creature started to stagger. Almost at their feet, the creature finally collapsed.

'Ludbous, dead Ludbous!' Agai yelled, thumping his chest. 'We'll have a great feast tonight!'

Rinra bent over the creature and touched the warm flesh. 'I've never killed anything before.'

'Well, now you have, and it's a big carcass. This will make good eating,' Agai hefted their prey onto his shoulders. The animal's blood dripped down his back.

'I've been to other planets with Colu, more than anyone else on the Orthama space station,' Rinra fell into step beside Agai, as they walked towards the skip. 'You're so strong.'

Agai realised his face was reddening.

'We've seen other places Zorn bullies. I don't like to be bullied by anyone,' Rinra rushed on, to cover the awkward moment.

'Yeah,' Agai reached the skip and secured their prize in the back. 'I come out here on my own often. Mother is a bit, um, well demanding.'

'You mean bossy,' Rinra smiled.

'Yeah,' Agai was taking a few minutes to recover from the effort. He was sure footed and strong, but the load was heavy. He didn't want Rinra to think him weak, so he'd struggled on. He managed to carry the carcass the distance.

'Gardt knows how I feel. Sometimes I come out here to spend the day on my own, just swimming in the lake, exploring the forest.'

'It's a beautiful planet,' Rinra looked around, breathing deeply of the fresh clean air.

'The people from Gardt's world are so used to being told what to do. Even though these ones are prepared to start a colony and do all the setting up, I doubt without my mother's suggestions and practical guidance they could have managed.'

'You should wash that blood off.'

'Good idea. Let's go for a swim, a quick one. We'll need to get our meat back soon so it can be prepared for the feast.'

Rinra admired Agai's physique as they both peeled off their clothes and dived into the lake. Agai took several strokes out into deeper water.

'How long will you be here?' Agai asked.

'Depends on how things develop,' Rinra grinned and kicked out. 'This is fun.'

'We must be getting back soon,' Agai reminded his new friend. 'I might have been a bit,' he hesitated.

'Rude,' Rinra finished his sentence.

'I guess I'm like my mum, I don't know how to be...'

'Kind,' Rinra prompted.

'Gardt tells me I should be more aware of what others are feeling,' Agai turned and swam towards the bank.

'You were being bossy before.'

'I'm not a good teacher,' Agai sighed.

'We can all learn.' Rinra scooped up some water and aimed it at Agai. They playfully splashed until Agai and tried to dunk Rinra, who spluttered and headed to shore.

'This is a day of firsts for me,' Rinra shook off the water then sat on the bank. 'First time I've been on a skip, first time I've shot a gun, first time I've killed an animal, and first time I've had a swim.'

Agai grinned, and pulled on his top, 'this is a first for me too, sharing a hunt and a swim in my own swimming spot. Maybe we can make sure you have more firsts.'

Rinra did hope so.

CHAPTER THIRTY-THREE

# Zorn's Mining World Xamba

Zorn let blood drip down his chin while licking his fingers. He snapped another bone off and waved it in the air.

'Now, is there anyone else questioning my plans?'

The soldiers nearby shook their heads and stood sourly nearby.

'Good.'

He continued to disembowel and demolish his former aide.

'The profits from the mine have been well spent in acquiring ships we need to battle our enemy, my Lord,' the little bookkeeper ventured to say.

'So, we have an attack force. Now, what information do we have on our enemy?'

'As you discovered my Lord, the planet Orthama is barren, laid waste as testified to by the survivors on the space station above. There are traders among their number that have dealings with several planets that are yours, my Lord. As they have only traded for waste materials. They are no threat.'

'Why do they trade for rubbish?' Zorn snorted, 'and what do they trade?'

'They trade these,' a big dark purple person stepped forward and handed a few small boxes to the big man. Zorn looked perplexed. 'You press the screen with the light on and it makes music.'

'Humph.' Zorn pressed the screen on one and heavy metal music blared out. He pressed another and classical music filled the room. 'Rubbish for rubbish.'

'It has been popular, and sold well, my Lord,' the purple man added.

'What else?'

'These are for sport they said,' the purple man Gu-hamp bounced a ball then handed it to the disgruntled leader.

'Sport?'

'It is for recreation. An activity people do to relax and play games. They put up a ring on a wall and showed our young ones how to throw it and put it through the ring. It is a skill that can be worked on.'

'Like we practice hand combat games, they do this?'

'Yes.'

'Music,' Zorn turned another small box over in his hand pressed the button and a haunting trumpet blasted long strong notes into the air.

'Who are these traders?'

'We deal with two that come from Orthama, and two that travel from a distant world called Earth. That is where Rakal now lives.'

'And the person Vashla has with her, this Gardt Ness. What of his world?'

The purple man shook his head.

'That is where the mine workers came from, my Lord,' the little bookkeeper answered. 'The ones in the ships we originally purchased, they were taken back by Vashla have gone to live on Vashla's world.'

'I did know that!' Zorn snapped. He stood up, pushing aside the remnants of his meal.

'We believe Rakal has visited Vashla, in fact that he is there now,' the purple man Guhamp explained.

'They could combine their efforts against us?' Zorn growled.

'It is likely, they have little defence against your attack, my Lord,' the bookkeeper bowed.

Zorn paced about the room growling, occasionally standing still to stare at the view screen.

'Rakal, that is a familiar name. Had a brother, who liked a fight, if I remember. It was long ago, before our parents sent us separate ways.'

He thumped his hand on the control console.

'How far apart are these planets along the grid?'

The bookkeeper pushed another weedy-looking man forward.

'The distances are vast, my Lord. I can show you here,' the small man raised a clear window from the control panel, pressed the screen to show dots, and a line joining the dots.'

'Orthama?'

'Here my Lord, nearest to your own world,' nervously the little man pointed to a glowing red dot at one end of the panel. 'Here is the planet Vashla now lives on.'

He pointed further along and followed the line halfway across the panel. 'This is the planet that provided us with workers for the mine, it as you may notice, is not far from our current position.'

'And the one that Rakal protects called Earth?'

The little man followed his finger along the line to the farthest corner of the panel in the lower corner, then tapped it. He moved quickly out of the way as Zorn moved close to inspect the map.

The purple man was by now edging towards the door trying to leave without being noticed.

'Do not leave!'

Everyone in the room froze.

'You,' Zorn pointed his bloody finger at the purple man. 'Come here and tell me more about these traders.'

'I don't know much,' the Guhamp gulped as he shuffled a few steps forward.

'Come here, tell me what you can.' Zorn put his massive arm across the shoulders of the unwilling guest.

'Where is your planet among this vast projection?'

'I will show you, my Lord.'

'You will,' Zorn turned to the bookkeeper and yelled, 'clean up this mess.'

'Yes, my Lord,' the bookkeeper nodded towards two drones to help remove the remains of Zorn's former aide.

'We will strike this one first,' Zorn commanded, 'we will see if they have any defences. One dead planet and a small space station should be easy to conquer.'

'My Lord, we have five fully equipped and manned ships ready to attack, the rest of our fleet, as mentioned previously,' the small man shifted from one foot to the other, 'they are finding out more information about those other planets.'

'Fear not, squirt,' Zorn sneered, 'I'm no longer hungry. My former aide did say I had too few ships close to home. I now think five will be enough to launch against Orthama. The other ships, by then, will be back to regroup. Then we can set about attacking these other worlds. I mean to have them all.'

'Yes, my Lord.'

CHAPTER THIRTY-FOUR

# Vashla's World - VaLinta

Agai noticed that when Rakal and Vashla were together they spoke in their native tongue. Even to him it sounded abrasive. How quickly he had adapted to the language and culture of the worlds they'd befriended?

'Our guests from Orthama are talking about going back soon,' Gardt said, looking at Agai for a reaction.

'Yes,' he replied flatly.

Rakal followed them out into the garden. They sat at bench seats beside a long table. Vashla put a tray laden with salad and cold meat before them to savour.

'I will be returning to Earth shortly,' Rakal carried a tray of drinks and put it beside the food. 'You people have much in common with the humans of Earth. This is just what Tam's family do, eat outside and soak up the sunshine in the evening.'

'You're going too?' Agai took at a seat and began to load his plate.

'Rakal will return,' Vashla sat beside her son, 'he needs to get back to Earth.'

'Everyone is leaving. Rinra, Colu and the others say they need to go back to Orthama.'

'It's been good having guests these last few days,' Gardt smiled as he ambled over to the table and sat down opposite Rakal, beside Vashla on the other side to Agai.

'I had a message from Tam, I must go back. You can come with me if you like. I must admit you remind me of Kat when he was younger.'

The youth shifted uncomfortably in his seat. He couldn't bring his eyes up to look at any of the adults directly.

'Mind you, Kat, has had a few relationships but now settled down,' Rakal remarked. 'The woman is a soldier, already a mother, and she is getting the reluctant pacifists in the Davidson family, to train in self defence.'

'I'd rather go with Rinra to Orthama if you don't mind Rakal. Who knows what Zorn is planning, or when, or where he'll attack? I think it's a vulnerable target. Fewer people to retaliate, and from what they've been telling me, weapons are few. They do have one big gun, but, it's too much. They need assistance in planning defence and attack if Zorn goes against them,' Agai announced. He gave his mother a side glance.

'I'm sure Rinra would be happy to have your company,' Gardt said with a knowing smile.

'Really?' Vashla turned to look more closely at her son. 'It's a good suggestion. They need to have a defence. The Elders had the opportunity to listen to defence suggestions by the human Anthony. He had some good ideas, but few were put in place. You could go and see what needs to be done to escalate this.'

She turned to Rakal, 'how old is Kat now?'

'He's twenty-five, only a few years older than Agai,' Rakal replied. He stood and walked around the table to slap Agai on the back. 'Rinra would like the company.' He winked at Vashla over the young man's head.

Gardt almost choked on his food when he saw Vashla's look of alarm.

The next day Rakal left and so did the Orthama contingent. Agai went with Rinra and the others.

'We'll stand out among our peers when we get back,' Colu happily announced.

'Why?' Agai asked.

'Because we've had sun on our skins and we've coloured because of it. We all feel the fresh air has done us good.'

'Oh, I guess. I've never thought about living on a space station all the time. You and Rinra have been to other worlds and traded. The air must be just as good on those worlds.'

'Not always,' Colu sat down beside Ty and Arda, 'some smell and are dirty.'

'We'll be at Orthama shortly. The Elders have been advised you are joining us. Do you know how long you'll be able to stay?' Rinra was at the control panel. They slipped into the grid in Rakal's wake and were now speeding towards their home world.

'I'm not sure how long I'll need. Can you tell me what defences Orthama has in place now?' Agai watched Rinra set to work accessing the information he needed on the small vehicles' computer.

'We don't have everything here, this may help though,' Rinra tapped the screen.

'What's wrong?' Rinra could see by Agai's slumped shoulders and sour expression that he was unhappy with what he was reading.

Agai continued to read as they travelled. He rubbed his eyes as he pushed the data pad away.

'If this ship was captured by Zorn, we'd be easily over run,' Agai sighed. 'That Anthony had a few good ideas for defences of Orthama.'

'He did,' Rinra agreed.

'I've got a few ideas too.'

'Good, we'll need all we can get,' Colu now sat beside Rinra at the helm.

'I don't think any of you know what you're up against,' Agai stretched while watching the view of the majestic space station large on the view screen.

'What do you mean Agai?' Ty asked as he poured himself a drink. 'Want one?'

Agai just shook his head.

'You may as well say what's on your mind Agai, we are looking to you for help with our defences,' Rinra prompted.

Agai sighed and started pacing about the control room. 'Like the Davidson's on Earth, you are pacifists. I've seen what my mother and her kin are capable of. She had been bought up, as Zorn and Rakal had, with no re-gard for the lives of those they conquered, with greed and self-obsession the only goal. They have a natural aggres-sion and viciousness. Both my mother and Rakal have changed their ways but, I have witnessed things you would say are gruesome.'

'You forget that Colu and I, with Maya and Shea, have travelled and traded with many people on different worlds. People on those worlds are uneasy about Zorn, but I've not witnessed anything other than bullying,' Rinra glanced up from the control panel. 'We'll be docking soon, sit down Agai. We have time to make plans.'

'They fear Zorn,' Colu pointed out, 'we can see that.'

'We need to know what Zorn might be thinking, and, in case of attack, be prepared to hit back,' Agai sat down. The small craft was expertly manoeuvred into the dock. 'We'll need a diverse range of attack and defence mechanisms.'

Rinra stood up and smiled at Agai. 'We are a resilient people, and with your knowledge of space pirates we will create something amazing.'

Agai smiled back, 'perhaps, if we are all truly descendants of the Ancients', our shared diversity, and working together could be our greatest asset.'

CHAPTER THIRTY-FIVE

# Rakal's World - Earth

Rakal, the former space pirate, was speeding to the opposite end of the galaxy along the grid. His thoughts were of Tam and the family he'd sworn to protect. His ship slipped out of the grid on the dark side of the moon. He looked over the small fleet of spacecraft he had in stationary orbit. He'd plundered these in his old life, now he would use them to augment the security on Earth. He'd kept them there so as not to alarm governments on Earth. He would bring these ships into Earth's orbit, have them manned, and armed as a first line of defence. This would be a priority, Rakal knew Zorn would not be patient and to underestimate him would be folly.

He landed in the paddock beside the Davidson's main home. Tam rushed out of the house with little Mata running ahead. Rakal left his vehicle striding down the rampart to meet them. He pulled Tam and Mata into a crushing embrace. They silently clung together for some time. When they did pull apart Tam wiped away fresh tears.

'We miss you too much when you go away. Next time and every time, we'll be with you.'

Rakal planted a fervent kiss on Tams willing lips.

'Me too,' Mata nodded.

'Very well, we'll always travel together. I don't wish to be parted from my heart.'

They walked savouring the moment. Their soon to be eight-year-old child, held Rakal's hand, the small fingers nestled inside his own, while Tam snuggled under his arm. Soon they were through the little wrought iron gate at the side of the house and treading the path to the kitchen door.

Richard and Davrew sat at the table and both greeted Rakal with appreciative smiles.

'It's good to see you back. What news do you have for us?' Richard asked.

'Please, sit down and tell us,' Davrew pushed a chair out and smiled at their grandchild, 'come child, sit beside me.' Mata nodded and happily took up the offer, especially as a huge plate of biscuits was within reach on the table.

'We all went to Orthama, they have some defences in place, but not many. Agai has gone there with the group that came to see Vashla's world for themselves. He will strengthen their defences and work on a retaliatory means of attack that doesn't involve destroying a planet.'

'It's good to know Agai has found his strengths,' Tam remarked while sitting down beside Mata.

'I bought some captive thoughts from Vashla's library, there are several clues as to Zorn's make up and battle tactics.'

'You didn't bring her library with you I hope,' Richard pushed the plate of biscuits towards the child who took one and happily began to devour it.

'No heads, just their memories,' Rakal took a biscuit and smiled at the child. 'Agai is a few years younger than Kat, about twenty I believe.'

'Twenty -two,' Tam corrected.

'He's a strong young man and always trying to prove his value to his mother. That's no mean feat,' Rakal reached for a second biscuit.

'Speaking of Kat, your first-born son is heading this way with his wife Emily,' Tam said, 'he rang earlier today.'

'It'll be good to see him,' Rakal mumbled through his full mouth. 'I told Vashla that Emily is a soldier, still in the Australian Army.'

'I'm glad her tour of duty in the Middle East, is over for now. Although experienced it's always a worry for Kat when she's away,' Tam grinned, holding Rakal's hand tight. 'Did you tell Vashla, Emily took time off to have adorable baby Tia, and has taken extended leave?'

'I said she was a mother as well as a soldier,' he replied.

'You know Emily started and exercise regime for our family. She's a joy to have around,' Richard rolled his eyes and winced. 'We're all feeling the effects of the training. I thought it best to let you know.'

They all laughed.

'Good, I'm glad the practical training has begun,' Rakal nodded and clapped his hands together. 'First things first, I have about fifty small ships in stationary orbit on the dark side of the moon. I think young Mica will need to do some fancy talking to persuade the governments of the world that we are putting in place a first alert and defence system. With help from your family members willing to take the trip, I intend to bring these ships into orbit around Earth. Some have weapons but are not hugely powerful. If Ash will put his mind to the task, we need to upgrade our weaponry, both around Earth and on it.'

'There's no chance, as you see it, that Zorn will leave Earth alone?' Davrew asked.

'I may remind you that I ate my brother after defeating him in battle on my first visit here. Zorn is a cousin of mine. He knows nothing of compassion and everything of greed. He will come.'

Davrew visibly shivered. Richard stood up and threw an extra couple of logs on the fire before walking to Davrew and putting a comforting arm about his shoulders.

'Whatever happens, we must prepare as best we can,' Richard nodded.

'I'm too old to see my family threatened, even though I know it must be,' Davrew reluctantly agreed.

CHAPTER THIRTY-SIX

# Orthama Space Station

Agai walked into the hall of the Elders pod aboard the vast space station. He looked out at a sea of faces. There among the crowd of Orthama residents was one set of eyes he wanted to impress. He found Rinra smiling at him and allowed himself a huge grin in reply. Then he became serious and began to start what he came to do. It was time to prepare for battle, in more ways than one.

'I'm not a speaker. I've just come to tell you a simple message. Right now, we need to concentrate on the defence and attack systems of the space station, and training of every citizen for the imminent threat of Zorn's forces. Everything else, including the breeding programme, should be put aside for a while.'

There was an up-swell of noise from the audience, angry shouts from many corners of the arena.

'Agai, I'm sure your suggestion is well intended,' Vini of the Elders was standing and speaking strongly and loudly to quell the gathering disquiet, 'perhaps you could explain your reasons. What you're suggesting is such a radical departure from our whole focus of life. We need to be convinced of the need and then put the plan under consideration.'

'Put it this way,' Agai continued, 'if Zorn strikes now, there won't be a breeding programme to work on. Orthama will be just another of his conquests.'

'Why do you think this is likely now?' another Elder stood to challenge.

'Come on, you were here when my mother Vashla and Gardt explained the reasons. Have you heard of a planet called Canqellee or one called Hequenit? No, because Zorn wiped them from the grid line years ago, vaporised them, gone and forgotten except for the memories of some of my mother's library heads, and because she helped him take those planets out.'

Feeling frustrated Agai raised his hands and began to tick off the reasons on his fingers. 'Reason number one, he's a space pirate and used to getting what he wants. Two, he was pursuing my Mother for marriage, but she turned him down. Three, Vashla and Gardt thwarted Zorn's efforts to get new slaves for his mine, so that, brings Gardt's home planet Ghaur into the mix. Four, Rakal is Zorn's cousin, and he wants to get the better of him. Reason number four, or is it five, is that currently you are an easy target. Six, some of you have been to Vashla's World, it has clean air and lots of space. He wants it. Seven, your last contact with him was basically bluff and bravado, he's sure to come back just to see if he can knock you over for the fun of it. Eight, nine and ten, you don't live far away from Zorn by the grid. Let's face facts, Orthama, is three or four generations away from being marginally habitable. You've become used to living in a space station and not living on a planet, both the planet and your current home here would add to his achievements. We need to make plans now to save Orthama so that you can continue to work towards the time you are ready to re-colonise.'

'What have we to gain by this alliance to your scheme?' a third Elder was on his feet.

'Do you have to ask? We would all gain the freedom, to remain autonomous, sharing manpower and weaponry,' Agai knew he sounded abrupt.

As the audience became more boisterous, Vini raised his arms to quell the crowd.

'We will receive a report from this excursion,' Vini again took charge. 'Colu and Rinra have already indicated the visit to VaLinta was productive. What do you suggest we change? We have a weapon of destruction. We are preparing ourselves for defence should we be boarded.'

'Firstly, you need an alert system, a defence strategy, more than one type of weapon to confuse the enemy,' Agai quickly summed up their needs.

'We do have some defences. Allow us to show you what we have now perhaps we can build on this,' Vini suggested. 'I think we should reconvene tomorrow after some research into our present defences is actioned by our guest. We would be appreciative of your knowledge, as we did agree with your mother and Rakal that we would assist in the security of all our planets.'

'I think something must be put in place right away,' Agai nodded to the audience and allowed himself to be led away.

Rinra had to wait until Agai had been given a tour of the Elders facilities and a briefing on the space station defences before being able to see him.

'Rinra,' Vini greeted the youth, 'it's time Agai was taken to his accommodation, it is on level four, please show our guest the way.'

'Yes, of course Elder Vini,' Rinra replied.

'We are implementing some of Agai's suggestions now. They seem reasonable. We will be announcing this to the general population tomorrow. It would be best not to speak of this until the details are released.'

Rinra nodded agreement. They walked together, Rinra leading the way, and didn't speak until they were away from Vini.

'Are you Okay? It took so long before I could come to you,' Rinra squeaked trying not to tremble.

'I'm fine. I sure do hope they put the first part of the plan into action tonight. I left an extreme outer monitor for early alert in place near the grid. It had to be activated, that's all. I don't think anyone here really gets the urgency.'

'Zorn did follow Colu and I back from our last trip with our cousins from Earth. He could have just as easily gone in that direction,' Rinra turned and took Agai's arm in his.

'Any direction Zorn goes will be trouble,' Agai looked at Rinra and smiled, 'I'm weary, but not too much, to talk.'

'Good, I'd love that too,' Rinra waved open the door with his thumb. 'That reading the thumb print is a security measure the human Elder Anthony introduced. He believed in personal security of every person on the space station.'

'Is there any danger here?'

'Not much, when Davrew was here there were some bullies about. Anthony saw that there was no way of people here locking their doors, or even having a private place. He said it was essential.' Rinra led the way inside the room that was comfortably furnished. 'Are you hungry?' Agai nodded.

'Interesting, there could be some useful people here, some willing to go against the mould, be a little courageous.'

Rinra handed Agai a mug of hot brown liquid.

'What's this?'

'Coffee, from Earth,' Rinra smiled and took a step closer, 'may I remind you that some of us have been very adventurous already.'

'Don't I know it,' Agai grinned as he planted a firm kiss of Rinra's pliant lips. 'Tomorrow I'll expand the early warning system.'

'That can wait until tomorrow,' Rinra snuggled into Agai's arms.

Agai soon got to know the layout of the space station and the trainee pilots. He drilled them with target practice while getting the crafts that were available battle ready. The time passed quickly with Rinra keeping him company and watching as a defence mechanism for the space station and the planet below were prepared.

'You've been busy Agai,' Rinra smiled as they settled down to relax in their room after a full day of activity.

'The medical staff are now much more prepared for the possible injuries that may occur.'

'Good, I've no doubt we will need that,' Agai rolled his shoulders, stretched then lay full length on the soft bed. 'I only hope we are prepared enough.'

A few hours later a clanging gong rang through the space station.

'What's that?' Rinra rubbed sleep filled eyes.

Agai shot out of bed and pulled on crumpled trousers.

'It's the early alarm system, Zorn is on his way.'

CHAPTER THIRTY-SEVEN

# Rakal's World - Earth

Rakal was alerted by the alarm on the panel of the control room of his spacecraft.

'What is it?' Tam was at Rakal's side in a heartbeat.

'It's the early warning beacon, the one Agai put in place near the grid entrance to Zorn's planet. Orthama is being attacked.'

'You only just returned from Vashla's a week ago. How can it be this soon?'

'Who knows what Zorn has on his mind? None of our early warning systems are buzzing, it sounds like they are the first ones to be attacked.'

Kat joined them running with stealth-like silence into the room. Rakal smiled at his son who now matched him in height and build. His hair was mousey brown-blonde, like Tams, and his features were refined, so he was still an easily recognisable Davidson.

'Do you think your lovely wife, Emily, has had enough time, to whip the family into shape?'

'Not really, but her regime has certainly made an impact on everyone.'

Rakal laughed, 'it looks like we may be put to the test sooner than planned, Orthama is under attack.'

'I can hear her laughing from here, is Emily just outside?' Tam quizzed their son.

'She has such a wicked and infectious chortle. It's hard not to join her,' Rakal smiled.

'Even when she's putting the family through a punishing assault course, her laughter keeps everyone smiling,' Kat nodded.

'How on Earth did you meet and marry a career soldier, I can't imagine,' Tam rolled his eyes. 'And our grandson son Ty is so much like the twins Saz and Skye when they were younger, always getting into mischief.'

Kat laughed.

Rakal looked them both in the eyes and pointed at the star map on the control screen. 'This alert is no laughing matter. I'll contact Agai and find out what the situation is. I may need to go out and take a few ships with me with the best of our pilots as back up to flank Zorn's ships if needed.'

'Would that leave us vulnerable?' Tam asked nervously. 'We are building more weapons and skips in our make-shift factory across the road. Pat and Bill's old barn is proving useful, but we've hardly a fleet ready to repel a large-scale attack.'

'I'm thinking that Zorn will not want to spread his resources too far either. I've been told by various associates of our trading trips, that Zorn has sent out spy ships to find out details about our planets. He may only have a small fleet to attack Orthama. We could do some real damage to his chances of success if we defeat him soundly on this first assault.'

'What will happen if he comes back at us, we are still so ill prepared?' Tam was pacing about behind Rakal.

'That's a chance we might have to take.'

Tam stopped dead and looked directly into Rakal's eyes. 'If you go this time, I'm coming with you. And you can't stop me!'

Rakal looked back, then quickly away. 'Fair enough,' he grunted.

Kat just whistled and left to speak to his wife.

CHAPTER THIRTY-EIGHT

# Orthama Space Station

The Space Station suddenly filled with anxious faces and frenzied activity. Agai and Rinra ran into the control room to find some of the Elders, bleary eyed and confused, milling about the screens.

'Where are they? How many ships? What size and description?' Agai asked.

'Where did you set up the beacon? We have nothing on our scanners yet,' Vini stood behind the operator trying to detect the direction of the attack.

'It was just before entering the grid above Zorn's mining planet. It should give us a small opportunity to prepare. If you don't have them coming through already, they won't be long. I hadn't completed the warning network.'

'We can set up the satellite weapons,' Vini suggested.

'Perhaps we should discuss this,' another Elder faced Agai, 'we have no proof of Zorn's attack.'

'Come off it, this is no time to talk, it's time to act,' Agai retaliated.

Vini nodded toward a younger Elder to start releasing the weapons into space around their planet below.

'The pilots should be at their stations and ready to surround the station as guards within minutes,' Vini continued.

'Who authorised such action?' The objecting Elder raged. He stood over Vini in stature, but the smaller man held his ground.

'I did,' Vini replied calmly, 'and our pilots have been preparing to defend our position for many weeks. You know we are a ready and close target for Zorn. Naturally, all the precautions we've set in place should be utilised.'

The alarm continued to sound its clanging gong.

'I can see no attack. This is just a noise set up to frighten us,' the taller Elder continued.

Agai just rolled his eyes. 'By the stars, now is not the time to argue either. I thought you knew what we were up against.'

The space-scape surrounding the station was displayed, in three-hundred-and-sixty degrees vision, on the screens before them. The familiar aura of a hazy atmosphere on the planet below that glowed orange. The black void around it made it even more spectacular. The released orbs painted a gradual line around the planet.

'There,' Rinra pointed to a change in the image at one side of the room.

Agai was at the panel scanning the scene.

'Five, large battle cruisers. The type my mother used to prefer for attack. Spacious on board and can be operated by minimal attendants, so that the attack force can do their job.'

'We are getting a message in from Rakal,' The control panel operator announced.

'Put it on the view screen,' Vini ordered.

'Rakal, you call at a busy time,' Vini stared into the face of the burly dark-haired alien.

'I call because we hear the warning alarm. Agai did a good job of putting that in place.'

Agai nodded. 'There are five ships so far, large battle cruisers. They're in formation moving rapidly towards us. I doubt they know we've been alerted.'

'We are launching the satellite orbs now, they can strike if the planet is breached, although the atmosphere is still not sufficient to sustain life, they may try to land and use it as a launching post for further attacks. We can't permit that to happen,' Vini stated. 'We have pilots and ships ready to meet this enemy.'

'Good,' Rakal looked at the young man and the frail looking scientists, 'we can be at their back and flank them but our arrival will be some hours yet, we are just leaving Earth, and even with the Grid it takes time to reach you.'

'I'll take the ships we have with the trained pilots and go out to meet them,' Agai advised.

'We don't want the space station compromised if we take the battle to them,' Vini agreed.

Agai stared older man on the screen, 'I share your concern Rakal, we will take the fight to them and trust your arrival will be in time to send Zorn away.'

'How many combatants do you have?' Rakal asked.

'We have twenty small craft with weapons adapted. They have been practising target shooting and some of them are quite good flyer's,' Agai tried to sound confident.

'Have any of them killed before?' Rakal was running his hands over his controls as he spoke.

'No. I've limited experience in battle. Mother always did the killing on her raids. I did occasionally assist,' Agai replied honestly.

'You've taken on an enormous task, Agai, and your early warning alert will save lives. I thank you for that, even if the Elders on Orthama, are unaware of the danger, I am. Be proud of what you've achieved so far. Our pilots are equally inexperienced but have been training well. We'll get there as quickly as possible,' Rakal nodded the screen went blank.

'Rinra you must help with the medical team to ensure any casualties can be cared for,' Agai turned to his companion. 'Vini, is that acceptable?'

'Of course. We'll need to have our best medical staff at the ready, Rinra is among our best.'

Agai nodded at the Elder, kissed Rinra briskly, then left.

The new pilots needed a leader and he had volunteered to be there. It was time to put words into action. Agai couldn't help but feel a buzz of exhilaration. He rushed into the landing bay, where the fleet of adapted battle ships were being prepared to launch. There was a hive of activity around the ships as the final tasks were completed.

He leapt up onto the highest vantage point, a loading platform at the end of the room. He took a deep breath, before raising his arms.

'Are we ready everyone?' A sea of familiar faces looked up at him. He'd become accustomed to picking the genetic line each one came from. Most of the best pilots here were from the original, more aggressive and tactical gene pool. He'd discovered that the original seven scientists were tough and capable combatants in hand-to-hand fights. They had honed their skill as an exercise medium and passed this on to their next generation clones.

'Right everyone. We must protect this space station and Orthama, now!' Agai jumped down and climbed into his craft.

'Open the space door, follow in tight formation,' he spoke evenly through the communication link to the small fleet, even though his heart was pounding. 'When we get within one hundred thousand clicks break off into groups of four, as we practised. Good luck all of you. Fire steadily and at the ships' hearts. We aim to disable. Surprise, that's our best weapon.' He wondered silently how many of these raw recruits would survive.

The small fleet of spaceships followed Agai into the black void and formed the tight V he'd had them practising above the skies above the dead world. They moved at a steady pace towards their foe.

'They will have superior fire power. Our strength is that we can dart in and out and hit them often. Keep the com open but don't say too much. They might be listening.'

Agai bought the formation around to face the enemy. Whilst Zorn only had five ships, they were large fighting vessels. The hope that surprise would give them the upper hand was soon dashed. The first torpedo from the battle-ships incinerated two of the small craft at the end of the formation.

'Break off and attack,' Agai shouted. Soon the little minnow ships were finding their own targets and avoiding the deadly slower attack. Ships were buzzing in and out and around the five larger craft using speed and agility to escape. The battle that ensued was fierce.

Agai stayed silent, almost holding his breath, the intensity of the battle was so strong. Two more of the small crafts and the new pilots were damaged and broke off to return to the space station and Zorn took his aim and destroyed the limping craft before they could reach sanctuary.

'We're down to fourteen ships now, Commander Agai,' a controlled yet concerned voice sounded a warning in his ear.

'We have to hold on. Keep getting close, hit them where it hurts, aim for the life support, weaponry and navigation areas we discussed in the brief,' Agai replied.

The dark void was a virtual light show of flashes of fire, darting ships about the ever-menacing larger ships that continued towards the space station. It reminded Agai of the games he used to play with Kat when he was younger. The toggle control was the same and he'd insisted that the trainee pilots use the shooting game in their leisure hours to help prepare for this day. Two damaged ships had made it back to the space station. Now the remaining twelve ships valiantly darted in an out around the larger craft, shooting and hitting, zig sagging away from the retaliation. Two of the larger ships had slowed almost to a stop. The other three were increasing speed and moving too close to the space station for comfort.

'Regroup and go in for the kill,' Agai barked.

Three groups of four small craft turned about, launched a final fatal blow to one of the severely damaged battle ships.

'Good work! Now again,' Agai urged. The little ships swung back and attacked the other three large ships from the opposite direction. He led them, taking his remaining squadron members with him. They continued to dart about the larger vehicles dodging intermittent fire. The larger ships had now stopped attacking.

'We've disabled the weapons on those two ships,' Agai yelled.

'But sir, the other ships are more fortified. We may as well be shooting lights as the shots just glance off,' a young pilot answered.

'They are getting too close to the space station. Keep attacking. We must stop them,' Agai urged his pilots on.

The large battle ships were almost indistinguishable from one another, only the markings on the middle one made it clear it was the leaders. That ship had been flanked by the other two craft but now it pulled away.

'Stop him getting too close to the space station.'

All twelve-little craft, having made a final run at the other two ships, turned to take Zorn head on. The large ship rebutted the insignificant attempts the small craft made to breech its defences. When Zorn launched his assault, it was with a brilliant and wide arc beam that swept two of the little ships away. Like a large feral cat tossing a mouse about, the little ships were caught by another arc and sent in the opposite direction. Zorn let loose a guttural growl and maniacal laugh through the com line.

'That's a tactic my Mum used, it's meant to be intimidating,' Agai told his remaining troupes.

'It is intimidating, he's tossing Baz and Mims ships about like they're toys. What's more they are now being flung towards the space station,' a pilot on a flanking ship replied.

'Keep firing, we have to wear him down,' Agai urged.

Agai charged his little craft full tilt at the larger ship and fired rapid bursts into the hull. These bounced off the surrounding bubble of its shield. Zorn laughed more menacingly.

'Agai, you should not be in this battle. You are my dearest Vashla's child.'

Agai ignored the taunt.

'My Mother will never be your dearest anything.'

More rapid fire this time towards the weapon array, then he dashed away again and swung round to fire back on the two lumbering giant ships. He found his target there. Two of his companions followed suit and soon Zorn had only his flag ship and one other in the fray. The others were moving slowly back towards the grid.

'Your ships are turning and running Zorn, perhaps you should do the same,' Agai retaliated, but regretted it immediately. Zorn laughed again and fired his laser beams and torpedoes at once hitting three more of Agai's small fleet. Two were left disabled and hanging, waiting to be picked off at will by Zorn's superior firepower. Agai had been hit but was ignoring the warning signals on the screen as he turned again, the other remaining ships in formation behind him, all using rapid fire at the same target Agai hoped to disable the weapons on the opposing craft.

'We need more ships,' Agai heard his companion say, 'but we can give him all we've got.'

'That's it Bre, keep firing as we turn about,' Agai continued to urge them on.

They turned again, the five ships kept formation and they fired again.

'We are really putting on a show for those on the space station guys, keep it up!' Agai looked out the view screen at the space station, they were getting too close. He realised two more ships had been launched and were coming to join the battle. 'Who is piloting those ships?'

'Commander Agai, Nin and Aja here in the old trip ship. It's been fitted with all the firepower we can muster. You need help and we are here to do just that.'

Agai took a deep breath. These two newly developed clones were from the original fabric of the genetic research. They were only days old. Although fully developed adults, they'd not lived at all.

'Very well, all into formation,' there was no time to argue, Zorn continued his assault. Two of the small ships nearest him had been thrown out of formation and catapulted towards the space station. Agai realised the two new ships were in between.

'We can push them away with our shields. These are older ships with surprises in store for Zorn,' Nin announced. With that, the two out of control ships, started slowly to move back towards Zorn's battleship.

Agai whistled long and slow.

The annoying clanging in his ear was an alarm sounding. He checked his controls and saw that the life support had been hit and the cramped cabin was sparking live wires in several spots. The large ships from Zorn's original strike force were coming back. If they had managed to repair their weapons and strike, the little force he had put together would be done for. They simply were underpowered, too few, and with barely penetrating fire power.

'Drat, I'm hit,' Agai muttered, undaunted he put on a pressure suit while manoeuvring the controls. 'Follow me.'

The little ships held formation and the two new arrivals joined them at the rear. Agai smiled, he thought they must look like an arrowhead. He wondered if the people watching from the space station would think that. He wondered what Rinra was doing. He hoped that his lover would be too pre-occupied to watch the battle. 'Give all you've got, guys!'

The rapid fire from all seven ships hailed down in a concentrated position on the hull of the larger ship. Then Agai realised the reason the other two ships in Zorn's fleet had returned. There behind them coming out of the grid was Rakal and a fleet of ships that were firing at the larger ships.

'Rakal, by the stars, glad you could join us!' Agai shouted.

'I'm happy to give Zorn a kick,' Rakal replied. The ships from Earth quickly zapped, dived and harassed the two ships ahead of them until they joined Zorn's other remaining ship.

'We're being hailed,' Rakal said. 'Agai, can you view this?'

'Yep.'

'Good.'

'I am Zorn and I will crush you!' Zorn snarled.

'Not today, Zorn,' Rakal began to laugh. It was a familiar guttural laugh. 'We'll allow you to leave if you promise never to return.'

The ships around Zorn quickly took the opportunity to leave. They limped away as best they could. Zorn did not try to stop them.

Agai suddenly felt hot. The ship he was in was falling apart. He pressed the transport button on his wrist and was enveloped in a white light, shortly after he appeared beside Rakal.

'Orthama pilots, I'm now on Rakal's ship, return to the space station and tend your wounded.'

'Nin and Aja here, we'd prefer to stay until Zorn leaves or is otherwise dealt with. We just joined the battle.'

Messages came in from the other ships. Two were in bad shape and returned to the space station but the others remained.

Zorn's huge disc shaped battle cruiser stood out against the black of space, its shining dark metallic blue cover still ominous.

They could hear Zorn growl, a slow guttural noise that grew louder with each passing second. There was an image on the floor of the control room in front of them, shrouded in white light. Zorn stood before them.

'You may think you've won cousin, but this is just the beginning.'

'It's a hologram,' Agai assured Tam who was going a shade whiter than his already pale complexion.

Rakal stood face to face with the hologram, 'go now Zorn, while you can. There is no profit in this dispute.'

'No profit, but I have so much to gain.' He growled again. Then the white light vanished, and so did the huge battle cruiser. Agai felt the hackles on his neck rise. How did Zorn do that?

'Rakal!' Tam was clearly shaken. 'I must be a complete fool.'

Rakal shook his head. 'What do you mean, my love?'

'You and Zorn, you look so much alike, the same dark shock of hair, dark eyes, build, and stance.'

'We are cousins.'

'Cousins, I can't believe I've thought you could change. Look at you! You are just the same lumbering space pirate you were when you came to Earth all those years ago! All I could see when you and he were face-to-face, was the image of a crashed space pod among school grounds, with you cursing in any number of dialects and me part of the crowd of curious students watching.'

Rakal took a few steps towards Tam and put his arms around his shivering companion.

'That was long ago.'

'Tam, my Mother has changed, and she was far more aggressive in her activities. Rakal was someone she often referred to as soft.'

Tam had pulled away from Rakal's embrace and was staring at him as if he were a stranger.

'Lover,' Rakal moved closer to Tam, 'I am your heart, and you are mine. We have a family. Right now, Kat, our son, is helping his wife train more pilots. We are all working together to keep our planets safe, Earth and VaLinta, this space station and Orthama too. How can you doubt me now?'

Tam closed his eyes, put his hand either side of his head and held them there for a moment and then looked up.

'Oh Rakal,' Tam sighed. Rakal pulled Tam into a tight embrace. 'You know the funny thing I just thought?'

'No, what is that my love?'

'Back when I was at school, it was the sixty's, no mobile phones, I don't think the school had a computer. The only phones were in the school office. We kept your visit a secret from the world. Nowadays kids would have images on You-Tube and Twitter within seconds. I guess things do change, and people do too.'

Tam relented, but still stood a little distance from Rakal.

Agai cleared his throat. 'We'd better get my ship back to the space station for repair.'

'We'll tow it,' Rakal nodded and pressed the tractor beam on. 'I didn't realise the ships you had were so small. Zorn only came with a few ships. He was confident he'd easily win.'

'He had five ships at first. Maybe he was just seeing if we would put up a fight.'

'Maybe,' Rakal looked out at the space station and the small craft making their way home. 'Zorn and I used to play together as children. We do look alike; our mothers were sisters. Back then when our families had a home planet, we lived together. We did mock battles and the families did raid and plunder in other worlds. Somehow that changed and our home-world was destroyed. Zorn always played to win, and he would change his tactics to do it. You might say cheat to win. I can't see he's changed that much since then. We must expect him to redouble his efforts and maybe attack in a different way.'

'The view of Orthama is impressive,' Tam said while sidling up to Rakal. 'I guess, it's just a shock. You are so much like Zorn. I just can't believe it.'

'No one wants to know that the face of the enemy could be their own,' Rakal agreed.

Agai met the chief mechanic Ey when he returned to the space station. The small fleet of ships were being overhauled by the team of mechanics. They had been doing that job for years. Now there was an urgent focus to their tasks.

'Agai,' Ey greeted him with a warm handshake, 'an Earth tradition I know. You all did a mighty job. We lost two ships in that last battle, but the others are all repairable.'

'Good, I'll leave that with you, I need to get to the hospital,' Agai left the docking bay and headed back along the now familiar corridors of the space station.

When Agai walked into the hospital he was assailed by the smell of sweat, disinfectant and the sounds of muffled crying. He looked about at the beds laden with burnt, bleeding and barely alive pilots, his heart sank. He couldn't see Rinra.

A while later, Rakal caught up with Agai and Rinra.

'Vini, and the Elders, are meeting to arrange a memorial service for the two young pilots, and their crews that died today,' Agai wanted to bring Rakal up to date with the results of the battle.

'Gid made it back here, his partner and children were able to say their goodbyes. With burns to ninety percent of his body, we had him soaking in cool gel, only his face protruding,' Rinra sighed, 'we were able to make him comfortable in the end.'

'The ships were totally destroyed,' Agai added.

Rakal looked uncomfortable.

'Is Tam with you?' Rinra quizzed, 'I thought you were both here to fight Zorn.'

'We are,' Rakal replied, 'Tam is just having a rest aboard our ship. We came off light, our damage minimal, and will be repaired. Some of the other ships, yours included Agai, need a full refit. I'm glad you transported to our ship when you did. It was ready to fall apart.'

'I was suited, I would have made it to the escape pod had it got worse.'

'Well, your Mother would feed me to the monsters in the lake on VaLinta, if you had got into trouble, bad enough that Tam is in a mood with me.'

'We need to regroup and work out what to do next,' Agai took Rinra's arm and headed for the door. With Rakal following they made their way to speak to the Elders.

CHAPTER THIRTY-NINE

# Vashla's World - VaLinta

Two days later, Rakal and Vashla were sitting in the sunshine in her garden on VaLinta.

'We won that battle, simply by turning up at the right time. Agai and his little group of pilots had almost lost out to Zorn's superior weaponry. I came here to see if we can get more ships.'

'We've the ten ships the colonists arrived in, they're carriers not fighters. I have my own small fleet of twenty ships from my plundering days, stored in a huge cave on the other side of this planet. I hid them there so Zorn couldn't find them. The colonists do have a few good pilots among them. There are more on Gardt's home world, but these people are planning a new colony. They have many skills, and some show promise in personal self defence. We are a long way from having combatants. There is a security contingent with a security chief, mainly for self-regulation of the colonists, certainly not for interplanetary warfare. Although misguided, they have technology and are willing to learn.' Vashla poured two large glasses of honey mead and handed a glass to Rakal. 'Did I nearly lose my son?'

'It was close, Zorn only had five ships. He was testing us all out to see how far we could stretch ourselves,' Rakal raised his glass and savoured the sweet flavour of the cool refreshing liquid. 'I've reliable informants that tell me, Zorn is having trouble with the mine workers on his planet Xamba.' He picked up some of the sweet biscuits Vashla had put on the table.

'A diversion from them, in the form of an uprising, would be good for us right now,' Vashla suggested, 'it would do a lot to distract Zorn from attacking us.'

'Hmm,' Rakal took two bites and demolished his biscuit. 'We've no idea where or when Zorn will strike next. The early alert system has been enhanced though, so we should have some warning.'

'You said his ship just vanished. Did he cloak it or transport it?'

'We don't know,' Rakal shrugged and sat back in his chair. 'This sunshine gets into my bones, it's like this on Earth. I've grown used to being comfortable.'

'These people from Ghaur, they've come to depend on me. I feel responsible for their future. In our life before, we felt responsible to no one. We took what we wanted when we wanted, the price for this was a solitary life. I know now I don't want that life anymore. I value Gardt and his commitment to me. Is this the same for you and Tam?'

Rakal just nodded.

A roaring siren broke their reverie.

They both stood and rushed to the control panel in the house.

'One ship, above VaLinta, much larger than the battleship he used to attack Orthama. It's almost as big as Orthama space station, and it's firing up,' Vashla looked up at Rakal with a pained expression. 'Zorn is attacking this planet!'

'The firepower could do tremendous damage. Can we fire back from the satellites?' he asked.

A huge bolt of fire from space shattered the tranquil world.

'He's aiming at the village,' Vashla gasped. 'I must make sure everyone gets to safety.'

'You have bunkers?'

'The Linta people had a huge underground cavern for storage, the new villagers have been using it to store wine and food. They can shelter there. I'll also need to get those space ships off the ground, immediately,' she nodded at Rakal as she touched her transport bracelet. Rakal did the same. Instantly they were on the outskirts of the village. The mayhem that greeted them, with people running for cover from falling debris, while the bolt of destructive light from space, was carving up the buildings, shattering everything in its path.

'Get the ships airborne and use what firepower you have in defence. Each ship has been fitted with a cloak and shield,' Vashla instructed Rakal.

Gardt ran up to them.

'I haven't died for a while; I really don't want to do it again today.'

'You still have the Ancients' restoration chamber?' Rakal asked.

She nodded.

'Yes, it's hidden. I promised Gardt I would never use it ever again. Now the villagers need to get to the safety of the cavern. I hope I won't need to restore anyone, but, I may need to.'

'Some of the villagers are running that way now,' Gardt pointed to the people moving away from their homes toward the cavern.

Rakal and Vashla ran towards the houses. A beam of fire cut a building in two and it causing shattered debris flying in all directions. They ducked and continued. Gardt was running in their wake.

'This way,' Vashla yelled above the calamity. 'The villagers are going in the the right direction. The cavern is over there.' The noise of falling crashing buildings, fires igniting, and exploding, made it hard to be heard. Vashla pointed the way.

'Who's that?' Rakal shouted back.

'The Security Chief Rymus, he's moving them towards safety. Hurry, we need some pilots to get those space-ships airborne,' Vashla ran to the man's side at the entrance to the cavern. 'We need pilots,' she yelled over the noise.

He nodded and motioned for them to follow him inside. Rakal paused as he saw a tree nearby that had been split and falling in the direction of the cave entrance. He used his personal shield to deflect it. The entrance was still clear.

'It's not safe here,' Rakal shouted to Vashla. Gardt scrambled over some branches and entered the tunnel behind them.

'Its safe inside,' Gardt replied.

'There's food and water here, enough for everyone,' Vashla calmly reassured the frightened villagers. 'We'll need to defend our home. I need six good pilots to get the transport ships into space.'

'I'll lead the way,' Rakal beckoned the reluctant volunteers.

'I wish Agai was here,' Vashla sighed. Rakal nodded and ushered the group of volunteers to follow him.

'Wait,' a beautiful brunette woman called after Rakal. 'I was with Tam before, he'd taken a group for a walk up towards the lake, over an hour ago. They haven't returned.'

Rakal looked at the faces within the cavern.

'Tam must be here,' he said.

The woman shook her head from side to side.

'Get the ships airborne Rakal, I'll look for Tam,' Vashla pushed the big man towards the entrance. 'Go now, I'll find Tam,' she repeated. The group moved away with Rakal in the lead.

Vashla took a quick head count and guessed there were still a dozen or so unaccounted for.

'Stay here,' she advised. 'I'll bring anyone else I can find back here. Be prepared to tend the injured.' She headed for the entrance.

The noise outside had increased as the village had become a burning ruin. Vashla saw Rakal take the other group towards the spaceships. She was unsure if there would be any vehicles left to save, but she prayed to the stars there would be.

'Curse you Zorn. This was such a beautiful village. You'll pay for attacking my planet,' she moved through the village wreckage, looking for survivors.

She heard a faint cry for help, a young boy was behind a wall, the only upright part of what had been a communal hall. Vashla realised all her elaborate technology could not save this child, rescuing him was up to her. She grabbed a nearby cloth from a building that had been split in half.

'Keep low,' she called to the boy. She covered her head and ran through the flames, dodging falling debris. She reached him and tucked the lad under her arm. Jumping over rubble she ran back to the cavern. It was cool inside. The boy was gathered up by a big woman. Vashla's mind turned to Tam. He could be anywhere. She needed to get back to her own house and take her skip to do a wider search.

'The boy will be alright,' Vashla said. 'I'll search for more. Take a full head count and make a list of those you think may be missing. I'll search and return with more survivors.'

Vashla touched her transport bracelet, instantly she was back in her own garden. It had barely been touched by the carnage that rampaged nearby. After sending out an alert to her allies to come to her aid, she jumped on her skip and set out to look for signs of life. She used her night vision and heat image scans to search in the places that were impossible to see with the naked eye. Guiding her ship at low altitude she found two women unconscious. She hauled them onto the skip and made a quick return trip to the cavern.

'Oh, by the stars, they're alive! Thank you, Vashla,' a plump woman cried when she returned to the villagers.

'We've done a head count. There are still six missing. Three children and three adults, including Tam,' Sergeant

Rymus, the security chief advised her. 'The attack has moved away from the village.'

'Yes,' Vashla replied, 'the main barrage is now over towards the lake. I'll do a search of the outer walkways, perhaps, that's where I'll find them.'

'I did find one body on the other side of what remains of the hall. I'll get it out of the rubble and bring it here,' Rymus rubbed his forehead.

'We need to know where everyone is, don't be concerned about the dead, I'll take them to ensure their recovery,' Vashla replied. 'If you find anyone else, bring them here and tend their wounds.'

'How can you heal the dead?' Rymus asked.

'Never mind that, be assured I can,' Vashla looked around the faces in the cavern. 'Did anyone see which direction Tam went?' She asked again, now anxious about Rakal's partner. She owed Rakal her life and would repay him by finding the one person who'd made his world complete.

Vashla continued to scour the village surrounds. There were now huge tracts of overturned soil, felled trees and foliage splinted and shattered, with rocks strewn about as though they'd been tossed in a salad.

On one of the many paths leading away from the village, she could see three people. When she got closer, she could see two children and a man limping along. She stopped to pick them up.

'Have you seen Tam?' she asked them.

'Yes, Tam and my sister were heading towards the lake,' the man replied.

'Quickly, get on board. Hold on tight children. We'll get you to the cavern and safety,' Vashla lifted off and made the journey to the cavern.

'Head for the lake, I'm sure that's where they'll be,' the man suggested as they disembarked.

She nodded and took off again. This time with a solid starting point to search, the lake was wide, deep, and frightening. She'd never revealed her secret to anyone, not even Agai, her son knew that she could not swim.

Vashla skimmed over the lake and around the edges until she reached a high point where a waterfall cascaded down the side of the mountain into the lake. Then she saw a limp body on the rocks below. The closer she got, the clearer the figure became. Tam was lying in an unnatural way, broken, and crushed upon the rocks at the water's edge.

CHAPTER FORTY

# Zorn's Mining World Xamba

Mele and Dua whispered in the shadows.

'We've got support,' Mele was facing the mine corridor, his eyes searching every crevice for spies.

'We had support last time,' Dua snorted, 'look where that got us.'

'We've learnt a lot more about this Zorn person since then,' Mele turned to his friend, 'we know we don't belong here.'

'We know he's obsessive, controlling, and an egotistic sadistic dictator. We know he controls lots of traders through fear campaigns. We know he wants mine workers and he doesn't care where they come from.' Dua turned back to pick up his hammer and chisel. No new age equipment here, strictly old sweat and muscle labour. 'We know we are here because Ghaur's would be colonists were freed, and we, the death row prisoners, soon to be dead, were traded as replacements.

'We didn't know anything about him when we first came here. How could we know how this prison mine worked? Now we do,' Mele continued undaunted. 'We know that he's starting wars and spreading his resources pretty thin.'

'So, what good is that? We're still his prisoners in this disgusting dark, dank hole in the ground,' Dua picked up his tools too. 'We lost twenty good men in that riot. The guards didn't care how many they killed either. I think they enjoyed it.'

'What I'm saying is, that maybe a confrontational re-volt, was just a foolish start. Now we should work our way into his good books. We could provide him infor-mation, and work at defeating him from the inside,' Mele raised the huge hammer to his shoulder.

He was a head taller than his companion. Both men were muscle toned from the work, and taller than many of their guards. They both stank from lack of hygiene, but the smell was hidden behind the stench of the acids in the air from the mining process. The food they were handed once a day was as stomach churning. They were weak from hunger but too afraid to stop.

'There's someone coming. Let's go!' Dua and Mele attacked the walls with their picks. Working hard to not alert the guards to their plans.

Several hours later they made their way to the com-munal cavern where the meals were handed out. They had to be careful now. Dua went over and joined a few friends that had helped in the original riot, while Mele joined a group of younger men who had been too afraid to do more than talk. The guards walked in and the at-mosphere in the cavern filled with silence and venom.

'Sit apart you lot, no congregating!' The guard clubbed two men to make them separate.

Obediently the prisoners moved. Mele looked about as he forced the revolting gruel into his mouth.

Later, back at work thumping the walls of the caverns and filling their carts along the mine wall, Mele caught up with Dua.

'I overheard two guards talking about Zorn coming here.'

'Really,' Dua lost his rhythm and looked up at his friend.

'Yep,' Mele took up position nearby and began chipping at the face of the tunnel. 'The guards moved away before I could catch anything else.'

'So, we may get a chance to see this creep,' Dua stopped to scoop the ore into the buckets nearby.

'Guess so, although why he would want to come here? I can't imagine.'

Several sleeps later, they found out the answer to that question.

When eating an equally vile meal in the same cavern, they were amazed when a dark haired solidly built man was escorted by a group of heavily armed guards into their midst. They slunk back to quiver by the walls, while watching the intruder as the guards shoved the prisoners aside. One small and weedy man scuttled along beside the big man with a note-board in hand, talking to Zorn as they walked. Zorn appeared to be listening. He stopped in the centre of the chamber. He looked at the prisoners, listened for a short while, then grunted.

Mele noticed everyone had continued eating but kept a wary eye on the visitor. He wasn't as big as he thought he'd be, but he was imposing.

'You,' the escort guard beside Zorn pointed, 'and you!' he pointed to Dua, then Mele, and three more of the original rioters, who'd escaped punishment until now.

Mele almost gagged on his half-eaten mouthful of gruel. 'Come now. Lord Zorn wishes to speak to you.'

Five wary prisoners stood and defiantly walked to the guard. Mele was not about to let this Zorn intimidate him.

Then they heard it, a deep guttural growl growing to a deafening crescendo. Some of the others began to tremble. Mele held his nerve. Dua did too he noticed. The growl changed to laughter, menacing and almost lashed their skin with its power.

'Bring them,' Zorn demanded as he walked towards the cavern exit.

The five prisoners were taken out of the cave complex through unfamiliar tunnels, and into bright sunshine. Mele held his hand in front of his eyes, he along with his companions, who were temporarily blinded by the brilliance of the daylight.

'This way,' the guard pushed them along.

Zorn strode ahead. They all followed in fearful silence. They marched up a ramp and into a spaceship. They were forced to their knees in front of Zorn when he sat down.

'Now, I need to know all you can tell me about your home world, Ghaur. I need to know all you know about Gardt Ness too. Speak, I will listen.'

'Gardt Ness, the one who returned from space in disgrace?' Mele gingerly asked.

Zorn nodded. 'Go on.'

'I only know what I saw in the media at the time. His mission was a failure and all the other members of the expedition were killed. He made out he was a victim and that the government and the I.S.C.C., the money men funding our colonisation programme were lying to us. No one believed him. He was branded a non-citizen and left to live a solitary life.'

Zorn began to laugh a deep and resonating tone that hurt Mele's ears. He held his hands to his head and noticed his companions were doing the same.

'He was not lying, and you were misled. Vashla held him captive. Now, tell me about your world, its people and government,' Zorn walked close to each prisoner, inspecting them intently.

'The government controls everything, food, transportation, even who and how you associate with. We, who have nothing, are kept that way. While those with money and power, get more and more. We are over-regulated and have no freedom to express ourselves,' Dua explained cowering.

'It is run, this government, by one or many?' Zorn demanded.

'I don't know,' Dua answered honestly, 'more than one, and the I.S.C.C. have a big stake in what happens.'

'I like a well-regulated world, management are often very pliable and agreeable to my demands,' Zorn started strumming his fingers on the table before him. 'Indeed the I.S.C.C. had been very accommodating in providing mine workers, the ones you called colonists, the ones I paid to get. Still, you have been more than satisfactory replacements.'

'Can we stand?' One of the other prisoners dared to ask.

Zorn turned and smiled at him. The evil intent in his eyes shattered the man's bravado. With a quick flick of his wrist the man standing looked shocked just before his head toppled from his shoulders and rolled to the floor.

'Bring my meal to me,' Zorn ordered the guard, who obediently brought the body of the prisoner to Zorn's desk. Zorn proceeded to rip the man's limps off and chew on the bones.

Dua and Mele looked at each other and gulped. 'Continue. I need to know everything I can,' Zorn demanded as he pointed a bloodied bone at his captive guests.

## CHAPTER FORTY-ONE

# Vashla's World VaLinta

Vashla landed beside the crumpled and bloodied corpse. She looked at the horizon. The space-based attack had continued to gouge huge furrows of destruction across the landscape. Her only hope of restoring Tam to life was in the path of the current bombardment. Heaving the still weight aboard the skip, Vashla decided to return home and put Tam on ice. Later she'd make her way back to the hidden place of the restoration chamber if it weren't buried. There would be a way to stop her cousin's anguish, right now though, nothing more could be done. They needed to stop the attack and ensure all the citizens of her world were safe. She turned the skip back towards home.

Vashla did what was necessary to preserve Tam's body before going to the control panel in the house.

'What's the situation? We are still being bombarded down here.'

'We're about to get to the heart of the problem,' Rakal replied, 'is everyone there safe?'

'Most of the people are in the cavern, there are a few on the outskirts that I rounded up. Will you be able to stop the bombardment?'

'We're onto it, Mother, don't fret,' Agai joined the banter. 'You sound a bit, um, you know wound up.'

'You are here, son,' Vashla smiled with relief.

'Of course, I heard there was a little trouble this way, and came to join the party,' Agai jibed.

'I'm fine, just stop that ship! I've got some missing people to find and having to dodge the assault isn't making the task easier.'

'Okay, we're going in for the kill now,' Agai concluded.

'We'll be back planet-side shortly,' Rakal added as he broke off communication.

Vashla returned to the cavern and removed the dead for safe keeping. She didn't tell the colonists about the restoration chamber. With the number of missing under a handful she went searching again. Her immediate thoughts were to travel beyond the area she found Tam. She suspected Tam had been out rounding up any stray people when the attack began.

She'd recharged the skip power supply, while talking to the villagers. Now the attack from space was more distant. The line from the giant spaceship, a constant point for the attack, as the planet rotated the bombardment reached new ground. From the distance Vashla could see the rising smoke and debris. She flew close. The steam coming off the lake was a gush and so noisy that even from her vantage point some distance away, the rising water droplets were falling back on her face. There were three more children and two teens missing. She rushed on past the base of the waterfall, through clouds of steam, over gouged furrows in the land that could have been put there by a giant plough. The former villagers, the Linta had used ploughs in their fields, and the new inhabitants were rediscovering these ancient tools.

On the grasslands that stretched ahead, she could see no signs of life.

'Where could they be?' Vashla muttered to herself. She scanned the horizon. There were caves at the beginning of a small mountain range ahead. Perhaps they had sheltered there. After crossing to the rocky outcrops, she began to shout, 'is there anyone out here?'

She continued over a ravine, around a ridge. Surely, she had travelled too far. These curious young people would not have managed to get so far from the village on foot. That's when she saw it. Another skip, at the base of a rocky slope, there were caves above it.

'Is there anyone there? Your family have sent me to bring you home.'

Suddenly the constant barrage ceased. The ground stopped trembling. The sky began to clear. She breathed deeply. The attack was over.

'Come out, I am Vashla, and this is my world you live on. I can return you to the village.'

Moments later, she saw frightened eyes looking at her from the cave entrance. Two or three faces. With relief, she landed her skip beside the other and clambered the steep slope till she reached the cave.

'There you all are,' Vashla greeted the children and the two teens.

The older boy stood up and nodded.

'We came out looking for blueberries to pick. Tam came out with us. When the attack began, we were near the top of the waterfall. We all clambered to safety, but Tam didn't make it.'

'I know. We must deal with that later. Come, we'll return to the village. Can you still drive your skip? I will not be able to carry you all on my own.'

The young man nodded.

The youngest of the children came towards her and without saying a word he took her hand. Vashla blinked. These people relied on her. She felt somehow that she had let them down. They were lucky, only a few had died and the injuries to the people were not too severe.

She sat on her skip with the three youngest clinging to her and the two teens on their skip. When they landed, they followed her into the cavern.

'It appears that our fighters have halted the attack.'

The people inside were keen to return to the village to see the extent of the damage.

The older boy, Vashla had returned with, walked up to her.

'Have you told Rakal about Tam?'

'Not yet, I'm hoping there will be no need.'

'What do you mean?' The youth spluttered. She didn't answer.

'I'll go back to the house and find out what's happening, do not mention that you saw Tam die.'

'Okay,' the youth replied.

Rakal and Agai had beaten Vashla back home. All she could hear as she approached the cottage was a roaring anguished cry.

'Noooooooooo!'

Vashla cursed, now she would have to work hard to stop Rakal doing something stupid, like trying to kill Zorn on his own.

Rakal was rampaging around the garden kicking over pots, chairs anything in his way.

'Rakal,' Vashla said in a sweet but demanding tone, 'RAKAL, calm down.'

Rakal looked at her as though she was insane. He began to growl and found Vashla joined him in an ever-rising pitch until the crescendo almost shook the walls of the little house.

'Stop that, your deafening!' Gardt yelled.

'Mother Tam is dead, and so are several villagers. You have them in the cool room.'

'Yes Agai, they are all dead,' Vashla grabbed her son by the arm, 'must I remind everyone that I have a restoration chamber?'

Rakal stopped dead in his tracks.

'Why haven't you restored Tam then?'

'The planet has been bombarded, the villagers needed to be taken to safety, the stragglers found and brought back. I've been a little busy.'

Agai looked at his mother and began to laugh.

'What's so funny?' Rakal shouted.

'You two,' Agai replied.

Gardt was smiling, 'I know what you mean.'

'Do you?' Vashla shook her head and sat down perplexed.

'There's nothing funny here,' Rakal picked up a chair he'd knocked down and sat down.

'I think Agai means, you being responsible for other people, not like the old way you were as pirates,' Gardt put his hands on Vashla's shoulder and began to massage some of the tension that had her in tight muscles. 'Do you think that there will eventually be peace?'

'This is my planet, I want my planet safe,' Vashla snorted.

'It is funny,' Agai said, 'but not funny at the same time. When can we restore Tam?'

'Soon, but I need to know what happened. Was it an automated or manned drone that did this? It looks like that the ploughing ray was set to destruct and just gouged the surface as the planet rotated? There didn't seem to be any variation from the line of attack the whole time.'

'It was minimally operated, could have been an automated drone,' Agai replied.

'We blasted it to bits, does it really matter? We need to restore Tam now,' Rakal was back on his feet pacing.

'Agai, you and Rakal must go and check if there are any more of these drones about. Earth could be the next target.'

'Or Ghaur,' Gardt gasped, 'it's closer, and with the population covering almost every segment of the planet's landmass the damage would be horrendous, and the loss of life unimaginable.'

'Agai, take Rakal. I will get to the restoration chamber and restore Tam and the two other villagers too. We can't sit by idly thinking Zorn will give us a reprieve, he's just not going to.'

Gardt nodded. Rakal was still in a state of shock. Agai took his arm and led him towards the spaceship they'd just arrived in.

'Mother will deal with Tam, she is right, we must check to see if there are more of these attack drones about. We must destroy them if there are.'

'You will restore Tam?'

Vashla just gave Rakal a scathing glare as she stood up. Without another word, she walked into the cool room.

She thought it best not to tell anyone that she thought the restoration room might be buried under half a mountain of rubble. She would do all she could. Rakal had become a firm friend and ally and the thought of having him brooding over his lost love was unbearable, almost as bad as the thought of losing Gardt or Agai.

## CHAPTER FORTY-TWO

# Zorn's Mining World Xamba

'Lord Zorn, I did your bidding and brought the prisoners to you today. I can see no value in wasting time with them,' the aide stood a head higher than his leader. He spoke as he would to a friend, but realised all the while, the danger in being so frank. The weapon hidden in his sleeve was there for self defence.

'You are my bodyguard, Amar, not my keeper,' Zorn rounded on the bigger man. 'I will decide what is useful and what is not.'

'Of course, my Lord,' Amar replied, 'the prisoners, do you wish me to return them to the mine?'

'Keep them comfortable somewhere safe for now, I may have more to ask. These are troublemakers and may need dealing with in a way which you may find entertaining, but for now let me dwell on the facts they have already presented.'

'The attack on VaLinta commenced as you ordered my Lord. The drone ship had only two personnel, their loss was not significant.'

'True Amar, but the damage to the planet was minimal. I have launched three other drones, but the surprise is no longer there. They will be alert to this danger.'

Amar agreed, Zorn was a masterful warfare tactician.

'Do you think they can withstand a full force attack?' Zorn asked the man for his counsel.

'They are working together, but their planets are far apart. If we attack on all fronts, I believe they will fail, my Lord.'

Zorn nodded agreement. 'You may go, I have much to prepare.'

Amar bowed and backed out the door.

Zorn sat digesting his meal and the information he had on his enemy. In his youth, he had played with both Vashla and Rakal, on a world that was green and full of life. His parents and theirs had used that world as a home base. They would make raids and take the adolescents with them to see what could be gained from pirating. Each of them trained to be prepared for anything, but he alone, learnt the benefit of using fear to control people. He had employed this strength and become influential on many planets.

He pressed a button to open a shoot and he threw the last of his meal down it. He watched the bones slip away. He had grown to enjoy the look of surprise and horror on the faces of those he controlled. He still relished that. His father had begged him not to kill him, he savoured the grovelling snivelling way his father had acted, right up to the moment the blade he wielded sliced his throat. They had given him all he needed, except what he craved most, power.

Now he needed a large strong army. Fear would help him enlist, willing or otherwise, an army that would be obedient providing he was able to offer a reward at the end. What better reward than new planets and people to plunder.

Xamba, was brown and grey, a continual stench from the foul air and dust blown sky made it a loathsome place. It was his planet though, and he wanted many more. Vashla would not be his wife, so she would suffer, and her planet would be his.

This other planet Ghaur was something entirely different. A huge population of people willing to be controlled, that was very appealing. He had the benefit of a contact on that planet.

'Damera,' the screen in front of Zorn held the image of a robust man with a crinkled face. He also had a mass of grey hair and a greedy twinkle in his eye. 'Lord Zorn,' the man greeted. Zorn was pleased to be addressed correctly.

'I believe you have more colonists ready to move,' Zorn smiled a thin-lipped smile.

'Yes, my Lord,' Damera replied. 'Gardt Ness has contacted our planets Politicians. They are alert to our dealings, so things may be a little more difficult.'

'You can still provide me with these people?'

'Yes, my Lord, we have that situation under control,' the man paused and adjusted himself in his seat. 'I do not wish to go the way my colleague, death at the hand of that Vashla person.'

'You will live. I now need more from you,' Zorn watched the other man squirm and he smiled as he outlined his plan.

Zorn was trying to decide what best to do. He could use the drones, but he didn't trust technology. Now that his enemy knew of their existence and how to destroy them, they were best kept as a secondary offence.

Zorn thought back to the days of his youth.

He recalled the day his fears were crystallised. It was when he was quite young, on the planet his parents used as home base. His uncle's family lived nearby. Zorn had a pet Arnachiapat, it was a creature that ate insects and had a hard shell, it fitted in Zorn's hand. He took it everywhere with him.

His father has asked him to get his brother to discuss their next raid. As often happened Zorn walked across the communal area of the complex and saw that his uncle was working on his latest gadget. He was always tinkering with machines.

'Uncle, Father wants you to join him. Can you come over please?'

'Sure Zorn, but first, help me complete this experiment.'

Zorn rolled his eyes and sat in the corner of his Uncle's workshop playing with his pet.

'This just needs something to test it on,' his uncle looked thoughtful, with his hand on his chin. Then he walked over to Zorn and picked up his Arnachiapat. 'This is the very thing.'

'No,' Zorn cried.

His uncle, without a care, put the animal in on a space at one end of the machine and pressed a button. Zap! The pet Zorn had moments before been petting began shaking uncontrollably then fell over.

'Not quite right yet Zorn. I'll go over to your father now.'

Back to the present Zorn realised that his plan had to be something no one would expect. Then he reached for the musical trinket that the purple traders had given him. It had sat on the corner of his desk for some time. An idea that was delicious sprang to mind. He could use these and their musical melodies, to control the minds of his enemy. He'd used hypnotism before very effectively.

After playing around with different types of downloads Zorn decided he had something worth testing.

'Amar,' Zorn called his guard, 'fetch a prisoner from the mines, I will get you to return him after I've spoken to him. Then Amar, I want you to have him watched, his every movement, the guards are to report to you directly. Do you understand?'

Amar duly went to the mine and looked around the nearby work force. After speaking to a few guards, he selected his target, a plump and sluggish worker.

'Is he a poor worker?' Amar quizzed the guard.

The guard replied with a surly snort and pushed the man towards him.

'You will come with me.'

The man gulped and shuffled after the massive man.

'Where are you taking me?' the dirt ridden prisoner squeaked.

'You will be returned,' Amar led the man back aboard Zorn's command craft. He was surprised to watch Zorn make the man put on earphones and listen to music for some time. It seemed like an age before Zorn dismissed them both.

The next day Amar reported back to Zorn.

'The man is refusing to stop working, even for meal breaks, he says he can't. He will kill himself within a few days if he continues without sustenance or sleep.'

Zorn began to laugh, a hearty resonant laugh.

CHAPTER FORTY-THREE

# Vashla's World-VaLinta

Vashla jumped on the skip again and returned to the site of the restoration chamber. As she'd discovered the day before, it had been buried when the drone beam ploughed up the surface of her planet. She was angry at herself for having to use the manual tools, all she had at her disposal, to unearth it. Still, she had the technology. She simply needed to use it carefully. Lining her skip with the particle dissemination beam, she aimed at the rock. Slowly the rocks were peeling away, layers of debris with each swathe of the slicing ray.

Meanwhile above the planet, Agai sat at the controls of his small spaceship, Rakal was beside him. They were scanning space for any other ships, hoping Zorn had not decided to attack again.

Agai watched Rakal closely. He was merely going through the motions.

'Rakal, you can let go. I've seen a lot of horrible things happen to people about me. Mother was often the cause. She will restore Tam. You will have your partner back.'

Rakal seemed to freeze, his hand hovered above the keys, his face a blank mask.

'Gardt's hailing us, Rakal, let me initiate the transmission,' Agai had to move Rakal aside to touch the controls.

'Gardt,' Agai breathed out as he saw the older man's image light up the screen. 'What have you found?'

'There's no sign of more drones this side of the planet. I've been in contact with Orthama and they have not had any sightings either,' Gardt replied.

'I think for the moment, Earth is safe, merely because of the distance, but I'm concerned about Ghaur,' Agai spoke too quickly.

'So am I,' Gardt wasn't looking at Agai. 'Rakal, what do you think Zorn's next move might be?'

'Rakal,' Agai nudged the big man, 'Gardt asked a question.'

Rakal looked up at the view screen noticing Gardt on the screen for the first time.

'Zorn was always clever, traitorous and aggressive, even as a child. He will be enjoying leaving us guessing what his next move might be.'

'We could take the attack to him,' Gardt watched Rakal's face for a reaction.

'That would be walking into a trap,' Agai was shaking his head.

'Perhaps, I don't want to leave here right now,' Rakal muttered.

'Mother will restore Tam. You will be able to return to Earth together.'

Rakal glared at Agai and walked out of the control room.

'Agai, keep an eye on him. It would not be good to have him go crazy,' Gardt shuddered as he said it.

'I can't stop him doing anything, any more than I can change my mother's mind. They are both *space pirates* as the media on Earth branded them,' Agai shouted in frustration.

'I know son, I'm going planet side now. There's a lot to repair. VaLinta was gouged over a third of its surface. Vashla will need me there to help,' Gardt's face vanished from the view screen.

Agai pressed a button to call Orthama. He needed to speak to Rinra. Suddenly he felt losing someone so close, who meant so much to him, would be unbearable.

Rakal paced in the corridor between the weapons store and the escape pod. His mind was a whirl. He tried to clear it. Stomping further along the corridor of the small ship he went into the sleeping chamber. He didn't think sleep would ease his fears, but right now he was so very tired. He lay down and was soon asleep, overcome by exhaustion.

Soon he was dreaming.

'Tam, where are you?' Rakal was running through the forest near the Davidson's home on Earth. Mata was calling out too. Then he heard the voices of Richard and Davrew. He ran ahead. Somehow the foliage was thicker than he recalled it being, and he was crashing through, breaking twigs and branches as he did. The other voices were well behind him now.

'Tam where are you? You need to come with me, come home,' he kept calling out and hearing no sound. The forest seemed to become almost impenetrable. He was tearing his way through the shrubbery, but he was blocked at each turn. There was no reply to his calls. He was alone.

He woke up sweating. How would he tell young Mata or Tam's parents? How could he go through another day? He needed to do something. Without a word to Agai, Rakal went to the weapons store, took out several weapons, jumped in the escape pod and flew over to his own ship in orbit above the planet. He would not contact Vashla until he was well on the way to Zorn.

Rakal sped with stealth to his main spaceship, secured the pod in the hold so it couldn't be traced, then ran to the control room. His ship was a triangular black ship with three magnetic propulsion thrusters, emitting a golden glow from the base. The ships control room was at the heart of the ship. It was a thin wedge that Rakal now launched at full speed towards Zorn.

Back on the ship he'd just left in orbit, Agai was talking to Rinra on Orthama.

'I'll have to get Rakal back in here. We need to make plans,' Agai pressed the internal intercom.

'Rakal, come back to the control room.'

After several minutes with no reply Agai went searching. When he discovered the weapons store raided and the pod missing, he cursed.

'Mother, I need to speak to you immediately,' Agai despaired as his mother had become difficult to locate.

Vashla was busy, the job was only half complete, unearthing the restoration chamber would have to wait, again. The colonists were demanding her time. Yes, things had to be put back in order, Gardt had returned and he was helping, still, so much more needed to be done. This is her world, and she wanted to enjoy the freedom of living on it, unhindered by the responsibilities she now faced.

After a frustrating morning of helping families in the village rebuild, or, demolishing the ruins to make way for new homes, Vashla returned home, going straight to the communications room. Agai had left several messages, she returned his call.

'Agai, you want to speak to me?'

'Mother, Rakal has gone after Zorn.'

'I thought I told you to keep an eye on him.'

'I did, but he's angry. Have you restored Tam?'

'Not yet, the colonists demand time and assistance.'

'What's stopping you putting the dead in the restoration chamber?'

'It's buried.'

Gardt walked in covered in dust from his labours, he overheard Vashla's reply.

'By the stars Vashla, why didn't you tell me?'

'Yes mother, it would have been good to know the reason for the delay,' Agai scolded. 'I can't help you because I need to get back to Orthama. Rinra needs me, although there appears to be no immediate threat, the Elders are demanding more discussion. I can look out for Rakal on the way.'

'Agai, go then, but take care. Zorn is not finished yet.'

'I will contact you as soon as I get to Orthama.'

'You've done well, son,' Vashla sighed and looked at Gardt.

'You wanted him here,' Gardt pulled her into an embrace.

'He's grown into a man who will do what he wants. The colonists are adults, why do they demand my help? They are capable of doing repairs without me.'

'They've come to rely on you Vashla,' Gardt kissed her gently. 'Now, where's the chamber? I can help you excavate it.'

'With your help, another half day, we will uncover it,' Vashla returned his hug. 'I need to get the bodies there as soon as I can now, they are starting to deteriorate.'

'What about Rakal, should we go after him?'

'He'll have to take his chances.'

CHAPTER FORTY-FOUR

# Zorn's Mining World Xamba

Rakal sat at his control room station, tears streaming down his face. He'd logged his destination as Zorn's mining planet. It made no sense to go after his enemy on his own. He knew it was courting trouble. His mind was filled with Tam, always being there. Always bringing his big ideas into perspective, always smiling and teasing, always being a great parent, teaching Rakal how to be with Mata the way he missed out with their first born, Kat, who'd become a friend as an adult, with Tam's encouragement. Wiping his hand down his wet cheeks he barely noticed the blimp on his view screen. Then he saw it, and another. He was surrounded. Zorn had him trapped. It was a stupid move.

Zorn gloated. Rakal snarled at him.

'Rakal, you've managed to get yourself lost in my territory. Why?'

Rakal said nothing. The room was bare, only the desk Zorn sat at with a window behind him. The view was of a dull and dreary grey sky, with orange sandy soil and brown hills bare of foliage or vegetation. Lifeless other than the perpetual stream of Zorn's guards.

'Did you think you could spy on me? See what my strengths are and report back to your shabby group of allies?'

Rakal continued to brood in silence.

'Take him to the courtyard, chain him to the rail. Leave him there, at least until the sun bakes his skin,' Zorn began to laugh.

Amar hoisted Rakal roughly to his feet. He was tightly bound and could not escape. The aide had to push and drag him to the courtyard.

'Zorn can see you from his room,' Amar grunted while chaining his victim to the post.

'I'm like him, aren't I?' Rakal starred back with dark cold eyes.

Amar said nothing more. It was unnerving for the aide to see another so like Zorn. To know they were somehow related, and yet, bitter enemies. He turned and left knowing that soon the suns above the parched soil would rise in the rank sky, to beat down unmercifully on the chained man.

Zorn was laughing. He had an idea. A deliciously good one, he walked about the room with the little music trinket in his hand. He would take his time to make sure the plan worked. His cousin would soon be pliable. He sat at his desk and worked on the box, ensuring it had all he intended within it. Amar arrived at his masters' call, he found Zorn laughing still. That was disconcerting.

Usually when Lord Zorn was on this planet, he was foul to be around. He loathed the place.

'Bring me the two prisoners from the cell. They will assist me putting my plan in action.'

'Yes, my Lord,' Amar nodded dutifully, rushing out to perform his task.

## CHAPTER FORTY-FIVE

# Vashla's World-VaLinta

Vashla and Gardt worked well together and gradually uncovered more of the spaceship that housed the restoration chamber. They managed to reach the entrance hatch. It wouldn't open.

'Can we open it another way?' Gard stood at Vashla's side as she pounded on the door opening device. Taking a deep breath, she stepped away from the vehicle and nodded.

'Where?'

Vashla clambered over the remaining mound of soil and aimed the atomiser beam again, not far from where he stood. Gardt jumped on his skip and followed her lead. Gradually, more of the craft entrance was exposed.

Without further ado, Vashla jumped off her skip and ran to another side portal, this was smaller, and opened with a swish when she found the indent key.

'This isn't an entry, it's too small,' Gardt was baffled.

'It's a waste release station, expulsion rather than entry. However, it gives us access to the inner opening mechanism of the main entry,' Vashla sent in a remote orb to the entrance control to open the main door.

They went inside once it opened. There was a lot of damage to the vehicle. Gardt sent a silent prayer to the Ancients in hope that the restoration chamber had survived the attack. Shortly after he realised his hopes were dashed.

'I don't know how to repair it,' Vashla yelled and kicked the chamber wall.

'There must be a way,' Gardt was trying to sound convincing, and failing miserably.

Vashla started pacing. 'Do the people on your world have Ancient technology?'

'No, not unless the I.S.C.C. have kept the knowledge from us,' he replied as he lent against the wall of the ship.

'The people on Earth, the Davidson's have great technological expertise, they will help.'

'They will be devastated to know Tam is dead,' Gardt pointed out the flaw in the suggestion.

'How about Orthama, they are closer in linage to the Ancients, they must have someone who could help.'

Gardt nodded, 'it's worth a try.'

Back at the cottage they contacted Agai on Orthama station.

'Agai is discussing our plight with the Elders, we have to wait for help to come,' Vashla slumped into the nearby easy chair. Long shadows cast from the trees outside covered the floor of the room. Gardt drew the curtain.

'It's dusk. We've been at it all day, time to rest now, Vashla my love.'

Vashla allowed the exhaustion she felt to swallow her up. She curled up in the chair and was soon asleep.

Zorn stood at his window looking out at his mining world.

Amar had returned Rakal to his spaceship. He'd been taken back into space above Zamba. The exact place Rakal was in before he'd been captured. In his own small craft, Rakal was in a deep drug-induced sleep. Amar had followed Zorn's instructions and made certain the earphones and listening device on his prisoners' head was working, before leaving. He reported that he had set Rakal's vehicle on automatic pilot on a course back to VaLinta.

Zorn nodded at his aid and began to laugh, the menacing guttural laugh, the aide recognised as trouble for his enemy.

Rakal wasn't sure how long he'd slept.

When he woke, he tore off the music device without even thinking where it came from, realising he was in orbit over VaLinta. Rubbing the sleep from his eyes he pressed the communications console. He called Earth, with a sinking feeling, knowing the news he was to deliver would devastate the Davidson's. It was time they knew Tam was dead.

Agai, Rinra and the Elder Vini had returned to VaLinta.

'Rakal is back,' Agai pointed to the sleek craft on the view screen, 'he's been gone for over a week.'

'Your mother is hailing us,' Rinra opened the comm.

'Agai, you are back, and you've help with you?'

'Yes mother, Elder Vini has bought all the scientific research that Orthama has on the Ancients. With the information they have on other Ancient artefact's, Vini believes that our engineering knowledge will be enough to repair the restoration chamber.'

'Good, I have frozen the bodies so they cannot deteriorate.'

'Mother, did you know Rakal is back?'

'He's not responding to our calls,' Vashla replied. 'Bring our guests planet-side. I'm sure Rakal will soon follow. He may have had time to cool off his bad temper.'

'Does he know about the restoration chamber?'

'Not yet,' the screen went blank.

'Does that mean trouble?' Rinra asked while taking Agai's hand.

'It means we have two angry and frustrated former space pirates to pacify. It's good that Gardt is with my mother. Rakal is another matter. Tam was the only one I knew who could calm him down,' Agai blew out an exasperated breath.

'Where could he have been for a week?'

'Only the stars know,' Agai gave Rinra a quick hug, 'let's go.'

## CHAPTER FORTY-SIX

# Vashla's World-VaLinta

Rakal did return. He hardly spoke. Vashla offered him a meal.

'I need to tell you Rakal that we have had a delay in restoring Tam. We will be able to do this as soon as the Chamber is repaired. It was buried during Zorn's attack.'

'Tam is still dead, and you cannot change that,' Rakal snarled.

'We have resources to repair the damage. We will bring Tam back to life for you.'

'Don't bother, I've told the Davidson's on Earth. They know your treachery.'

'Treachery! Grief has taken your mind! This was not deliberate. I've been working for a week to recover the chamber, and to restore Tam. We'll do this very soon,' Vashla tried vainly to keep her voice from rising.

'I don't believe you. My children are now without Tam, and so are the Davidson's,' Rakal stood up and pushed his chair over as he stormed out.

'What's got into him?' Gardt asked the question the dumbfounded Vashla had on her mind.

'He's not himself,' Vashla sighed. 'We have to plan our next course of action. We need Rakal to be with us in this.'

'So Vini, Rinra and Agai had better get that chamber repaired quickly,' Gardt picked up the overturned chair and pushed it back under the table.

'I'll call Earth. I want to let Richard and Davrew know what's happening,' Vashla strode over to the console. 'Tam will be restored.'

On Earth, Richard took the call.

'Vashla, Rakal told us that Tam is dead. He seemed matter of fact about it. Is it true?'

Vashla nodded.

'However, Rakal is not himself. I should tell you that I have a restoration chamber, Ancients' technology. I've used it many times to bring dead back to life. Gardt will tell you on our earlier and my wilder days, I would kill him for pleasure then restore him. He is, as you know, very much alive today.'

'We've been planning a funeral,' Richard had blood shot red eyes, clearly distraught. The image Vashla saw on the view screen broke her heart.

'The chamber was buried during the attack by Zorn's drone. Half VaLinta was gouged and it has taken time to uncover the chamber. We will restore Tam. I assure you there is no need for a funeral.'

'Then why did Rakal put us through this anguish. He knows each member of our family, especially Tam, was adored by us and their children. How could he be so heartless?'

'In his state of grief and anger Rakal went off to face Zorn alone,' Vashla shook her mass of long dark wavy hair away from her face. 'He's just returned. We've no idea where he went or what happened to him. He has hardened after seeing Tam dead. He is not himself,' Vashla paused, should she reveal the truth? Gardt nodded at her as though reading her thoughts. 'The chamber is uncovered but damaged. We now have scientists and engineers working to repair the damage. Tam will be restored.'

On Earth the sun shone in a delicious expanse of blue sky. The bitter smell of freshly cut grass assailed the occupants of the garden. The grounds had been freshened from overnight rain. It was beautiful. Davrew had gone outside to the special place they often came to sit and find peace. The rock beside the fishpond was cold and it sent a chill through every part of his body. Richard could see Davrew shivering so he sat down and snuggled close. Silently they watched orange and gold slithers dart about the pool.

Miri walked out through the back door, drawing her cardigan tight about her. Seeing her parents sitting together, Miri stood silently for a moment, and let the sun warm her. Unwilling to interrupt, she stayed that way, until at last, Richard looked up. At that moment, he beckoned her forward. Miri moved slowly towards them.

'Peter has gone to fetch Mata. Kat's on the way too.'

Davrew began to sing an evocative hypnotic tune. Miri remembered the last time she'd heard Davrew sing that song, it was the day Bon had died.

'Parents should not have to go through the anguish of losing one child, let alone two,' Richard whispered.

'We will speak to everyone, please alert the family for a gathering Miri,' Davrew looked up into the face of their eldest child. 'Vashla is saying she can restore Tam. Rakal was so brutally adamant that we would not see Tam again.'

'Grief can create harshness, Davrew, my love. Vashla said Rakal was filled with anger,' Richard leaned close to his partner. They held each other up.

'I'll let everyone know, we shall honour Tam this evening. Whatever happens, it will be good to have a gathering,' Miri tried to smile but felt her heart incapable of the effort.

Peter pulled his station wagon into the drive Mata leapt out of the car the minute he stopped. The child ran straight over to her grandparents and they all sobbed, clinging to each other for comfort.

Peter climbed out and walked into the house after his partner, Miri.

Back on VaLinta, Gardt and Vashla were sitting watching the control panel.

'What do we do now?' Gardt asked Vashla.

'Wait to see what Zorn does next.'

They didn't have to wait long.

CHAPTER FORTY-SEVEN

# Vashla's World-VaLinta

Ria ran from the village as fast as she could. Breathless at Vashla's door, she knocked once then rushed in.

'Gardt, Vashla, Ghaur is under attack. Father is on a rampage. The President contacted him.'

'What kind of attack,' Vashla demanded. 'Ria, stop rambling and tell me.'

Gardt pulled out a chair and gently pushed the flush faced woman into it.

'Father said there were a fleet of ships above the planet. If they do the same to Ghaur that they did here it will be catastrophic. There are no wide-open spaces, every part of the planet is built on and any hit will cause untold destruction. It will be mayhem. The order the government hold dear, will be obliterated.

'I don't see that as a bad thing,' Gardt remarked dryly.

'Mother is still there,' Ria squealed.

'Yes, of course she is, along with your cousins, aunt and uncle and the younger children.'

Vashla was already at the communication screen contacting the planets that had become her allies.

'Zorn keeps taking the first step. We must be able to block his way and fight back,' Vashla thumped the console in frustration.

'We have been busy recuperating from the attack here,' Gardt reminded her.

'Yes, busy. While he has been preparing his next assault at his leisure,' Vashla growled. 'Where is Rakal? We need him here to help prepare for battle?'

The answer came swiftly when Rinra barged into the house unannounced.

'Rakal has damaged the restoration chamber and knocked out Vini. I only just got away on the skip. Agai is there trying to reason with him.'

Vashla growled, a full body, deep and resonantly deafening roar. She stormed out of the cottage with Gardt chasing after her.

Ria began to sob. Rinra, not having met the woman, sat down beside her. Wiping away her tears with the palm of her hand, Ria began to talk.

'I'm one of the colonists from Ghaur, I wasn't supposed to be here,' Ria explained. 'That doesn't matter. Ghaur is under attack. Zorn has a fleet of ships above the planet. My mother and family live there. Only my husband Bru, and two of our older boys are with us here.'

A shocked Rinra grew paler. She walked over to the communication screen and resumed the link Vashla had initiated.

'I'll finish what Vashla had started, we must contact all the planets in our alliance and make plans to retaliate.

Normally, Rakal would be the one to lead us with Vashla.'

Ria nodded and composed herself enough to join her new friend at the console.

Vashla had jumped onto a skip with Gardt getting on behind her. He held fast to his feisty athletic woman. He knew there was trouble ahead. They headed towards the restoration chamber site.

As they skimmed low over the treetops, Gardt noticed how the scars carved into the land from Zorn's attack drone, were already healing. The foliage was sprouting and the planet recovering.

He thought of his own home world, Ghaur. It was so built-up, barely a square of ground was free of construction of one form or another. Unlike this planet, it had few green spaces, and rare expanses of water, as most of this liquid was delivered from underground water caverns. An attack, like the one here, would be far more devastating and the government there, less adaptable, or capable of assisting the masses. The main aim of the laws there was to control, contain, and maintain order of the large population. Exploration of space, and the hope of colonising other planets, was the only glimpse of release from this oppressive regime. No wonder the average citizen on Ghaur was pre-occupied with the thought of colonising new worlds. The I.S.C.C. fed upon their need, making deals with Zorn and their expense.

As they approached the Ancients' remarkable recently uncovered spaceship, he spotted Rakal.

'There he is,' Gardt pointed, he could feel Vashla tense her muscles.

'Take over,' she yelled into the wind. Suddenly she was free falling away from their skip. Gardt floundered moving forward to take hold of the controls of the small craft which pitched perilously. He regained control and landed near the spaceship.

He couldn't see either Vashla or Rakal, but he could tell where they'd been. There was a dent in the wall of the spaceship about Rakal's size and scratch marks on the wall opposite, where Vashla had tried to gain a hold. A battle was taking place, but the opponents were not there. Gardt ran inside the spacecraft and looked about carefully. Vini was on the floor near the restoration chamber. He quickly went to check the Orthama Elders' vital signs. Thankfully Vini was alive. Gardt saw Agai come in the entrance and he let out the breath he'd been holding.

'Thank the stars you're Okay,' Gardt looked up at his son. 'Where are they?'

'I couldn't get Rakal to calm down, so I led him outside away from Vini. Mother landed on Rakal and bowled him over with her dive from the skip.'

'I got a shock when she jumped off,' Gardt admitted.

'Rakal quickly recovered and they started wrestling. They went over towards the lake. Mother was yelling, speaking their native language, growling a lot. I've not seen either of them like this for years.'

'Help me get Vini onto the skip and back to the house.' Gardt lifted the unconscious man under his arms while Agai raised his legs. They put him on the skip. 'We've got to do something quickly, Ghaur is under attack. We need both your mother and Rakal to get working together to defend the planet.'

Agai nodded, said nothing, jumped to the skip controls and took off with Vini slumped and buckled in.

Gardt returned to the spaceship to see what damage had been done. He took a mental note of the repairs that would need to be done, on his way to the control room. There was one way he could help Vashla. He only hoped he could do it in time.

At the spaceship controls Gardt looked for the two fighting warriors. A quick body heat scan located them. He pressed a button on the control panel, instantly the larger of the two opponents was pinned in position like a statue. Gardt saw the image on the screen of Vashla as she slumped to the ground. He ran outside to check her injuries.

'You still have the knowledge of the battle,' Vashla smiled at Gardt. 'I'll tie Rakal securely, even though he's pinned. We must get him back to the spaceship. He must see sense. We need his help.'

'Ghaur is a planet unprepared for war,' Gardt agreed as they lifted Rakal and carted his heavy weight back the way they'd come.

## CHAPTER FORTY-EIGHT

# Gardt's World- Ghaur

'They're not as unprepared as you might think,' Vashla added as they released the pin on Rakal who was now secured behind a force field aboard the space craft.

'Ghaur, has some defence?' Gardt asked.

Rakal growled.

'Wake up Rakal,' Vashla shouted, 'we need your expertise.'

'I need Tam.'

'We will restore Tam, providing you've not done irreparable damage. You will have your partner with you again. Vini was doing repairs when you knocked him out.'

Rakal became more subdued.

'I'm going to leave you to think for a while cousin,' Vashla turned and quickly went back outside.

'We need to find out what's happening on Ghaur,' Gardt could hear his voice crack.

Vashla nodded. They both jumped back on the remaining skip and soared quickly across the treetops to their cottage home.

Vashla greeted her guests, with a curt nod, as she walked into her house. Rinra was still at the communication station. Vini sat in a chair at the table, with Ria beside him. Both were drinking a steaming brew. Gardt had followed Vashla inside and he walked over to Rinra.

'Vashla, I've contacted all our allies and a few that may be new to you. They're all willing to assist,' Rinra explained and showed Vashla the contact list.

Vashla nodded and smiled. 'Good, now we have to act. As I mentioned, Ghaur is not entirely defenceless.'

'The report I have from Ghaur is that Zorn has three large ships above the planet. We think these are drones. There's another thirty battle ships of different sizes in formation that have just joined the original three large ships,' Agai moved to the table and took a seat. 'All of them sit in stationary orbit, intimidating the authorities on the planet. We believe the people of Ghaur are unaware of the danger and their government is trying to negotiate with Zorn.'

'Ha,' Vashla slid onto the bench seat beside her son.

'What about Rakal, will he join the battle?' Ria asked.

'He will stay where he is. I don't think he's capable of reason right now. We need the thinking, tactical fighter, not this madman.'

'Do you think he went mad in space?' Gardt shook his head.

'I don't know,' Vashla shrugged, she'd regained some of her composure. 'He's not himself. The Rakal I know would never hurt any of the Davidson's, especially his children. He's always been proud of Kat and adored doting over little Mata. When Tam is restored there'll be trouble.'

'Mother, I think we need Rakal in the battle. The people on VaLinta know his strengths and look up to him, they will think it strange him being kept away.'

'Son, you speak wisely. I don't trust him as he is, but we can't afford not to have such an experienced fighter with us in this battle.'

Vashla poured herself a cup of dark brown liquid.

'Coffee from Earth, a stimulant I believe,' Vashla raised the cup in salute. 'I will get Rakal tomorrow. To-night, we rest. By then our friends will have their fleets of ships gathered. We can make our plans with clear heads.'

The next day, Vashla woke beside Gardt in their huge comfortable bed in the home she'd built for her family. She hadn't slept well. Her head was spinning with plans. It was early. Gardt slept soundly, breathing deeply. She slipped out of their bed and went to wash. She took some time to brush her mane of black hair and tie it up into a braid then bun on her head. She admired her reflection in the mirror. A little fuller in figure than in previous years, her breasts were large and still alluring. Her fighting clothes hugged her body, without covering up her assets.

Today all the preparations for battle would be put together. The allies would be amassing, and she would be the one everyone would look to for leadership. Kat had said she would be the General. That was one of the highest ranks in the Armies on Earth.

'Don't think you're slipping out of here without me, woman,' Gardt teased her as he drew her into a deep embrace.

'I wouldn't dream, of going anywhere, without you, now, Gardt,' she kissed him passionately, then just as quickly, pulled herself away. 'I must get Rakal. We have the first of many battles to face today.'

'I'll get everyone ready for your return. We'll leave immediately for Ghaur. We've delayed enough.'

Vashla nodded and left.

Rakal returned with Vashla and seemed to throw himself into getting everyone organised for the battle.

Vashla was busy making sure the rendezvous with their allies could be met. They came up against small delays. Although the ten ships on VaLinta had been fitted with weaponry, they were hardly big guns.

'What's the delay? We should be on our way!' Vashla shouted in frustration at the Security Chief.

'We had a mix up with finding some of the armoury supplies, we've found them now. We'll be ready shortly.'

'Thanks,' Vashla muttered a little curtly.

Soon the small fleet were heading for their allies' assembly point. When they arrived at the co-ordinate, they were surprised to find no one there.

'Mother,' Agai hailed Vashla from one of the other ships. 'It appears Rinra was told to meet at a different co-ordinate, I've put this in our navigation array, and we'll be with them in a short time.'

'I was specific, why would they change the meeting point?'

'I believe they were given the change by Rakal this morning.'

'Oh,' Vashla started to realise what was going on, 'and, the other contingents of our allies' ships?'

'I've contacted them all. They were all given different places to meet.'

'Very well, we now have the correct location for all our ships,' Vashla had immediately moved to her control panel and pressed a button.

'Yes mother.'

'You will go to Rakal's ship. He is pinned. Tell his crew to carry on as normal. Bring Rakal to this ship. I wish to keep him near.'

'You believe he sabotaged our departure and rendez-vous,' Agai said. 'That's not Rakal.'

'Not normally, no, by the stars I've allowed him free-dom,' Vashla yelled. 'Bring him here.'

Shortly afterwards Agai appeared with Rakal. Vashla now wore her full hand-to-hand combat arms, and the look was unmistakable. Rakal was pinned and secured.

'You don't trust me cousin.'

'Not with your addled brain,' she said nothing more. There was no time for idle chat.

Agai turned to farewell his mother and wish her well.

CHAPTER FORTY-NINE

# Battle for the Worlds

Vashla returned to the task.

She was now with her massed fleet of allies. Her own small stash of plundered craft, only ten were battle-ready. In total, there were the ten, armed and converted craft from the Ghaur colonists, and thirty from Orthama. Vashla knew they were being piloted by inexperienced youths that had been training for action. From Earth, a further forty battle ships joined the fleet. Some of these ships were ones Rakal had plundered previously. Other craft had been built on Earth, by the surprisingly ingenious engineer Ash Davidson. This was hardly an armada, however, Zorn had many enemies and the traders known only to her as the purple dealers from the planet Ozer, had joined with an assortment of twenty more ships that appeared to be very much more battle-ready.

They slipped into the grid, in rapid succession, all about to arrive above Ghaur.

'Mother,' Agai's voice sounded on the comm.

'Yes son.'

'I believe Rakal may be using some communication device to contact Zorn.'

'I had noticed.'

'Perhaps Rakal should be sedated,' Agai suggested.

'He doesn't know all our plans. Or the planets security system I've already put in place. His misinformation could be beneficial.'

'He knows how many ships we have, and when we will be there,' Agai reminded his mother.

'He doesn't know everything.'

'We will arrive through the grid in moments,' Agai knew he could say nothing more.

They had arrived.

Vashla ran her hand over the control panel. She hailed her fleet and Zorn.

'Zorn, cousin, I'm here to escort you away from this planet. You have not attacked this world, and we insist you don't.'

They could hear Zorn growl then laugh.

'Vashla, cousin, you cannot stop me. After I have all I need from this world, I will return to yours, then to Orthama, and the other planet Earth. You will not stop me!'

'Ah, so you say. But we've been a day behind your arrival here, and you haven't attacked the planet so far,' Vashla began to goad her opponent.

'I was waiting for your arrival. You can now witness the destruction of this world,' Zorn started he deep throated growl.

Vashla began to laugh. Her laugh was every bit as menacing as his growl. She cut communications with Zorn but continued to speak to her small fleet.

'Watch my friends as Zorn creates his own demise.'

She said nothing more.

Zorn had hundreds of ships, and he spread them around the planet Ghaur. Six massive drone ships were now positioned at intervals about the planet, and Zorn arranged his smaller ships in an orbital line between.

Gardt hailed his partner.

'Vashla, my love, this is going to be a massacre. My people, my planet of origin, will be decimated,' he pleaded for the survival of the planet.

'Have faith in my plan, my love, you will see. We will be the victors.'

'There is a communication coming in from Ghaur.'

'We're willing to do whatever you want, Lord Zorn. Please don't ruin our world,' the President was standing pale-faced behind a lectern. 'We're a peaceful people. We could offer you a great deal.'

Zorn began to laugh again.

'You have nothing I need. My need is only of another planet, free of vermin inhabiting it, to secure your soil, produce and resources. I will take it, now!'

'We're helpless to stop him, Mother, we're not enough in number or firepower,' Agai added, equally concerned. As they had so few trained pilots, they each had to man different ships.

'Watch and learn, my son. Have faith, my love.'

'We will watch, is that all we can do?'

'Gardt, be patient.'

They watched.

## CHAPTER FIFTY

# Battle for the Worlds

Zorn set his drones to work first, a huge deadly swathe of light issued from each craft, and his fleet was quick to follow suit and fire at the planet.

One by one, the drone beam of fire returned from an invisible barrier and caused the ship of origin to disintegrate. Each ship was firing deadly weapons that rebounded on themselves. The space in front of Vashla's fleet began to look like a mass of explosive firecrackers, erupting in an almost rhythmic sequence.

Vashla began to laugh.

The sound of Zorn's scream filled the room. 'Cease fire!' His ship, having held back to watch the attack, had not fired.

'Now, my friends, it is time for us to close in for battle.'

Vashla swung her battleship about and took aim at Zorn's ship. The others from her fleet were quick to follow. Some of Zorn's mercenary ships were not too damaged and when they turned, they didn't all join the fight, instead, they headed for space away from the planet. Away from the grid, as Vashla, and her combat ships were in the way.

'Cowards!' Zorn yelled.

'There are still more, undamaged, ships remaining,' Gardt said anxiously, as he swung his ship about firing on a fleeing ship.

'I've got your back,' Agai yelled, as he shot rapidly at a small ship, rushing towards Gardt's craft.

Vashla had swung around again, destroying another small craft on her way back to her main target, Zorn. His ship was sending torpedo bolts out into her motley group of fighters. The purple people and friends dived into the fray, quickly forcing the larger ship to turn away from their persistent bombardment. They lost several ships in the encounter. The drones had broken up quickly, but many of Zorn's battle ships remained. Now they joined the fight firing at will.

Recklessly, Shea and Maya, rushed at a group of Zorn's ships. They had with them four more ships in a diamond formation, they fired bolts in unison.

'Great shooting!' Agai shouted. 'You've been practising that. Come on guys, let's clean up!' He fired again taking out another of Zorn's fleet.

Vashla smiled, but she had no time to wallow in parental pride. She was close enough now to Zorn's ship, firing three torpedoes rapidly into his side and two more at his weapons array. Then she set her battleship on auto pilot with tractor beam on Zorn's massive hull, setting an automated continual fire of her cannon. She took a quick look around the control room, then left.

Rakal was stunned to see Vashla in his chamber.

'We're in battle. Shouldn't you be fighting?'

'I am,' she replied.

Rakal was still immobilised, so she pulled him to his feet, quickly patting him down.

'This will do you no good now,' she held a small communicator in front of his weary eyes.

The instant she touched her bracelet a white light shrouded them both.

They were aboard Zorn's battleship. Vashla pushed Rakal, bound and on a levitation device, towards the main control room. There were two guards at the entrance. Before they could react, she drew her scabbard and quickly dispatched them both. The guards lay slumped where they fell.

They entered the control room. Vashla pushed Rakal into the first crewman that turned her way. The dead weight of the big man fell on him. She fired at other man, felling him. She leapt across Rakal, to slit the throat of the hapless crewman pinned beneath him. She rolled Rakal, still pinned and inactive to trip the next crewman trying to intercept her. Silently she turned to see that there was only Zorn and a navigator remaining in the control room. She shot the navigator and the door mechanism in quick succession.

Zorn engrossed in watching Vashla's battleship, as it fell apart under his determined attack, now realised he himself was under attack. Vashla had evaded death.

He began to growl making the air around the room vibrate. He flung himself at Vashla, launching into hand-to-hand combat. She was ready for him sliced his chest with her scabbard, slammed metal-covered knuckles into his head.

'While we're chatting cousin, you could tell me what you have done to Rakal. He's not himself.'

Zorn was only stunned by Vashla's attack. He grabbed her arm, getting hold of her, and he flung her into the chair he'd recently sat in.

'He came out on his own, landed in my lap. So, naturally, cousin, I gave him a present. A twist of thought, a persuasive memory, he helped delay you, he relayed information.'

'Not enough it would seem, cousin,' Vashla rose and sidestepped Zorn's lunge, giving him a swift hard kick behind his knee, sending him stumbling.

'You excite me when you are fighting,' Zorn was drooling.

'You make me sick, cousin. To think, I ever contemplated union with you!' She caught Zorn another swipe on his arm, with her scabbard. She unsheathed a small sword and attacked with both blades. Zorn lashed out and caught her with a body blow, then another to her head. Vashla caught herself before she slipped to the floor, planting her sword deep in Zorn's leg. Then she lifted her scabbard to Zorn's throat.

'Tell me, now cousin, before I slit your throat, and add your memories to my library. How do I reverse the damage you have done to Rakal?'

'I'll never tell you,' Zorn squirmed and kicked out at Vashla.

She retaliated with two swift swipes of her blade, severing Zorn's throat. Then she completed the task, severing his head from his shoulders.

Rakal had rolled over. He was looking at the door. Zorn's henchmen were cutting through her hastily created seal.

'Time for us to go Rakal,' she lifted him roughly to his feet, pressing her bracelet as the door was breached.

On the bridge of Gardt's ship, Vashla arrived in a dishevelled state. He took one look at her and pulled her into a smothering embrace.

'I thought you were still aboard your ship. It's been destroyed.'

Within a short time, all the ships in Zorn's fleet had left, as quickly as they could. Zorn's battleship had mysteriously disappeared.

'There will be another attack from Zorn's men,' Rakal shouted.

Vashla glared at her cousin, touched the control panel, immediately, Rakal was again, paralysed and unable to speak.

'Don't mind him, Gardt. Zorn has damaged his mind. Now, when we return, Tam will be restored, and we can work on returning our Rakal to us all.'

'Agai,' Gardt hailed their son, 'your mother is alive.'

'By the stars, Mother, you know how to leave us guessing. What of Zorn?'

'We have another head for our library.'

'When did you put up the repelling barrier? Mother, no one knew you had.'

'A girl has to keep some secrets,' Vashla smiled.

Agai laughed. 'See you back on VaLinta.'

Vashla placed Zorn's head in storage, ready to put in her library when she returned home. Somehow, it didn't give her the rush of exhalation she usually felt after a kill, especially, such a mortal enemy. Zorn's ship had disappeared. Who was controlling it now? She wondered, was the threat still there? Had she changed so much, that killing was no longer an adrenalin rush? Vashla looked at her reflection in the glass surrounding Zorn's head. The answer was yes.

CHAPTER FIFTY-ONE

# Battle for the Worlds

Back on VaLinta, Gardt had prepared refreshments. A gathering of friends and allies was taking place. No formal requests had been made, they simply arrived. Vashla had gone to change and freshen up. Her combat attire was no longer required. She'd returned in a subdued mood, Gardt had picked up on this and wondered why she wasn't jubilant at defeating Zorn. She came back out looking casual and alluring in an aqua silk dress, with body hugging plunging neckline and straps on the shoulders. She walked over to Gardt, leaning into him for a hug. Then they went outside into the garden, to the guests.

'Friends, I am glad we are all here,' Vashla poured a glass of wine and raised it in salute. 'We have much to discuss. There needs to be a way forward for us all.'

'Surely mother, now that Zorn is dead, we can return to our peaceful lives?' Agai voiced the thoughts of everyone at the table.

'Not quite,' Vashla said, as she looked about at the faces of her friends and family. 'Tam and those who died here, on the attack we suffered on VaLinta, are almost restored. Rakal is still imprisoned. His mind has been altered by some tampering on Zorn's behalf. I'll be able to find out how by delving into his memories, I have his skull in my library. However,' she paused to savour the sweet taste of the beverage, 'Zorn's ship disappeared. Do we now face another adversary?'

Richard and Davrew had travelled through the grid to join them in celebration of Zorn's defeat. Tam and Rakal's son Kat, and his wife Emily, also sat on a nearby garden seat, enjoying the warmth of the sun. Rinra had returned, with Agai and Vini representing the Elders, from Orthama. Two extremely tall and purple men, from the planet Ozer, were sitting in the shade, squinting, the sunlight. They were unaccustomed to the bright sunlight, so an umbrella was hastily erected.

'I've asked our Security Chief to join us today, he came from Ghaur. He'll be here shortly,' Vashla continued.

In a surprisingly high-pitched voice, one of the purple traders spoke. 'We have news of the planet Xamba.'

'Please, go on,' Vashla urged.

'There is a native population on the planet, they have for many generations mined their world in a sustainable way. Zorn changed all that and created a polluted world. They are willing to fight Zorn also.'

'Zorn is dead,' Gardt reminded their guest.

'This was before today's battle, however, the battle-ship disappearing, may mean that Lord Zorn's aide Amar, has taken over where his master left off. He did seem capable of this when I was taken into Zorn's confidence,' the purple trader concluded.

'You've been to Zorn's planet, and spoken with him?' Vashla quizzed.

'Yes, and it was then I knew we must fight. Zorn is a madman, ruthless, killing without regard for the lives of those around him who suffer.'

'What did he ask of you when you went to his world?'

'He asked about the devices we traded for; the little music boxes intrigued him. Also, he asked where and at what point in the grid our planets are. He learnt a little about each world. I had no choice but to speak the truth. I saw Zorn eat a man who dared to speak out of turn.'

'This brings me to another problem I've been pondering,' Vashla looked into the dark eyes and wrinkled face of the trader. 'I think we need to formalise our association of our planets.'

'You mean a treaty?' Richard offered.

'Yes, a formal alliance arrangement, so we know where we stand. We are friends, I for one am glad of that. I don't want to be responsible to every world or sector of space. Right now, I wish only to offer a haven as a new colony to the people of Ghaur, who wish to make it their home. I want nothing more than to make this home a good place to be. Perhaps my drive to fight has left me.'

'Now that's saying something,' Agai shook his head.

'If Earth agrees to this suggestion, believe me, there are huge political hurdles to overcome. With many governments on diverse continents with differing cultures, an agreement to align themselves with other planets governments, is a difficult concept to accept,' Davrew pointed out. 'There's no single planet wide government and the organisations' they do have such as The World Health Organisation, directs and suggests, without real power or authority. The United Nations, overseers of peace treaties on Earth, again it's not a power base, rather a director of allies armies to contain unrest and promote peace.'

'We do have a brilliant diplomat in our seventh born Mica. Rakal is testament to his abilities, having travelled Earth, meeting many governments and cultures, he was the linguist in the earliest days of Rakal being on Earth,' Richard concluded.

'I hate politics,' Gardt added. He began clearing away some of the dishes.

Vashla smiled.

'Ghaur, your home world would be equally full of obstacles to overcome.'

'What you're proposing is a formal alliance with each of the planets, including Orthama,' Vini summed up.

'Yes. This planet VaLinta, your planet Orthama and its space station, Earth and all its governments, Ghaur and all its politics that Gardt hates, four planets at least?'

'We have two home worlds,' the purple trader added. 'Ozer is our main world with its satellite moon.'

'I hope, Xamba can be added to the mix, when the people there are liberated. Even the death row prisoners from Ghaur, now miners, could have a second chance,' Gardt shrugged.

'You want a pact with all these planets,' Kat elaborated, 'stating each will look out for each other, and, agree to abide by the laws of that planet when they visit.'

'I think it would be wise for the generations to come,' Vashla nodded. 'I know nothing of politics, I've always ruled my ship, my planet, as I wished to. No one has ruled over me.'

'So,' Richard pushed his plate with barely a scrap remaining from the meal, into the centre of the table. He held up a device for everyone to see.

'This little gizmo is an adaption of the latest iPod on Earth. I can type up a document and we can all sign it. It links to computers on Earth and can register our agreement there immediately.' Quickly touching a few icons and displaying a document page, Richard was ready to go. 'What did you want to say?'

'Something simple and clear,' Vashla suggested.

'Legal documents, this is the realm of huge words and repetition that no one understands,' Gardt sat back and scratched his head.

'There are those on Orthama who have expertise in the Ancients' contracts,' Vini suggest, 'perhaps we can trace these origins to draw up some agreement.'

'They have 'legal eagles' on Earth too,' Kat chipped in, 'my experience of them, and I've had a few run ins due to failed relationship's and greed. Is that they bind everyone up with so much legal gobble-de-gook that only the fancy solicitor or lawyer can understand what they say. And usually they get the cash, and the client gets the bill.'

'Why don't we just make an agreement?' Emily suggested. 'Say who we all are. What planet we represent. That we agree to respect each of our planet's wishes on their planet of origin, and, we all want to remain friends working together in harmony. You know, for the good of all our planets, against any threat we may perceive.'

'Like the Federation in Star Trek!' Richard blushed at the acknowledgement of a long time favourite TV show. Davrew nudged him in the ribs.

'I think that's a good idea,' Agai agreed.

'Perhaps it could be as Emily suggests,' Vini nodded.

Richard typed up a simple statement, and each of the people at the table signed their names, next to the planet they represented. After which they then all drank and ate some more.

'Excuse me everyone,' Vashla said as the chill of the early evening had started to settle. 'I should go to check on Tam and the others being restored. On the way I'll go to the library, to find out what I can, from Zorn's memory, of his treatment of Rakal. I'm now certain he was captured. He's certainly not the Rakal of old.'

'Do you think he'll be Okay? He's my old man,' Kat tried vainly to not sound anxious.

'We'll restore Rakal's mind. To be honest, Tam, once restored, is the best person to help with that.'


Vashla felt very uneasy when she returned the next day from the restoration chamber with Tam and the two colonists. She had something to tell her new allies, something she discovered in her library while accessing the mind of Zorn. Right now, she was delighted to be able to reunite families. Her world had become one of responsibilities and a source of great joy. When Richard and Davrew saw Tam, they hugged and cried, holding each other tight. She hoped seeing Tam would help Rakal, however, she had her doubts.

CHAPTER FIFTY-TWO

# Battle for the Worlds - VaLinta

The next day Tam sat in Vashla's garden. She'd done as Gardt suggested and left her friend alone for a time to think. Now the morning sun was warm. She loaded a tray with some iced tea in a jug and two glasses, another habit she'd picked up on Earth during her many visits. Without a word, she sat down on the bench seat beside Tam, poured a glass of the refreshing liquid and handed it over.

Tam smiled briefly.

'Zorn isn't dead?' Tam asked again.

'No, as I said to all our friends yesterday, when I went to the library to delve into the memory of the Zorn I killed, I found it was just a clone. A new one at that, his memories were limited.'

'Everyone left right after you said that,' Tam continued.

'I apologise for that, Tam, you would have liked more time with your parents. The fact that we are all still in danger made their departure essential.'

'Rakal doesn't seem to even acknowledge me. He doesn't believe I'm alive,' Tam gulped down the tea, trying to cover and overflow of emotion.

'We will rectify what Zorn has done to him,' Vashla tried to sound reassuring. For the time being, no more words were spoken. They sat beside each other, in silence, sipping tea.

'The Ozer traders have a lot to offer,' Gardt was speaking to Dreece, from the communication console inside the cottage. 'You found the journey to Earth a good one?'

'Yes, those purple men from their world, have interesting technology and outlook. But here, I can't believe all the things I'm seeing. Some are so like what we have developed on Ghaur, and others are so amazingly different. Ash Davidson is a dynamo of ideas.'

'I'm glad you agreed to go with Richard and Davrew. The planet Earth is one Vashla talks about all the time. I've yet to visit.'

'To think this trip was suggested because Vashla misses shopping,' Dreece was oozing enthusiasm. 'Have you spoken to Ria and Bru yet?'

'No, I'm just about to call them,' Gardt smiled. This was the first time in years he'd seen Dreece look excited.

'The villagers want their extended families to join them. Ria and Bru have missed the younger children dreadfully, they'll be glad to see them again,' Dreece looked up at the sound of a door closing nearby. 'I've got to go, there's new space-ships being built, new skips for

VaLinta, new defence systems being proposed. It's all happening. Give my love to Ria, Bru and the children.'

'I will.,' Gardt nodded as the screen went blank.

Moments later Gardt was calling Ghaur.

'Hi Ria, you look well,' Gardt smiled at his former wife.

'You too, considering the journey, Agai is quite a pilot, he was showing off a bit I think.'

Gardt laughed. 'Did he do some fancy flying?'

'You could say that.' Ria wore her comfortable clothes and her hair cut was new. She looked relaxed.

'It's good to be home,' she smiled. 'Mother is well, she's afraid of being bored without the children.'

'You're coming back to VaLinta?' Gardt felt his body release some tension. 'Of course, the boys are there, and frankly, I think the fresh air, and everything, it will be a much better place for our little ones to grow up.'

'Dreece sends his love,' Gardt relayed the message.

'I was surprised he went to Earth instead of coming here,' Ria turned away from the screen for a moment. 'Bru is talking to the President and the management of ILD about what we can do to defend Ghaur. He's reminding them not to be complacent.'

'Good, that's what they need.'

'While I've got you, Gardt, there was one thing I wanted to bring up. You know housing is a precious commodity, especially given our population. Well, since we've been back, the ILD want to control everything. We're having none of it. If we want to travel to VaLinta, Orthama or even Earth, it shouldn't be up to them to tell us what to do.'

'Go girl,' Gardt couldn't stop himself saying.

'We need a base here on Ghaur. We've set up a group to show potential colonists what it's really like on Va-Linta, just how much they need to do, and how little of the comforts they are used to will be available to them. Our home was rented out when we didn't return. Mother took the children to her place. She wants to leave that home. I hope you don't mind, I suggested we all move to your old home. The authorities can't place anyone else there because it's still your home, your property, Gardt Ness the former pilot. It's rare to have a vacant home to go to.'

'Of course, I don't mind.'

'Mother came to live here yesterday. The the children are really looking forward to seeing their big brothers and the planet we keep raving about.'

'Does your mother want to come here?'

Ria shook her head her blond hair swayed. 'No, she does want to keep busy though. She wants to help tell the people wanting to travel, all about the new worlds. She's been fascinated by what we've said.'

'She could come and visit, to have first-hand knowledge,' Gardt suggested. He rotated his shoulders and waited for Ria to answer. His former mother-in-law was a strong and independent woman. 'Her help in getting people to see the realities of space travel and colonising VaLinta, could be a blessing.'

'She might do that someday but, right now she'd like to make your old home an information centre.'

'Is this going to be a problem for the ILD and authorities?'

'I don't think they will want to get on the wrong side of my mother. She can be determined and quite bossy.'

'Really? I wondered where you got those traits.'

Ria laughed. 'Seriously, you don't mind us being here, in your home and making it an information centre?'

'Of course not,' Gardt shrugged his shoulders. 'I still wonder about what might have happened, if things had been different, between us I mean.'

'Do you?' Ria rubbed her pointer finger along her eyebrow. 'I don't think we were ever meant to be. I think, Father pushed us together, we never really knew each other, and, it looked good for his daughter to marry the best pilot the ILD ever had.'

'I guess so, and now we get on Okay as friends, don't we?'

'Sure,' Ria smiled again. 'Agai is coming to pick us up tomorrow, so we'll be back on VaLinta soon, with all the children.'

'See you then,' Gardt closed the line.


Vashla walked through the cottage door. She savoured the feeling of belonging. Gardt was at the comm. She smiled and walked over to hug him. She snuggled close, comfortably under his arm resting her head on his chest. He led her to the couch.

'With everyone travelling freely, Zorn will think we believe him dead,' Vashla mumbled, too tired to let events ruin her day.

'Yes, we must be vigilant though,' Gardt whispered while lifting her chin so he could examine her face. 'You look tired.'

'I am,' She kissed Gardt gently.

'I do love you Vashla.'

'By the stars, I love you too,' she closed her eyes and listened to his heartbeat.

'We have to plan for more attacks?' Gardt reminded her.

'Yes,' she opened her eyes and ran her hand over his rugged face. 'Tam has gone to Rakal at the Ancients ship. I've kept him away from the village. Rakal is still, not himself.'

'I was thinking about that. Seeing Tam hasn't changed him, has it?'

'No.'

'That trader who was here said he'd been to Zorn's planet. He said that the small iPods Maya and Shea took to trade with from Earth, fascinated him. Perhaps, Rinra and Colu can tell us more about them.'

'Perhaps,' Vashla sat up. 'No one has been to Rakal's ship since he returned? The one he took off in?'

'I don't think so.'

'Good, I'll just take a quick trip there. If Rakal was under some mind changing manipulation, perhaps the device is still there.'

Gardt smiled as he watched Vashla rush out the door.


A short while later Tam returned in tears. Gardt poured his friend a wine and made sure they both sat down and relaxed.

'Vashla will be back shortly.'

'I yelled at him, I told him off big time for not listening to me. He still doesn't believe I'm alive.'

'You were dead for a while but, he should believe the restoration, he's seen the Ancients' technology work before.'

'I still can't get over that he told the family I was dead. Kat was stoic, until Mata was told, then they both crumpled, so my Father said. It was so cruel, especially when he knew I would be restored.'

They both turned when Vashla rushed into the room.

'Here, it's one of those iPod things that Rinra, Colu, Maya and Shea were trading. Zorn must have manipulated it and created a hypnotic message on it.'

'How can we tell?' Tam grabbed it from Vashla's grasp and turned it over in her hands. 'We have these all over the place on Earth. They just play music.'

'Zorn hates technology, but, he's not afraid to use it,' Vashla retrieved the device then went over to the com. There may be a way of deciphering what's on it without listening ourselves. We don't all want to become Zorn's vegetables.'

A short time later they'd decoded the message on the iPod.

'No wonder he's addled.' Vashla read the hateful hypnotic message.

'How do we reverse it?' Tam had been standing beside Vashla to whole time the device's message was being decoded.

'It was simple enough to put that message on. We'll replace it with another message and get Rakal to listen to it. He'll be back to help us with the next battle.'

'He'll be back to my Rakal?' Tam took a seat to stop from falling. 'Thank the stars!'

They worked for many hours on the iPod message. Rakal was sedated and the device put in place. Over the next twenty-four hours, the big man lay in a comatose state, listening, absorbing, as Tam watched anxiously.

When Rakal woke, he was bleary eyed. He looked up at Tam, ripped off the headset, and rushed over, smothering his partner, in an all-encompassing embrace.

'What have I done?'

'You've been Zorn's puppet.'

'I hurt everyone.'

'Yes, but, that's behind us now,' Tam kissed Rakal. They stood together, holding each other close for a long time, saying nothing more.

CHAPTER FIFTY-THREE

# Battle for the Worlds

'Guhamp hailing Vashla of VaLinta,' the hooded purple man was on the screen in Vashla's house.

'That sounds good, 'Vashla of VaLinta!' Gardt teased.

'It does,' Vashla laughed, as she moved to the console, to answer the call.

'Greetings,' the purple man spoke in his high-pitched tone.

'Hello Guhamp. Do you have news?'

'Yes. Zorn has assembled ships above Xamba, and above my own planet, and five others. They are many in number at each location. No one here knows where Zorn is sending them,' Guhamp looked uneasy. 'There's much speculation and fear on our planet.'

'I didn't know Zorn was such a direct threat to your world.'

Gardt was now at Vashla's side.

'There's a lot being said about how Zorn fooled you he is not dead.'

'He didn't fool us as much as he thinks. Thank you Guhamp for keeping us advised. You are still able to follow the plan we made before you departed VaLinta?'

'Yes,' Guhamp nodded with a smile.

'Good, thank you again. Your people are valuable members of our alliance.'

'Right,' Vashla turned to Gardt, kissed him warmly. 'It's time to put the plan into action. I'll alert the rest of our allies.'

Within hours, each planet in the alliance was preparing to defend their worlds.

'Ash, can you tell me where you are up to?' Vashla was speaking to the engineer on Earth.

'We've the planetary shields on each of our allies' planets, although Guhamp needs Zorn's ships to move away a little more before he can initiate the forcefield. We've built more ships and increased our numbers, with the other little trick you suggested. The ground troops are also on standby on each world, should Zorn's fighters get through. We're as ready as we can be.'

'Let's begin,' Vashla sent the final message out to the allies. 'This time we take the battle to Zorn.'

The ships in Vashla's fleet were greater in number. Rakal lead the more experienced pilots in one stream, Vashla led the other. They arrived above Xamba where Zorn gathered his battleships. They split into their two groups picking off the ships in stationary orbit as they travelled in opposite directions. Soon they were being fired upon.

'What trick is this?' Zorn complained waking to the battle above his planet. His ships were firing at the enemy who seemed to be shot through but still there. 'They are an illusion!' Zorn yelled. 'Wipe them out!'

'They are firing at us and making their mark, Lord Zorn. They are real,' his general stated. He was on a ship a safe distance from Zorn when he relayed this message. 'We are hit.'

Rakal aimed truly at his foe. His pilots dispatched several opponents, hitting life support, and weapons areas, while the small craft weaved in and out rapidly, avoiding the fire from the bigger ships. Vashla did the same with her squadron coming from the opposite direction.

'Zorn is hailing us,' Vashla advised Rakal. 'Don't answer, let him stew.'

They could hear the growl before seeing the face of their enemy on the view screen.

'We have many more ships, you cannot defeat us here,' Zorn growled again.

'Why Zorn, do you think we would be so foolish to think one battle could win this war?' Vashla replied, batting her eyes in mock innocence, taunting the big man's reaction.

'I will chew you both up and spit you out, savouring your last drop of blood,' Zorn spat.

'We've destroyed most of this group of ships, ruining this part of your plan,' Rakal goaded.

'Zorn, right now above each of the planets you have ships, the same is happening to them. You will not defeat us. We want peace. You do not,' Rakal touched his bracelet and was engulfed in a white light. 'You will not live to create more havoc.'

Zorn turned to see Rakal behind him, on the control deck of his own damaged battleship.

'I see we have disabled your weapons array,' Rakal smiled, as he unleashed an assault on his enemy. The machete sliced through the air catching Zorn's arm. He then head-butted Zorn and took another swing. They dodged overturned chairs and smoldering control panels, as the hand-to-hand battle continued. Zorn had his own solid blade carving dangerous swathes about Rakal's torso. A clanging warning siren wailed, to alert Zorn's crew of the damage, wires were hanging sparking in broken disarray. The combatants dodged the sparks.

'You have recovered your wits,' Zorn snarled. 'I had thought you would be my champion.'

'What havoc you caused has been undone. I am here to make sure you are driven away from the worlds you torment,' Rakal lunged and dodged. 'Where are your supporters, Zorn?' Rakal taunted as his blade reached its mark severing Zorn's hand above the blade. Without flinching, Zorn stabbed Rakal in the thigh with the blade in his other hand, forcing Rakal to push him away. With a sweeping kick Rakal knocked Zorn's legs from under him. He removed the blade in his leg and turned to swipe at Zorn again. This time it missed but caught the fabric of his shirt pinning him to the floor. Rakal took advantage of Zorn's struggle to be free, with one slice, his machete came down hard taking off his opponents' head. Blood spouted everywhere and Rakal stood to catch his breath.

'Is this another clone?' Rakal asked the empty room. He was surprised when he was answered.

'No, my Lord Rakal,' a burly soldier stepped forward. 'I am Amar. I was his aide. He was never to be trusted. He thrived on fear.'

'Don't call me Lord Rakal,' he replied as he shook the soldier's hand. 'I see you've had enough of his rule.'

'Yes, my Lord,' the soldier quickly corrected himself, 'Rakal.'

Rakal went to the control panel, quickly he checked out the ships capabilities to confirm it was still operational.

'Amar, you have damage to your life support and lost many of your crew members, however, it is repairable,' Rakal looked Zorn's former champion in the eye. 'You were waiting to see who would win?'

'I hope to be of service to you,' Amar nodded.

Rakal hailed Vashla.

'I have Zorn's head for your library.'

'The real Zorn?'

'Yes, I am assured this by his former aide Amar.'

'We have the fleet above this planet broken and surrendered. The ones who submitted are willing to put aside the battle. We need to look to the future for this planet and all our allies.'

'What of Rinra and Agai how did their battle go?'

'They also caught our enemy by surprise, above the planet neighbouring Orthama. As did Maya and Shea with the humans, who attacked above Guhamp's home world, the purple traders happily joined the battle,' Vashla replied. 'The report from Kat and his partner

Emily is equally good. They destroyed most of the fleet Zorn had gathered above Saturn.'

She looked at the soldier beside Rakal.

'Amar, we are only one part of an alliance. If you can join with the free people on Xamba, release the slaves in the mines to become citizens of the planet, you may be able to create a habitable and profitable world. The people on the planet would benefit from your leadership. The original natives of the world would be an asset helping you towards that end.'

'I will do as much as I can,' Amar bowed.

Vashla acknowledged Amar, deciding to trust him, for the moment.

'We would be grateful for your assistance. Can you tell us of any other plot, that Zorn may have had? Or of any of his associates that may try to take advantage of a weaker people, as he did? Zorn was a bully.'

'He was a solitary warrior,' Amar replied with his hand on his chest in salute.

'This ship needs to be repaired,' Rakal held the control panel to steady himself. 'If you agree, Amar, we can all be friends. I will return to my own ship now and let Amar take over this colony,' Rakal saluted Vashla on the screen, then Amar.

Zorn's former aid bowed his head acknowledging his new allies.

Rakal pressed his bracelet and again was enveloped in the white light, returning to his own ship. He immediately turned to Tam.

'I think I need my leg seeing to,' he said smiling at his lover, then collapsed unconscious to the floor.

## CHAPTER FIFTY-FOUR

# Battle for the Worlds

As the combatants returned home, Vashla took reports of the damage and casualties inflicted. She took note of all the ships Zorn had gathered, the mercenary pilots listed, their capabilities noted. She was fearful of another enemy emerging from this group. The repairs to the space craft and recuperation of the pilots and crews, also kept her busy. It was many weeks after the battle that the members of the new alliance gathered over a meal to discuss the events, the planning, the battle, and recovery progress.

Agai and Rinra were first to arrive.

'I've bought some of the sweet fruit you like from our hydroponic garden,' Rinra handed a large basket of the stone fruit to Vashla.

'Thank you,' she smiled at the young dual person, 'come and sit.' She put down the basket and linked her arm in Agai's, steering him towards the outside table setting. 'You are happy with Rinra,' she spoke softly to her son.

Agai just nodded.

'I will have to get used to this,' she whispered again.

Agai smiled broadly, slipped out of his mothers' grasp then slid into the seat beside Rinra, taking her hand in his.

'Kat is bringing Emily again,' Gardt put a huge salad on the table. 'I'll start cooking as the rest of our guests will be here shortly.'

'Guests,' Agai said, 'isn't this my home?'

'This will always be your home,' Vashla smiled. She put some glasses on the table arranged in front of place-mats.

'Vini is bringing four Elders here, and Dreece has been host to the President of Ghaur and his wife. They'll join us soon,' Gardt continued. 'I've set up a second table. I'm not sure if we'll all squeeze in.'

'Guhamp liked VaLinta so much last visit, he asked if he could bring his whole family, his wife and four children,' Vashla added as she pushed back a loose strand of her hair behind her ear. She turned around to arrange cutlery on stands at either end of the table. 'Richard and Davrew are on their way. I can't wait to see Rakal and Tam again.'

'Are they bringing Mata?' Agai asked. 'Inquisitive child, with Tams' fine features but Rakal's dark hair and solid build from what I remember.'

Vashla nodded.

'Sergeant Rymus, our Security Chief, is bringing his family also, his wife and two teenage boys. He will accompany The President of Ghaur.'

When they all arrived, the new allies were seated and enjoying the meal, all that could be heard was the clinking of cutlery and curious chatter. Many of the children disappeared when the parents began to talk about the battle. Others simply stayed in the next room playing computer games.

'Vashla, I've been wanting to ask you since the battle,' Kat cleared his throat. 'How did we manage that trick of making our little fleet seem four times larger? And how did we increase our fire power?'

'Good trick,' Gardt smiled.

'It was technology found in the Ancients' ship with the restoration chamber,' Vashla nudged Gardt out of the way as she put down two candles on the table. 'The holographic images of four more ships were projected around each single vessel. The best part of this was that in using the enhancement images, each ship increased their own fire power by four at the same time, appearing to come from the holographic images.'

'Literally making our fleet four times bigger,' Emily tapped the table triumphantly and looked up at Vashla, 'that's truly brilliant!'

'We couldn't have done it without intelligence from Guhamp and his friends,' Vashla raised her glass to the big purple man, who returned her salute.

'We're all fortunate,' Rakal added, 'the casualties were not as bad as they might have been if Zorn had launched his assault fully prepared.'

'Now that Amar has met and joined forces with the rebels on Xamba, and the prisoners have been granted some freedom, safer working practices and their own rights. They plan to work together to clean the atmosphere and make the planet habitable. The intention is to trade for better equipment to be able to extract the abundant ores from the planet,' Vashla smiled and raised her glass. 'Amar wishes to become a signatory of the alliance.'

'I'll drink to that,' Richard clinked his glass with Vashla, then with the others at the table, before swallowing the contents.

'I've been preparing some plants for reintroduction to Xamba. The soil on the planet has been damaged by acid rain, but with cleaner mining and environmental re-establishment of vegetation, the planet could become quite a good place to live,' Gardt said as he stood and started clearing away the leftover food platters.

'Gardt, perhaps this is something we can now do to Orthama,' Vini suggested. The air quality with protective suits is suitable for short visits. 'You know we have a team of specialists in our hydroponics garden working on the reintroduction of plant life to our dead planet. Perhaps it is your expertise with soil that we need to be able to move forward.'

'I think we can improve all our worlds with cooperation and trade between us and others we encounter,' Vashla agreed. She followed Gardt's lead and started stacking the plates. 'We have desert, and I think the children will return for ice cream.'

The President of Ghaur had been quiet. Dreece had been explaining all that each planet had to offer.

'Could we travel to these other worlds?' the President asked.

'Of course,' Rakal answered, 'on one condition.'

'What condition?'

'That we call you by name and drop the *'The President'* crap. We are all citizens of the universe, all descendants of the Ancients, all free people living on our worlds,' Rakal replied.

'My name is Sarnee,' the man replied with a nod.

'There are those on Earth that thrive on pomp and ceremony,' Tam reminded Rakal while taking hold of his hand. 'There will be leaders on all of our planets who are this way.'

'I know this Tam my love,' Rakal sighed. 'Greetings Sarnee,' the big man held out his hand to shake. The sharp faced politician shook it and smiled.

'Well said Father,' Kat rapped the wooden table, 'now for dessert.'

'You are always hungry,' Tam wailed.

Emily giggled, 'always hungry.'

'On Earth,' Davrew enthused, 'the range of foods is remarkable. The diversity in each area is amazing.'

'That's true,' Dreece added, 'with Gardts' garden here we could expand our variety of staple foods. Seriously, we should think about our future as an alliance and benefiting from what each planet can provide for the other.'

'Well, I agree with that. I would like to be able to go shopping. I really loved doing that on Earth,' Vashla grinned impishly. 'You enjoyed it too, didn't you Agai.'

'Oh, Mother, I believe you've had too much wine. You know I hated it.'

Everyone laughed.

'We do have many talented people here on VaLinta,' Ria chipped in. 'I gave Vashla these place mats that are hand made by one of the ladies in the village. The candles from another, and there is a man making basic tools from wood sourced in the forest. The skills of handcraft should be encouraged.'

'Growing the fresh produce, on every world, and exchanging them would be a wonderful way to get to know our many cultures. I would like to travel to Earth to see their techniques that I am told are carried out on a grand scale,' Rinra enthused.

'Earth is bordering on being overpopulated,' Richard joined in, 'there are many there who would love to travel to other worlds. The Olympics last year in London was a great success. Imagine what it would be like to have interplanetary Olympics. There are one or two billionaire tycoons who would like to cash in the race for interplanetary travel. We could all share our knowledge.'

'Is Earth ready for that, my love?' Davrew asked. 'I have seen much prejudice there, although they have adapted and changed.'

'Well, I for one am prepared to make a change here on VaLinta,' Dreece announced. 'With the population growing, the former colonists now villagers have been exploring a freedom they've never known before on Ghaur. They have suggested moving to other areas on this planet into some of the original Linta villages. Without a lot of skips, or transport, this would be difficult as they would be even more isolated in those settlements.'

Gardt whistled, 'Glad to hear you plan to stay. That's certainly an about face from your early days here.'

'I haven't encouraged re-settlement in another village because of lack of transport,' Rymus the village security chief said gruffly.

'Well, since the battle for the worlds, I've been in contact with Richard and Davrew's family on Earth, and their youngest, Ash Davidson who is a remarkably inventive. He's built a multi-person transport skip,' Dreece babbled with excitement. 'He will deliver this shortly.'

'So, you will be able to transport several people at once.'

'Yes, and if I travel from one village to the next regularly, there is no need for anyone to feel isolated,' Dreece concluded.

'You'll be the local bus driver,' Richard laughed. 'I'll drink to that.'

'I think you've had enough to drink Richard Davidson,' Davrew stood glaring at his partner. 'What this planet needs is all the basic retail outlets such as good hotels, for temporary accommodation, meals and beverage services, along with shops, cafes and hairdressers.'

'My thoughts exactly,' Vashla thumped Davrew on the back. 'Let's go inside and open another bottle.'

'It is starting to get cool out here,' Agai stood unsteadily.

The evening chill had begun to seep into the bones of the dinner guests who'd been at the table several hours.

'I'm going back to Rakal's ship. I don't want to be rude, Vashla, but I've had enough, and so has Rakal,' Tam hauled Rakal to his feet. 'We'll see you tomorrow.'

Soon after, the gathering of the new alliance, the members disappeared to their spaceships or the village houses where they stayed. Vashla and Gardt were left alone. Vashla smiled at the mess in their kitchen.

'This mess can wait till tomorrow. I've need for sleep, and, if I wake in the early hours, I'll have need of you,' Vashla grabbed Gardt's hand and led him to the bedroom.

'Tomorrow,' Gardt smiled, 'we begin building our new world, our place, our freedom, and our way.'
Without saying more, Vashla switched off the light.

CHAPTER FIFTY-FIVE

# Orthama Space Station

Davrew smiled. It had been over sixty years since he'd left Orthama, as an almost newborn clone in love. The view of the orbiting space station bought back mixed emotions. Although they'd been to Vashla's VaLinta since the end of the Battle of the Worlds', two years earlier, this was Richards first trip to Orthama since his abduction and incarceration there. Davrew noticed Richard was shivering.

'I'm excited. How about you?'

'It's a little daunting,' Richard admitted.

I know, it's much larger than it was when we were here. Don't be nervous, my love,' Davrew gripped Richards' hand tightly. 'This will be our last time here.'

They watched as the view of the space station grow larger as they flew around the exterior towards the docking station.

'We'll be docking shortly,' Ash, their sixth child announced. He was at the controls, 'I'm looking forward to seeing the whole space station. The new extension with the Unification Auditorium sounds impressive.'

'That's where the Ceremony will be?' Richard knew he'd been told the details before, but his memory was not what it used to be. His body, too, was becoming more fragile.

'I'm looking forward to seeing the new Library extension,' Mica, their youngest, was walking along the array of view screens. 'So much information has been gathered from all the worlds in the Alliance and from the Ancients' archives here on Orthama. I know I could get lost in there.'

'Don't get too lost, Mica. We need you at the ceremony,' Ash nudged his sibling as he walked past.

'It's good to come here with so many of our children and extended family, Richard. I'm looking forward to seeing some old friends,' Davrew smiled and squeezed Richard's hand.

'Like Vini?' Richard asked. 'I remember Vini and the kindness he showed you when others were not so kind.'

'Among others,' Davrew grinned again. 'It's so much bigger than it was when we left. There have been several extensions.'

'There's the latest addition now,' Ash pointed at the screen. 'We'll dock just past there.'

Other family members began arriving in the control room to enjoy the final approach. Richard grinned. The passengers lined up to see the view. He could imagine the same excitement building in those waiting on the orbiting platform above Orthama.

Richard and Davrew walked arm in arm through the entrance portal into the space station. Their family followed, chatting excitedly. Their children, generation after generations, had made the journey. How many of them had come? Richard had lost count.

'Agai and his Rinra,' Davrew whispered nodding in the direction of their hosts.

The boy they had once known as wild and reckless, was now a dignified and mature man. His athletic stature, so like his mother Vashla, made him stand out from a crowd. His brilliant blue eyes were mesmerising.

'Welcome back to Orthama, Davrew and Richard,' Agai shook their hands warmly. 'This is my partner, Rinra.'

'I recall we met on VaLinta at Vashla's after the Battle of the Worlds', Richard smiled. Davrew nodded. That had been a casual meal and had culminated in an agreement by the victors to form an alliance. This ceremony would formalise that agreement. More than a year in the planning, there would be representatives from all the planets.

CHAPTER FIFTY-SIX

# Orthama Space Station

Rakal and Tam had been on Orthama for several weeks assisting preparations. When Tam saw his parents, he dragged Rakal across the crowded entrance port to meet them. Tam bear hugged his parents, lingering with Richard, before pulling away.

'Tell me, it isn't true, Father?' Tam demanded.

'What?' Richard scratched his forehead.

'I understand that if you die, you have insisted that we don't use the restoration chamber to bring you back to life.'

'Oh that,' Richard's face set hard.

'I think the Alliance Ceremony is a more pressing matter right now, Tam, don't you?' Davrew interjected.

'Of course,' Tam paused, still holding his father's hands. 'It upset me when I heard that you'd made that decision. I just had to say something.'

'I'm old, Tam, I just had my eighty second birthday. I've lived a good life. I've seen my cousin Bill die, and our beloved child, Bon, be butchered, and many others die in the Battle of the Worlds. We have a great family, but I am tired, very tired. I really don't want to talk about this now.'

Tam nodded, dropping his hands. He moved on to greet his siblings, cousins, nephews and nieces and their families.

Rakal shook hands with Davrew, then Richard. 'You are smaller somehow, your face pinched and frail, my friend,' Rakal held the older man's hand squeezing gently. Glancing up at Tam. 'Tam is all too aware that restoration can give you another chance at life.'

'Thanks, Rakal, you have been a good friend to me and my family,' Richard let his hand slip away from the big man's grip.

'Agai and Rinra are about to take you on a guided tour, I'll let you go and catch up with Tam,' Rakal smiled at Agai who took the cue to lead them away.

'Everything is so much bigger than I remember it! To think this is where I grew, and lived before Richard arrived. It seems a bit surreal now,' Davrew smiled, linking arms with Richard, 'I can't wait to see the rest.'

'Did you have a childhood?' Richard asked as they followed Agai and Rinra.

'Not really. We were developed as people,' Davrew replied. 'I told you that before, my love.'

'I guess so. Perhaps I forgot,' Richard shook his head again. There was so much to take in.

Agai led them to the side entrance of the docking portal room.

'I'm afraid we must complete a formal arrival check of every person as we leave this area. It won't take long.'

A smartly dressed dual person sat behind a desk at a console, began the process, asking each person to place their hand on a screen to register their arrival.

'We know you've travelled through the grid. The journey is still a long one, so we'll keep the tour brief then take you to your accommodation so you can freshen up,' Rinra ushered them on after the formalities had been completed. 'We've a sumptuous banquet prepared for all our guests in the dining hall. When you are ready you can explore all the facilities yourselves.'

'The security official looks a lot like our Yankee mate, Cal Bennett,' Richard placed his hand on the cold screen and watched as it glowed, briefly warming to his touch.

'Naturally, he's one of the descendants of that sperm collection,' Davrew followed Richard away from the security console after doing a palm print.

'They're still reproducing clones. I thought there were enough people here now, and they could just rely on kids being born.'

A large entrance door slid open and all discussion stopped as they entered a huge domed chamber. The walls were lined with consoles, and the transparent ceiling offered a breathtaking view of orange Orthama floating in black space above them.

'This is the library Mica wanted to get lost in. It's amazing!' Davrew looked back at the rest of their party. Mica had already dashed to the side of the room to the nearest console.

'There was a resource room when we were here, but it was small compared to this,' Richard pulled his fingers through his grey, thinning hair, no longer thick and black as it once had been.

'We did have a depository of Ancients' information that no one really understood or investigated for many years,' Rinra explained. 'Rekindling our knowledge of our past and the historical records became a priority after the devastation of Orthama forced our people to look elsewhere to expand our race. We've now added the culture and knowledge of all our affiliated planets. Earth has a huge section, Ghaur another. Ozer, the planet of the purple people, has a section also. We've cultural, literary as well as historical records, and there are fictional works and a whole section on music from each planet.'

'I really could get lost in here,' Mica grinned, returning to the group. 'But for now, I'll join my lovely family and stick with the tour.'

The size of the Library was impressive, but when Agai and Rinra led them into the Alliance Auditorium they were astounded at the grandeur of the chamber. It had space scape portals along each side, and with the preparations for the ceremony well advanced, chairs were lined up with signs for each delegation.

CHAPTER FIFTY-SEVEN

# Orthama Space Station

At the appointed hour, a reverberating chime sounded throughout the space station. The smartly dressed dignitaries from all the planets began filing into the Alliance Auditorium for the Unification Ceremony.

'I can't stand this stiff collar,' Rakal complained to Tam. 'I could've worn my battle dress. It's comfortable.'

Tam shook a finger in Rakal's face. 'You'd be far too frightening for many of the younger members gathered today. I'm in my full traditional Dual Gender dress with styled hair. Your suit is very fitting.'

'Too tight fitting, and all this...' Rakal waved his arm and growled.

'Is what is necessary to formalise the agreement.'

'That Sarnee of Ghaur will be revelling in this,' Rakal gritted his teeth and nodded at the delegation from Gardt's home world.

'Here, this is our section, Rakal. Earths delegation,' Tam ushered Rakal into the second row behind Richard and Davrew. Their son, Kat, smiled as they sat in the adjacent seat, his wife, Emily, at his side.

'You scrub up well, Father,' Kat jibed.

'Not too bad yourself,' Tam nudged Rakal to prompt a comment then carried on when none emerged. 'Emily, you look stunning.'

The fit looking brunette smiled and blushed. 'You look amazing! The ceremonial attire for the Dual family is so...'

'Uncomfortable,' Mata and Rakal said at the same time. Rakal patted his daughter's hand.

'It takes a lot to get the hair to fan out, Father,' Mata let out an exaggerated sigh.

Those hearing this laughed. The chimes were still ringing as the hall continued to fill with guests.

Richard and Davrew sat in the middle of the front row. Miri, their eldest child, and her partner, Peter, were beside them, with their children and some grandchildren on either side. Their family alone would take up most of the seats allocated for Earth's delegation.

'I love the way the decorative ribbons cascade down the walls. It's very impressive,' Tam said to Rakal to distract him from his discomfort. 'The rainbow of colours is brilliant.' The podium on the stage was the only focal point. A semi-circle of seats fanned out from it, with a huge banner above proclaiming the names of all the planets attending.

The last to take their seats on the stage were the Elders of Orthama. Beside them, one representative from each world was seated. The general mumble of the audience became hushed as the last of the Alliance Leaders sat. The small table behind the podium now lit to show an open book. The agreement that had been debated for many months, carefully worded and prepared, was ready to be signed. Soon the proceedings would begin.

'Yes, there will be speeches,' Tam looked at Rakal sternly to silence his complaints.

'I'll just close my eyes then,' Rakal muttered.

'You will not,' Tam scolded and nudged him.

'My two will keep him awake,' Emily grinned. 'Thomas, you sit beside Pa, and Nancy dear, you sit beside me, with your brother on the other side.'

Tam put her fingers to her lips to hush their grandchildren, who were play punching each other.

The audience fell silent as the first of the dignitaries stood.

'I am Vini, an Elder of the Orthama descendants, living here on our orbiting space-station. This is a monumental occasion for all our worlds. On my right is the current President of Ghaur, Sarnee. Leaders Guhamp of the planet Ozer and, Mica Davidson, an accomplished diplomat-representing Earth. On my left is Amar, from planet Xamba, voted as their representative by the new citizens of the planet, then Vashla from her world Va-Linta, and finally our scientist and historian from Orthama, Rinra.'

'I didn't know Rinra held such a responsible position,' Davrew whispered to Richard.

'Nor did I,' Richard glanced at his partner and tried to keep focused on the stage.

'You look tired. Perhaps this journey was not a good idea,' Davrew clasped Richard's clammy hand.

'I wouldn't want to miss a chance to be here with all our children and their families,' Richard shook his head. 'I'll rest afterwards.'

'Today will mark the formal commencement of our Alliance with all these planets. The new wings of the space station have been completed and named in honour of this event. As is fitting for such an occasion we sit in the grand 'Unification Auditorium'. After a short address from each of the representatives, the agreement will be read and signed by all parties.'

'I know the President of Ghaur will go on, and on. Do we have to sit through all this?' Rakal grumbled.

'Yes,' Tam scolded. 'We're here to hear Vashla and support her. After all we've been through, sitting through a few speeches is not going to kill you.'

On the other side of the aisle, Gardt sat beside his son, Agai, who applauded wildly when Rinra was announced. Beside them Ria and Bru sat with their children.

Gardt lent forward to speak to Ria. 'Ria, Bru, it's good to see you looking so fresh after the journey.'

'We arrived only a few hours ago, we brought all the children, and my mother has joined us from Ghaur.'

'Ahem,' Agai smiled and nodded towards the stage. Both Gardt and Ria then turned their attention back to the ceremony.

The audience applauded the arrival of a new union of planets and the peace they hoped would ensue. The legal document was read and acknowledged, followed by the audience reading and repeating a pledge, to seal the proceedings.

Richard smiled and clapped but stayed seated.

'Are you all right, my love?' Davrew asked and clasped his hand tight. 'You look pale. I think we should go straight back to our room and rest. This has been a big day.'

Richard just nodded and allowed Davrew to help him to his feet.

'I'm tired, that's all,' he croaked.

They made their way towards the entrance of the auditorium, slowly through the exiting crowd.

'Father! Are you all right?' Miri had dragged Peter by the arm, over to her parents.

Richard nodded and continued.

A tall dual person approached.

'Please, use this hover disc to assist your travel,' the dual usher offered the disc to Richard and Davrew.

'Thank you. That's most welcome,' Davrew replied. 'Miri, you and your family can go on ahead of us to the celebration dinner. We'll be all right now. Your father just needs to rest.' Davrew turned on the hover disc and helped Richard step onto it, holding his hand ready to walk at his side.

'I'd like to come with you,' Miri replied. 'Peter can take the rest of our gang to the party. Most of them are already on their way.'

'That's fine by me,' Peter smiled. 'I've never been away from Earth before and everything here is so exciting. Please excuse me,' the former teacher, now the Davidson's property manager on Earth, bounded away. The three of them watched his grey head of hair bobbing along with the others of their family leaving the auditorium.

'Miri, I'm just tired from the journey. I'll go to our room and rest. Please, you go with Peter,' Richard waved their oldest offspring away.

'I'll do no such thing. Now you have a hover disc I can walk at a cracking pace beside you. I'll work up an appetite.'

'Stubborn like you,' Richard jibed, squeezing Davrew's hand.

'Yes,' they laughed.

'Did you see the youngsters from Ghaur teasing the young ones from Ozer?' Miri chatted. 'I hope they don't cause trouble.'

'Kids will be kids, wherever they come from,' Davrew shrugged.

Soon they arrived at their accommodation.

'The rooms are so well appointed and comfortable,' Miri remarked as she walked into her parents' room.

Richard wasted no time in going to the bed and sitting down. He looked up at Miri.

'Now go on with you. Thanks for coming back with us, Miri love. I'd be happier if you go and enjoy the celebration,' Richard swung his legs up onto the bed and lay down, closing his eyes.

Davrew walked Miri to the door.

'We'll be all right. We have a hover disc now and will use it to join you after we've freshened up.'

Miri hugged Davrew and glanced back at her father.

'Go on,' Davrew insisted. Miri left. Moving slowly and quietly, Davrew removed the layers of ceremonial clothes.

'Now, Richard,' Davrew started to speak, then fell silent. Richard he was already asleep. Davrew carefully removed Richard's shoes and loosened his tight collar. Then, very gently, got on the bed beside him, and snuggled under his arm. He tensed when Richard began to speak.

'Do you remember going to Tris and Tod in England to see Aur being born?' Richard whispered.

'Of course, it was a lovely day.'

'How many of our family died in the Battle of the Worlds?'

'Six, as you well know, including Aur, vaporised when they battled Zorn's battleships.'

'Was it worth it?'

'I'm certain we're in a much more secure place because of it, so of course it was. Richard, are you, all right?'

'My legs feel very heavy. Can you massage them for me?'

'Of course, I bought some of that tea tree massage balm you like. I'll get it,' Davrew jumped out of the bed and rummaged through their luggage to retrieve the soothing cream.

'We've had a good life,' Richard smiled as he watched Davrew struggle to pull off his trousers and commence rubbing the balm into his legs. 'It smells of home.'

'Yes. Your legs are hard. Perhaps I should get the medic.'

'No,' Richard shook his head. 'Just stay with me. You've always been there for me Dav, I love you more than words can say.'

'I know that, you, old softy,' Davrew smiled and continued a rhythmic massage of Richards' stiffening lower limbs. Soon Richard closed his eyes. After watching the rise and fall of Richard's chest for a time, he got up to wipe the oil from his hands. With a touch of a control pad on the bedside table, the lights dimmed. Davrew returned to Richards side.

## CHAPTER FIFTY-EIGHT

# Orthama Space Station – the final goodbye

'The acrobats from Ozer are astounding,' Peter enthused. 'Who would have thought that gangly purple people could be so lithe and athletic?'

'Now, now, that could be construed as prejudice, or not politically correct,' Miri nodded towards the crowd. Their own children and grandchildren had dispersed and mingled happily with people from the other planets. They all applauded.

'I know it's silly of me to worry, but I want to check on my parents, Peter.'

'We'll go now. Everyone is enjoying themselves. They won't miss us if we slip away,' Peter agreed.

Miri nodded and took hold of Peter's hand as they manoeuvred through the crowd.

'They were never going to come to the celebrations,' Miri voiced what they both thought.

'It's been a big day for us all. The younger ones will already be sleeping. Naturally, your parents need to rest.'

'Perhaps we shouldn't disturb them,' Miri stopped, and looked up into Peter's eyes.

'We're nearly there now, and, I doubt you'll sleep till you know they are all right.'

Miri lent forward and planted a lingering kiss on his lips.

'You know me too well.'

They buzzed the doorbell just once. Davrew answered quickly.

'Miri, I knew you'd call by.'

'We were worried when you didn't come to the party. You're crying, what's wrong?'

'I can't wake your father.'

Miri and Peter rushed into the room.

'Oh no! It can't be!' Miri wailed and rushed to the bed to lean over her father's still frame. Miri began to so. Peter took her in his arms. They wept together.

'We said our goodbyes,' Davrew whispered.

Miri and Peter, bleary eyed, helped Davrew arrange Richard neatly and called the medical staff to examine Richard's body. A procession of family members came to say goodbye and share many tears and recollections. The celebrations of the Unification Ceremony were dampened by Richards passing.

'He was eighty-two, and had lived a good life,' Miri repeated to the next in line, all people she loved and treasured, but whose faces were now just blurs. 'We were planning a special family get together when we get home, but it's not to be.'

'Davrew is sedated and sleeping in the next room,' Peter said as he came to Miri's side. 'We must rest ourselves and plans must be made. We'll be celebrating when we get back to Earth. Celebrating the Davidson's family patriarch's long and love filled life.'

Miri nodded and closed the doors after the last of the family members had left. They walked slowly to their own rooms. The silence around them was suffocating. 'Davrew wants to take him home to Earth.'

The next day a solemn procession followed the casket on a hover disc as it was taken to the stage of the Unification Auditorium. Quite a different ceremony from the previous days Unification Ceremony, was held.

Miri stood and tearfully read a eulogy.

'Richard Davidson was not only the patriarch of our family; he was a wonderful father and friend. He was always there for every one of his children, their partners, grandchildren, and great grandchildren with a shoulder to cry on whenever we needed it. Our hearts are torn with sorrow, but we know that we must go on.'

Mica stood and hugged Miri, wiping away tears like so many other mourners in the room.

'It was my father's dying wish that he be buried on Earth. For those who wish to travel with us to the grid, you are most welcome to join us. For any who thought to join us on Earth to say farewell, we appreciate your good wishes but ask that you stop at the grid entrance. We will complete this sad task on Earth with Richard surrounded by family and carrying your love and appreciation with us.'

Davrew, Miri and Peter walked beside Richard's casket, with Davrew often clinging to their arms for support, stumbling as they passed the sea of family and friends surrounding them, overwhelmed with grief. They made their way to the spaceship for Richard's final journey home. Throughout that long journey from Orthama to Earth, Davrew would not leave the casket where Richard's body lay.

'I'm taking you home, my love,' Davrew whispered.

## ABOUT THE AUTHOR

Jill, born in Victoria, has always loved reading, writing, and creating wonderful worlds.

After her marriage and birth of their son they moved to Queensland.

As a member of many writing groups she honed her writing skills by producing book reviews, articles, and interviews for various online magazines.

Her published achievements include contributions to anthologies for children with 'The Ten Penners', six short stories in 'Fan-tas-tic-al Tales' 2009, nine stories in 'Mystery, Mayhem & Magic', 2019.

Further success with Michelle Worthington's 'Share Your Story' Group, one story in 'Spooktacular Stories' Thrilling Tales for Brave Kids, October 2019. Jill has a new story 'Larrikin Lyle' accepted for this groups 2020 anthology 'Tell 'em Your Dreaming'.

'Dual Visions' is the first book in 'The Ancient Alien Series' with 'Vashla's World' book two, and the third in the trilogy 'Travellers' to be released shortly.

Jill is also working on a young-adults Science Fiction called 'Microworld'. She lives with her husband and one cat in Kirra, Queensland.

# BOOKS BY JILL SMITH

### Adults Science Fiction

***'Dual Visions' #1*** The Ancient Alien Series
***'Vashla's World' #2*** The Ancient Alien Series

### Children's Anthologies

***Fan-tas-tic-al Tales*** – The Ten Penners 2009
***Mystery, Mayhem & Magic*** – The Ten Penners 2017

### SHARE YOUR STORY Anthologies
***Spooktacular Tales*** – Thrilling Tales for Brave Kids
***Tell 'em Their Dreaming*** – Bedtime Ballads and
Tales from the Australian Bush

### Coming Titles
***'Travellers' #3*** The Ancient Alien Series

### Young Adults Science Fiction
Microworld / Microworld Undersea

www.ingramcontent.com/pod-product-compliance
Lightning Source LLC
Chambersburg PA
CBHW070431170726
48291CB00002B/454